Another Horizon

By
Randy and Charlotte Shepard
Christmasten@gmail.com

Copyright © 2020
Randy and Charlotte Shepard

All rights reserved. No part of this book may be reproduced in any form, except for the inclusion of brief quotations in a review, without permission in writing from the author or publisher.

Cover art by
Leonard J. Peck
1938-2012
Whom we love and miss

ISBN: 978-1-7343140-1-4

Printed in the United States by Morris Publishing®
3212 East Highway 30
Kearney, NE 68847
1-800-650-7888

Chapter One

Old Dreams

Dreams are so often real in quality. They take the moments from our past and those of our present and combine them to deliver a message which our mind or heart needs for that day or time to come. Sometimes dreams come upon us during our nights sleep or they are found in moment when we slip from our daily reality into the realm of simple slumber or that of a passing daydream. And so was this one, a dream which repeated itself periodically. Not daily or even weekly but enough to remind him he had dreamed it before. A dream with an unknown meaning or reason and yet somehow it held the key to what life was about, it's course and meaning. And so again, this old man dreamed it in the same clarity which he remembered from the days of his youth.

The ocean was a torrent of rising mounds and the darken skies resounded with the thundering roll which followed the silver forks of lightning. The wind howled, dulling the voices raised against the storm. Yet the worried eyes upon the deep spoke more than the ear of any man could hear, just as the weary heart expressed itself upon the brow.

A small boat is tossed in the seas with only six people aboard. It is a vessel unequal to the task. How this small group came upon the sea and found themselves in peril is unknown even to them. Dave, known as Cap by his family and friends, is young again and fighting natures onslaught with the skill of a seasoned seaman. Linda his wife, Tom and Sherry, along with a small child are likewise aboard. As Dave looks to the stern, he sees a crewman he had known in his past from a ship Dave had once commanded. His name was Sharky, he wondered why he was there. Dave and the helpless crew fought the waves trying to keep the small bow into the wind. Tom yelled over at Dave, "Are we going to make it?"

"I'm trying!" Dave yelled, "it's taking all my strength." His arms strained as he fought to hold the rudder in line. " I'm not sure I can keep the vessel on course!" Dave was surprised at his own statement, because he didn't know what course they were on or where were they going in this storm.

Suddenly a wave broke over the port side, it was full and violent, the saltine fizzing mixture stung both nose and tongue as it passed. Dave was shocked, he had been keeping the vessel head fast into the waves as best he could; this shouldn't have happened. When the water cleared from his eyes he saw that Sharky was gone.

"Where's Sharky!" he yelled. But no one answered. He looked over the side, he knew he couldn't change course to look for him, because of the storm's rage. He knew if he tried to move the rudder the small boat would roll over and all would be lost!

Suddenly the wind seemed to calm, everything seemed to be ok and for a time it was easier to keep the vessel straight. When seemingly from no where, another freakish wave hit them from the side and as the stinging, salty water cleared from his eyes again he saw that Linda and the small girl were gone. Pain, hopelessness, and fear filled his heart. The wind began to rage again and the waters became even more deadly than before.

My wife! My wife is gone! His mind screamed. "No!" Dave yelled, but his voice was stolen by the wind. He began steering the vessel wildly looking for her. The boat turned sideways in the swell and almost capsized. The small crew struggled to keep themselves from going into the water. The deck was so slick with saltwater it was nearly impossible to keep their footing. They were pulled down by fatigue and wet clothes, and the wind stung their eyes and pulled at their hair as painfully as if it were made of sand. The slate black waters threatened from all sides, heaving the small boat up one moment before bringing it crashing back down again. One more bad wave like the last and the vessel would not be able to stay afloat.

Tom yelled at him, "Stop, or you will turn over the boat and we will *all* be lost".

"Where is she?" Dave screamed into the howling wind . . . but no one answered. The fickle sea slowly calmed enough to be able to see more than a few feet once more. The waves were rough but became navigable and time seemed to pass slowly. There was no hint that the storm would die completely out and no one spoke as the waters and wind moved them quickly upon the deep.

As he looked, he saw other children on the boat next to Tom and Sherry who were not there before. They smiled at him but sat silent. He did not question where they came from, his only intent was to survive the storm and search for his lost love.

Suddenly another wave rushed over the boat and it tipped violently to the side before it quickly came back to its keel. As Dave looked, Tom was gone and as another freak wave assaulted them, Sherry too followed him and was gone into the sea. In the blink of an eye he wasn't on the boat at all. He was in the water swimming and he was pulling the boat with a rope. He looked up at the boat as he swam and everyone who had fallen over was sitting in the boat looking at him. A small boy swam up near him and began to pull on the rope as well. He stopped and handed Dave a piece of green glass and then swam off in front of him faster than he could go. Dave looked up at the people in the boat, they were covered in a light fog and he could not see them well. He yelled at them.

"Where are we going?" But no one answered. He heard a voice call out in front of him. "I know!" Dave looked, he saw the young boy who had given him the glass. He was now dressed in a dark suit, white shirt and tie and standing upon the water. The young man raised his arm and pointed saying loudly, "To the horizon!" As Dave's gaze was pulled to the far curve of the earth he saw the horizon ablaze with the brilliant glory of the sun. The clouds in the heavens seemed to encircle the vast scene like a great auditorium. The pillowy white columns of heaven echoed the golden royal arraignment of nature in the varied colors of the sky, reflected in it's shimmering brilliance upon the vast deep of the seas. Was it a glorious sunset or a sunrise? Regardless it was without comparison. He wondered then deciding said to himself aloud, "It is the rising of the sun!"

Cap woke from his sleep in the noon day sun and sighed wearily. A robin-egg-blue sky hangs over the old man sitting by the shore of Bear Lake Idaho. In his hand is rod and reel, in his mouth hangs a pipe, and his old, gray cap is set tightly on his head. He is dressed in an old Navy issue P- Jacket. It was dark navy blue with large black shinny buttons double abreast. Small whiffs of old, silver hair branch out from under the cap, unkempt by this traveler of long roads and lonely highways. His pants and shoes are now worn like a man who has walked every mile from where he was to where he is now. Beside him on a rock is an old, large, leather worn book. It was once a ships log which he now uses as a journal. His prized possession, a left over from a life time of living. Only a few unwritten pages are left much like the aged image of the man who possesed it. If the book were closed it's raised seal, a cargo ship, would be clearly visible on it's dark and tattered surface.

      The day of solitude quickly wore on and under the evening sky lit by the failing sun. The words on the pages dance with the flickers of light from a newly kindled fire. It's pages are opened and, like the man who writes his life upon them, this book is almost finished, all used up by time, life, and the miles traveled. Tonight he writes little. Tonight is a time for reflection, a time to add up what life has meant and how much it has been worth. The return of the dream in his mid day nap seem to be the sponsor of these feelings. The old man sat intent on rereading the record of his past, while at the same time, with a well-trained hand, he tend his fishing line bobbing quietly in the water. The sky is clear with a scattered cloud or two and the water of the lake moves gently ashore with a small wake. With posture and expression it can be seen that the old traveler is deep in thought. A seagull alights near the old man, looking for food and Cap, the nick name of this wizened character, speaks to the bird as if he is an old friend. The bird watches with a curious, but suspicious eye, as Cap turns a page or makes a note or two. For him he awaits the possible treat, as if the book might be hiding a morsel within.

"So you came to help this old man did ya?" Cap said with a smile. "Well Ok... I'm trying to figure things out, trying to understand my life. Why am I here and how have things lead me from what I was to who I am? I sit here like an old tramp yet I have money enough in the bank. This is a tough task isn't it? Trying to put all the years together, and find some sense in it. But, I'm also trying to add something to my life, some new pages about today which may change who I am tomorrow. Do you think it's to late for this old man?" He gave the bird a quick eye up and down, "But how do I start? What should I read in these worn old pages to help me understand today? And what should I add, if any, as I write down the pages of my life, summing things up, adding up it's worth or uselessness? I sometimes feel like throwing this book away and forgetting the whole thing. Yet something inside says this is who I am and that's got to be worth something doesn't it?" The bird just jumped to another spot to watch as if reacting to Caps question.

"Where is my *first* memory, my first thought about life here on earth, and how did it bring me so far?" The bird turns his head as if to listen. Looking at the seagull Cap asked, "What do you remember about your first day of life? A little white prison? Were you cramped within, both in body and understanding? And then suddenly, with a determined effort, bursting into a world you had never dreamed of, one you had never imagined was so large. What made you first think to break the shell and climb out? Did you know there was a greater world waiting for you outside? Do you remember your mother bringing you food when you couldn't care for yourself? Do you remember the first day, when you stood and felt your own legs below you or when you first leaped into the air and made the sky your home? But look at you now, you're an old hand at being a bird. Flight is old nature to you and you know where to go to get the best food and how to handle the wind and nature. When the world gets rough *your* dance is upon the breeze and song is in your heart. For myself, you might ask, I can recall brief flashes from my first years of life, at least at the time. When you first realize you are really someone, a person. Perhaps like you when you first realized you could fly,huh?" Looking at the bird directly now he said, "But even as I stretch to remember the times which mean the most to me were not when I was a young child. It was when I was young man and traveling the seas of this world. You know, I met a lot of your cousins then, perhaps a grandfather or two. By the way, did they ever mention me to you?" The bird didn't react to the question and just picked at a piece of bread which Cap had thrown to the ground. "I didn't think so yet look at me," he said with another thought. Cap looked up at the sky and the mountains and panned the skyline with his gaze. "Here I sit now in a place so far from the ocean and much closer to the sky than I have ever have been before. I'm sure you are used to such things yet in my heart I yearn to be closer to the blue of the deep water and the white of capped emerald waves rolling inward to shore. Such things I have grown up with and is, I might add the place I truly love. A realm made up of liquid reflections, a kingdom much larger than the land, a true access to the whole world, that is the place which I have called home."

Cap looked down at his footprints in the sand. "Bear Lake Idaho, how did I come to sit on it's shores? It's not a bay at all, it's a large oyster shaped lake, a high desert mountain oasis. It has a beauty of it's own I will admit and I sure wouldn't want to offend you." He glanced sidelong at the bird.

"Indeed, these mountains, this lake has it's own unique place in nature. But it's not a bay, it's not an ocean, it's not my home." The bird cocked it's head and gave him an eye. "I know! I know what you're thinking, I've made my point already. I keep harping and yes, I know it is water, it is large. I should be thankful. But even with its small wakes rolling like little beach breakers, even with its firm and standing mountains rising from its shores they all seem so alien to me, as if this is someone else's memory, someone else's place," Cap paused and looked around. With a sigh continues his thought, "that they hold dear. You must know though, what I mean. For me this scene hardly fills the yearning I have for the briny spice of salty air and the endless horizon. I can see it in my mind even as I speak. Can you catch my vision? The horizon, the destination in which we are all bound on a course of our own choosing. It is that distant unknown shore or place always just ahead, the next choice for which we are set, somewhere at the edge of your sight. The endless boundary that you can never reach, yet is the goal, the direction we travel. When we make it there it is that place where our vision first ended. That is when you find you have an entirely *new* horizon, rising before you, growing with each moment you travel towards it. Destinations without end which stretch to the edges of the earth and beyond." Turning, he looked down on the bird. "I sure wish you could see it." The bird gives out a throaty call as if answering him.

"The seagulls who fly here at Bear Lake seem somewhat out of place, the pelicans too!" He went on again, "When I think of you guys I think of the ocean. I must say I was surprised to find you here in a mountain desert. Yet when I hear you call out, when I see your wings spread upon the wind as you fly over the beach, your eyes keen and searching, both of you, the pelican and seagull alike, seem to me like a long time friend I'd once forgotten. It's like the face you remember and then see in a crowd. It's like a friend you have missed and yearned for when looking for something familiar. Yet, perhaps, it's like a friend who, once was found, is too busy to stop and say hello. Excluding yourself, of course. You have been a fine fellow thus far." The bird hopped closer to Cap and looked for more bread impatiently, "I must admit though, to be totally truthful, standing here along this shore feeling the wind in my hair and water near my feet gives me some comfort and some peace. It helps me think. You see today this old man has something which he thought he might never have again." Cap paused a moment, his eyes taking on a deep and thoughtful look,

"A choice. I face a new decision, a change in my life and a change in how I might view the world, perhaps in how I might even view forever and at my age you can't but help thinking of forever." Cap began thumbing through the pages of his book, lost in a thought. He stopped and looked back at his feathered friend, his voice suddenly intense. "This is a decision which, if true, may make life worth it's course and length, give it meaning and reason both in calm and storm. Perhaps though, with this one such choice, because I haven't yet made up my mind in these things, it gives me pause to wonder about my feelings.

Am I contemplating an *indulgence* in hope? A fantasy where I hope that I might once again find the things I have loved and lost? Things I want to find so badly, things I hope lay upon my course somewhere up eternity's road, waiting just ahead over the next horizon? *Hope* and *want* are not truth, but I know they can be the driving force which helps us find truth." With those thoughts Cap looked out over the lake as the setting sun cast it's colors upon the water. The shades of red and crimson were mixed with the colors of the lake and that of remaining light. A fiery blast of colors burst over the mountaintops, trimmed with the deep golden light of the setting sun.

As the lake reflected the light of the evening sky it brought back thoughts of his dream. In Cap's mind he could see an image coming slowly to view upon the waters. It was the figure of a woman, standing like a spirit upon the lake. In his thoughts he walked out onto the water to be near her; he was young and strong. He took her hand and in his heart he yearned; he looked into her eyes, and for a moment, he was not alone, he was with her again. The vision parted, and Cap looked again at the bird.

"Yet here I am," He said, his grasp closing on empty air. "I have to stop and wonder, have I lost everything in order to bring me here where I might find everything? I am old now, so very long in my years, does any change in my life at this point mean anything? Haven't I sown my fate with my faults and mistakes or gained what blessing which might be from whatever or wherever God might be? Or could it be there's more water ahead, a greater sea, another ocean, for this old sailor to sail upon than there was in what I have left behind in my wake?" As Cap talks softly to the bird and to himself, the sound of rocks turning under foot above and on the road meets his ears. Cap looked up and saw an older gentleman, like himself, walking down towards him. He seemed dressed well, and was neat and clean. In his hands he held a rod and reel, and in the other a fishing basket.

"Hello, catch any thing?" The old man spouted.

"Heavens no," Cap responded "I don't even have a hook on my line. I just find fishing a good way to sit and think."

"Good, because it ain't fishing season." He added with a laugh. "And it's nearly night, you ain't suppose to fish at night." Cap looked sort of puzzled at the man's statement, especially as he observed the fishing gear this old guy was setting up, so he had to ask.

"You can't be the game warden, unless you like to poach a fish or two yourself." The old man shuffled to the waters edge.

"No, Just wanted to see if you would care if I," In mid sentence the old man casts a line into the water. " cast my line in and I do have a hook." Like a pro his line went way out and set with a gentle plop into he water. Cap picked up his fishing pole and gently rolled his line back in.

"I don't care, but just so's I don't get taken as your partner in crime I'll just pull my line in."

"Suit yourself" The old guy chuckled. "All's the more for me." He gave Cap a quick glance, noticing his book and pencil, then asked. "What are you writing?" He didn't look up from his fishing, he kept his mind on tending his line.

"It's just my journal" Cap answered. "Kind of a daily add on to my old ships log. You might say at my age it's almost finished, already written in a way, just a line or two left to jot down." The old guy reeled in a little and then let his line bob.

"Well I guess, but I think it ain't over till it's over. Best to have fun before it's all said and done, you know, before someone throws dirt in your face down a six foot hole. Journals, huh, ships log? I've never had much use for such things. I never really cared or ever really wanted to remember the past. I figure, I'll do what I can do today, then stand up and yell at the setting sun, 'Watch out tomorrow, I'm on my way.' Ha ha!" He laughed loudly at his own thought, somewhat self amused and pleased with himself. But when he noticed that Cap only met his comment with a small smile, he added in a different tone. "Besides journals always seemed like girls stuff to me." Cap didn't know why he didn't enjoy this mans company; usually any excuse to laugh and yell with another person was good enough, but tonight his heart was set on making decisions, taking a new and different course and he really wasn't up to a lot of laughing and jokes.

Still though, Cap, being a polite man and never wanting anyone to feel uncomfortable around him, tolerated the intrusion. Yet he had hoped for a solid night of being alone with his thoughts.

"Well, it isn't girly at all," Cap responded not quite harshly, "and it's an old habit I formed from my seafaring days. Actually it's an extension of the very records I kept while commanding my own vessel and that's an older practice and tradition then even you or I."

The old man smiled, "Yeah I got it, you were a sea captain and a sailor, fine, I'm sure it was fun." His words seemed scoffing and harsh, but then suddenly the tone of his voice went back to a friendly 'I've known you all my life' type of speech. "Old huh, well not older then the both of us put together I would wager or even *one* of us perhaps." He began laughing again. Then asked unexpectedly, "Your not a Mormon are you? These hills are full of them and I think they are the most lost people on earth. I mean I don't really care if you are one, a person has to decide things for himself. Yet, even though I think there is a God and that He did create all things, it's not like he's our dad and we see him everyday giving us help. I mean, I've never seen Him. Have you? I think He let us alone to make our own way and our own decisions. If we are thankful it should be only because he created us and put us here to have fun and go fishing. Wouldn't you say? I think we are to keep out of each other's way and let be what is. I think that's the best guide for life. Besides, even if you live by the scriptures, you don't find the word Mormon in the Bible, ayah?!" He gave a wink. "Besides, as far as Christians go, they seem a desperate and unhappy lot. Cheating each other and calling themselves good and fair in their dealings and then going to church on Sunday as if everything is ok."

Cap smiled, "If you don't like Mormons why in the world do you live in Idaho?" The old guy reeled in his line for another cast.

"For the fishing, what else? It sure ain't the climate. Ice fishing in the winter, regular fishing in the summer, and poaching when you can." Cap laughed, he could only agree with his sentiment on the climate and then he answered the old man's question.

"No, I'm not a Mormon, but I do have friends who are and they don't seem unhappy to me. In fact some of my best memories have been with them." The old man began to reel in again after his last cast.

"Sure, that's the way it seems that is unless you live with them you wouldn't know!
They are great pretenders. It's only when you really get to know them you see they are really a suppressed, and I also mean depressed, people. Look around you at this place, mountains, sage brush, cold winters and bugs in the summer. Who would live here if they didn't have to?" Cap had been thumbing through his book while he talked and this man's words were getting a bit irritating. He really wanted some time alone. Socializing might be good for some other time, but

not right now. Still the old guy might be a blessing in disguise. He has lived a long time with these people in the mountains and he should know them, so perhaps his insight was what Cap needed? Then again, Cap had known one family who were members of the Mormon faith and he loved them. They once lived near him, across the bay.

As he looked up to ask the old man a question, he noticed he couldn't find him anywhere. He must have disappeared into the bushes to fish another spot, somewhere just beyond the fire light. Cap looked over at the bird who was still sitting close by.

"Well I'm glad your still here, the old guy was a bit much don't you think?" The bird shook its head and groomed its feathers.

Cap cast his line back into the water and then sat back down to open his book. He took in a deep breath of night air and looked up at the stars. He was grateful for the unexpected sudden peace so that he could once again turn back to his thoughts.

I feel the past, as if it were here with me now, he thought, *but what should I believe for the future?* As he read he remembered, he knew these words, they were not so long ago. He had set them on the page and once upon a time when they were new. Indeed these passages were but a few years old compared to the length of Caps life upon this earth. Ten or even twenty years seemed like yesterday, when

80 plus years had passed since your birth.

The pages read:

    The day has just begun, on this (written date,) of this (noted year); the early morning breeze has lifted up and off the shoreline. It carries with it a soft scent of brine cast from the gentle wakes of the waters of Emerald bay; it refreshes my mind.

    In each curl of the dark green which now rolls to land on this new morning, the slight but distinct savor, earth's living blood, makes it's way to the nostrils of this old man.

    This was the last time I stood on the beaches of the rocky shore. Today I head inland, not really knowing why, but listening to something in my heart, which drives me on. That silent something which calls me to the mountains of the West.

    Today I want one last look at the Sea, the ocean, my home.

    The waters stretch out from this point of land, where I now stand. Its volume becomes the distant sea, the ocean. For the rising sun, is cradled on flaming water, with the birth of each new day, and for the suns setting, it holds the golden orb for one last time in the eventide of all it's glory.

Yet here in this small enclave, which is in itself, more than a cove yet less than a bay, this is where I claim as my own.

In all the vast earth, the planet; I have traversed its waterways and seen it's sights, but this is where I found my place, the place I call home.

This half crescent shore, has stood as a testament to the trials of time, changing slightly as the tempest would direct; That uniquely designed by heaven, by the passing of each season; all the way back into the times of it's own memory, to when God had formed it's shores.

Suddenly Cap could see himself, on that day not so long ago, he could almost hear the waves, and smell the spray of the surf. Youthful eyes in a worn body glanced to the horizon, hands steady upon the pages of his life, this very book, now in his grasp. He continued to read:

With reflections fixed to the past, my youthful days, I jot down a thought or two as memory would permit. Contemplating and reflecting, watching the world from shore to sky, as I had done so many times over my many days on earth.

Skilled I was, in hearing the voice of nature, as it prepared for day and let go the night. Thunderous skies or calm breezes, this old man of the sea, knows them all.

A dark blue jacket, with large black buttons, hanging loosely from my shoulders, the same jacket I wear now. But this old Jacket, and the things I now wear, have been a fading testament; a declaration to what life has been. But no matter the raiment, coat, shoes and scarf, it wouldn't be Cap, if I didn't have on my old hat.

In memory as he read and also in the present Cap ran his fingers across his caps brim. He could feel the golden symbols of his one time rank. Once a symbol of his work and position, now darkened and hardly gold. Only to his touch did it still feel the same. Captain or master of his vessel he had been called and was still so titled, even to this day. Though now, in the twilight of his life, his rank was only complimentary, acknowledged by those who still honored his life's achievement.

The sea, this had been his home, the only real home he had known since youth. Like few men whoever dared Cap had found life aboard ship, those ocean bound vessels were all he had ever wanted. Early in his years, he had eagerly climbed the ladder from crewmen to Captain; in consequence, commanding longer than most ever did. Seeing the world from its' ports, and knowing little else of it, setting course and crossing the many years of life to it's final stop, retirement. In those early days he'd felt like the luckiest man on earth; often saying, "I have never worked a day in my life, because I have loved the work I do. To me, each trip across the deep was a new adventure, even though each voyage was planned and we were in the regular ports of call. Because when dealing with the ocean, each trip often became a new experience, even though it may be the same route and the same waters you had traveled before. Each time you ventured upon the sea, you never were sure what you might find, or see or experience." One such time he said these words stood out in his memory. He was in port chatting with the locals as he usually did, but he liked what he'd said next so much he repeated the words often in other ports:

"I have wondered, of all those who have lived on earth, how many have lived the magic which brewed within the deep of the sea. The magic which was known only to those like me, and by those who have been lucky enough to live like me, having the greater part of their lives unfold and take form, while riding upon the lifeblood of our world. To the eye of the land lover, this magic was only seen on chance or singular occasions. Caught by a lucky glance out of the corner of the eye, or found on a windswept beach. Or maybe they dreamed of it in the dreams of nights visions; those which pass like phantoms in the dawn, and are often forgotten quickly.   Those dreams formed from the sound of the crashing surf, or the scent of the waves when it would take flight upon the whipping winds of a misty morning. For those who had not cast their life and lot upon the green and blue, the magic is only for a moment, and often too quick for the eye to see, and the heart to understand. I would say, to those new and choosing this life, those I was privileged to introduce to the sea and our ways, those I had trained over the years,   'It is the way of the deep, when you love it like I do. It doesn't let you down, that is unless it wants to keep you. But you better know her voice,' I'd often add in a serious tone, 'learn it well, and understand her ways. It is on days when the wind is calm and the water is glass, and there's not even a shimmer upon her face from horizon to horizon, a person can then look down upon the mirror of eternity and see their soul looking back. If you belong to the sea it's then and only then, you will know it. For you see your reflection in her eye, the briny deep, as she *sea's* you. Life will change for you, and you will walk being a part of the main, rather than a visitor upon it or a stranger in an unknown land. You will long for her, if you are ever parted from her and you will return; perhaps not even remembering why, but somewhere in time, you will return. Though the skin may harden, and the hair turn silvery white, your heart will remain strong, beating like thunder in a stormy swollen sky like the thunder of waves against the rocky surf. Hence then, this will be said of you 'Here is a child born of the sea, here is a one tested of heaven and tempest, here is a sailor of the deep.'

    I remember well when I would tell this tale all would stop, even the old salts. Voices would quiet, work would cease while I spoke. In the hearts of all those who listened images of all seafaring men, young and old, present and past, would take form and play upon the stages of their minds. We were then brothers afloat on a common quest, with a common vision. Ships of wood and large sails would fill the eyes of our minds. The wind as it rushed across the decks, the wood as it groaned and yielded to the passing waters below filled our thoughts and memories. The voices of those on deck and the hum of lines passing through fitting and fixture, the sounds of sails being pulled taunt as they would catch the wind for the first time of the voyage crowded our senses. Voices echoing orders as the rigging is secured, and duties are shouted one to another up on deck filled our ears. Some claimed that as they listened to my oration my appearance would change before them. My voice like magic, seemed to light around me and I took on the dress, and mannerisms, and aura, of the ship captains of old.

A clear bond formed with all sailors then, those alive and those long since dead. Sailors from other times seem to be in the wind around them along with visions of their future life and lives at sea. It all served to satisfy their choice to live upon the waves. It was no trick, all Cap was saying was the obvious, and this magic allure of the ocean had lived long before him. It would be there, just as he knew it is there now, long after he was gone. It was not his power, nor the gift of a witty tongue, Cap knew, but the power of life as molded by the ancient turning of the tide.

Cap suddenly found himself in the here and now. The wind was a bit colder now and he pulled his jacket tighter about himself. He added some wood to the fire. The chill must have been what had brought him out of his memories. He hadn't even realized he'd been lost in them, staring off into the past and seeing nothing of the fading day before him. The Gull began to scratch at the sand and Cap grinned in amusement, "Think your a cat now, do ya?" As he watched the bird he suddenly noticed a rectangular shaped object just under the spot where the bird was digging. As he lifted it out of the sand and brushed away the debris he realized it was a book.

Odd, he thought, "Why would a book be left out here?" He wondered aloud. It looked new and undamaged. He realized with a start that, even though it was smaller, it looked a lot like his logbook and even had the cargo ships imprint on its cover. Cap quickly looked to where his old log book now lay, it was as he had left it. Intently he began glancing at the pages of this strange book as he whispered, "What is it you have found here old bird?" The words inside the book were in print, but they were like the words he had just wrote, and like the stores of his life, which he had placed in his own book years ago. How was this possible!? He could not help but read on. He hadn't gotten far when suddenly the old poacher he had talked to earlier came rushing out of the bushes. Cap, for some reason he couldn't explain, sat on the book, hiding it with his weight and the edges of his jacket.

"Have you seen my book? I lost it!" the old man exclaimed, "I must have dropped it when I cast my line in the water." Cap knew something was wrong. If the book itself were not suspicious enough he didn't remember seeing this old guy carrying a book and he would have noticed such a curious item. Despite his suspicions for some reason it didn't seem wise at this time to confront him about it or let him know that Cap presently had this book.

"No," and after pausing said, "Can you describe it?"

"Well!" the old man responded rudely, "If you haven't seen my book why would I need to describe it to you? Do *you* have it?!" he demanded. Cap felt the ridged edges of the book below him and he was puzzled. The man says this is his book, but it has Caps life in it and, never having given permission to anyone to read his log book or especially print it, it could not be this mans book regardless of how it came to be.

"I asked if you would describe it in case I come across it. Where do you live so I can bring it to you?" The old man growled.

"Well how many books do you think are lost on the shore of Bear Lake? I think you have it. Give it back right now or I'm getting the law." Cap sat tight on the book and looked the man in the eye.

"Get who ever you like! But I want you to know that with your attitude, your verbal attacks right now as things stand, if it were that I was sitting on it with my spanker gib and giving it a full press with my well earned weight, even if my fingers were tickling it's pages, I wouldn't cast an eye to help you find it! I don't like people like you so good day and goodbye!" The old man looked at Cap with a new rage in his eyes. As he glanced around Caps campsite it seemed that he was fervently contemplating his next move.

"Ok," he responded harshly. With a new confidence in his words he added,"I'll just take your log book until *my* book is given back to me." He then bolted forward to grab Caps book from where it was laying on the sand. Cap stuck out a foot to trip the old gent but he nimbly hopped over it. As he reached down to take the book suddenly the seagull, which had been standing near by, jumped up and bit the old guy's hand. He snapped his hand to his chest with a shriek and exclaimed, "Alright, alright!". And with a noticeable growl the man threw up his arms and disappeared into the bushes.

Cap looked down at the Seagull and smiled. He knew if he had jumped up the book under him would have been exposed and a fight most surely would have ensued. The seagull, he figured, must have thought the old guy was bending down to give him a piece of bread and bit him by accident. After all Cap had been feeding the bird all day and night, and though they seem a gentile animal, they can be quite mean if they are crossed the wrong way. Cap could remember when he had netted a seagull to try and remove a fishing hook from it's wing. The bird had flown right under a line while the fisherman was casting it out and had gotten tangled. The bird, who didn't know what was going on, put up a tremendous fight. Only after a few painful bites, and a bruise or two, the bird was freed from the line and let go.

Understanding the bird was easy, however Cap couldn't explain what he had seen in the book, so he wasn't going to give up until he did. He also felt he needed to understand how, suddenly, here and now this strange man, which he had never met before, was connected to his life. He sat up and drug the book out from under him

And I want to know why, he thought.

Chapter Two

The Journey Begins

He opened the book once more and began to read. It was odd to read about yourself in second person or as a character in a book. All in all, the information and accounts of his life seemed accurate and it followed his memories and his writings very well. He began and as he read a strange phenomena seem to occur. To his minds eye the waters of Bear Lake lit like the screen of an immense theater. Upon it played a panoramic display of the visions which each page brought to memory. It was better than his log as it had things Cap had forgotten, yet it was in harmony with all he remembered about his life. It made the following account of his life in a descriptive poetic language. Memories seem to rip open the vault of time and the past was real, as it was when it was, so many years ago.

"Dave," (Cap's real name)"Dave" A silent voice called from the cloudy images of thought where memories now live and the past is alive. "Dave, you old sea dog, how are you?" The voice was crisp and clear now and so was the scene which unfolded.

A busy seaport was the set on this stage of recollections, a port which changed little through time, with it's old wooden piers and docks. Small boats to large ships filled the harbor in a fashion to inspire the best of all artists and poets. It was the living bread of the nearby town of Turnbridge, nearly the soul resource for scratching out a life in this rocky tree filled terrain. There were some farms which added to the variety at the markets, but the shipping and fishing industries gave the local population the real taste of the world and it's abundance.

Dave was a tall, strong young seaman who, with his ruck sac in hand, bounded down the short gangway to the dock.

"Tom." Dave grabbed his hand in a firm shake, "I thought you were on your way to England."

"I was, " He answered. " But we ran into a storm. Mother Nature you know, and she wasn't happy I want to tell ya. In fact, she was down right mad! Our ship was battered so bad we were taking on water in the main cargo hull. We had to turn back, or sink, of course. The Captain choose the first." Tom exaggerated a little, but the repairs were necessary now. They had been trying to put off earlier, less important work and make the trip first, but the storm changed all that.

"Good idea," Dave responded, "can't deliver much cargo from the bottom," he chuckled as he fingered his vest pockets in an obvious search pattern.

Even though he was talking jokingly with Tom he had a disturbed look upon his face. Finally, however, he did obtain his objective and quickly pulled out a long green cigar from his pocket. Success and accomplishments were in his expression now. Fumbling a bit, he desperately tried to light the horrid green thing against the wind.

Tom watched on, he had a, "Not again," look on his face. He never did like the smell of those cigars and always wondered why Dave would smoke them. They looked awful, especially after being chewed on for a while. They smelled horrific, and could fill a room with a putrid odor in seconds. As far as their conversation went, and how the storm had been, Dave understood what Tom had described well. Everyone who had been out to sea, and even those good folks on shore, had been kicked around in that one. It came up suddenly and then vanished about as quickly. It was truly an odd one, but odd wasn't a bad thing, it just happened now and then.

Dave hadn't notice Tom's disapproving eyes as he continued to puff fervently while mastering a reddish yellow glow on the big green thing. When he finally got it burning good enough, he proudly puffed away as if it made him special or something. Dave had become proficient in his cigars. He could talk and smoke even in the same breath, answering Tom's comments with a full mouth of stogie, and not dropping a single word.

With a puff Dave said, "Yep, we got knocked about in that one ourselves, was quite a storm. But I got to say, even though it's a set back in both our schedules, I'm glad to see you."

"Yeah, even better then when we use to plan a set back or two in the old days on purpose." Tom snickered. They both laughed a bit as Dave let go a few gentle coughs. Tom looked at Dave with a curious eye.

"Perhaps you ought to cut down on those things, you didn't use to cough as much, at least as much as I can remember." But that didn't stop Dave. He acted like he hadn't heard him. He just coughed and puffed, all the while looking at the small community, and wondering where they might go first.

With another puff he added, "You know, with both of us in town, it's going to be a bit rough on this place." Dave smiled largely as Tom agreed with a grin and nodding his head.

"I can imagine," he replied, but it seemed that it was his turn to be somewhat distracted, and Dave noticed it in his voice.

Tom knew exactly what Dave meant about being hard on the place. In their youth, the both of them prided themselves in being a holy terror in any and every port to which they landed. Getting into trouble and finding successful ways of running from it, was their dangerous game. This, of course, was a risky practice considering some of the countries they would end up in on their travels. Some countries would have, if they could have caught the two rascals, thrown them in a deep dark jail and thrown away the key. Of course they had been lucky, on most of their encounters and managed to live life free from incarceration.

Of course adding a few extra years to their lives, and several hard knocks along the way, (not to mention an almost permanent stay in a Greek prison which cost a lot of money, but ended safely) caused both of them to mellow down some. Yet being responsible was still far more than they would want to admit to themselves. In all, Dave seemed to have mellowed more than Tom, but both were a little wiser than they used to be. But as Dave *might* now admit, they still like to think of themselves as 'the terrible two', even if nobody else did.

As they walked Tom and Dave shared stories about the storm and they also filled in the gaps of time since they had last seen each other. Dave noticed that as they visited and made their way towards the town's main road, Tom still seemed distracted. It was like he was looking for words to bring up some unknown or unpleasant topic. He seemed fidgety as they walked and Dave realized it got worse every time he puffed on his cigar. So he put his theory to a test, he inhaled long and deep and then puffed, casting a large billow of smoke, sure enough Tom fidgeted even more. Dave realized that Tom's uneasiness definitely had something to do with his cigar, so he puffed, Tom fidgeted, he puffed again, and Tom fidgeted some more; what an interesting game this was becoming.

Dave noticed that Tom was fishing around inside his coat, going from pocket to pocket to find something. He couldn't connect that what Tom might have in his coat had anything to do with his cigars. But Tom was looking for some object which he couldn't find, or at least couldn't get out. Finally Dave's curiosity was more then he could bear, and asked, " Did you lose something?" Tom stopped and looked up, he had a "what?" expression on his face. "Well" Dave continued, "You either have a terrible rash, or somethings wrong." "Here," Tom finally said, "The darn thing was stuck sideways in my pocket. I thought I had lost it aboard ship, but here it is and I don't want to carry it around any more." In Tom's outstretched hand Dave could finally see that he was holding a tobacco pipe. One, which seem to have something carved upon it. Dave looked up from the pipe and replied, "You know I smoke cigars, not pipes" "Yes, I know," Tom answered, "When you lit your cigar, it reminded me. It was in that horrible, blinding puff of smoke I saw a vision, I heard the call, that I have a life changing gift for you. I just had to be sure I hadn't lost it, or at least, I had to see if I could get the darn thing out of my pocket without breaking it. When I knew I could, and that I hadn't, I knew then I could mention it to you." Dave gave Tom a quick glance, "Don't you mean that you hadn't, and that you knew you could, in that order?" Tom gave Dave a disapproving glance, "Who cares about the order, we're communicating aren't we?"

The carving on the pipe seemed to rise above its' once smooth surface. Its image was intricate, with great detail, portraying several themes. It was truly eye catching, and obviously crafted by one who possessed a keen eye and skilled hands. As Dave quickly surveyed the surface he realized, mostly from Toms expressions, that this was Tom's work, a talent to which Dave had never known his friend to have.

"I thought I knew you," Dave remarked, "I never realized you were so gifted." Tom motioned for Dave to take the present, "Something I picked up from my dad." he proudly answered. "But, I must admit, he was much better then I am."

"Better then this?" Dave remarked questionably. "Can't see how" The pipe fell into Dave's hand, he realized that the image on it's surface was that of a sea Captain. The face, the hat on the images head, the pipe in it's mouth, had been keenly carved in rustic detail. Behind the prominent image was a ship, with its sails set to the wind. And on the other side was the figure of a lady, dressed in a long gown with long flowing dark hair. Her hair faded into the carving and became the wind, which filled the sail's of the ship on the pipes other side.

Tom smiled, "The Captain looks a bit like you, doesn't he?"

Dave grinned, but still maintained an expression of amazement "A bit older, and he looks better then me I'm afraid," Gently he took the pipe and held it up to the sun light, and examined the design more closely. It was strange, it seemed the closer he looked the more he saw.

"You put a bit of magic in this didn't you, but who's the girl?"

"I don't know," Tom, responded, "perhaps it's someone your going to meet."

"Oh" Dave replied, "A lady with wind in her hair, a windy lady. Sounds like someone I would like to meet."

It suddenly occurred to Dave, "What's this for anyway, it's not my birthday or anything?" Tom laughed as he formulated the best answer in his reply, "Well, during my last visit to Boston I happened by this old tobacco store. In the window I saw a rack of pipes; the owner had just set out on display and on sale I might mention. I saw this one, sitting somewhat off to the side, and then suddenly like a bolt of lightning coming straight out of heaven, this selfish thought took me. I thought to myself, 'You know, this pipe might be a good way to get Dave off those sickening green cigars!' Of course I did the carving. I thought it appropriate with your promotion and all."

"Well, thanks Tom," Dave answered, as he turned the pipe from side to side. Tom was better at whittling then Dave had realized, this was a real treasure, in fact it wasn't whittling at all it was a piece of art. Dave looked slowly back up at Tom, his brow took a questioning form, "The cigars were that bad, huh?"

"Yea," Tom responded truthfully, "and much worse than even this simple, but direct hint lets you know. Lets just say, I 'm saving your first command." Dave smiled as he turned the pipe over and found the words,

To Dave, Master of his own vessel,
So Angels may guide your course each day.
Not turn to run, to get away.

Dave grinned as he finished reading the little rhyme, "All right, you made your point. And since you insist so fervently and I see you do. I'll give this pipe a try."

"That's good" Tom responded, " And I want you to know that this pipe has got my blood on it, so it would be an unforgivable insult for you not to use it."

Dave looked puzzled, "Your bloods on it? "

"Don't ask," Tom responded. "Something about a moving deck and a sharp knife"

Dave smiled and stuffed his cigar in his mouth, he then opened his upper pocket and placed the pipe deep within. Figuring this lesson was over, and thinking Tom would follow, he hoisted his ruck sac on his shoulder and turned towards the Shoreline Inn.

Tom started off with him, but he stopped shortly without warning, he wasn't quite done with Dave. Grabbing Dave's arm, and then seizing his hand, Tom turned it over till his palm was up. Reaching quickly into a pouch, which he kept on his belt, he pulled out a small white bag and dropped it into Dave's waiting hand. "Just to be sure you don't forget, here's some tobacco to fill it with." Dave looked at Tom with little or no expression; he reached slowly into his upper pocket like a man who had a gun to his head. Gently he pulled out several cigars and with a quick snap of his wrist, tossed them into a near by oil drum. Then as he smothered the lit one on the soul of his shoe, he murmured quietly to himself, "I had always thought these things made me look tough and manly." "Only in your own mind," Tom laughed. " and only in your own mirror." Dave then looked down at the small cloth sack of tobacco, "You really don't like those cigars do you?" "Dave, my friend," he answered as they started off again, "Nobody does! And I see it's up to me to protect your image." Giving Dave a solid swat on his shoulder they laughed as they walked into the clouds of yesterday, and as it faded from Caps view once more he sighed.

Some of us define our lives by our past, those days when we were young. Cap was no better; yet it is when the here and now suffers from our yearning of the past, that it is wrong. But Cap, as a confident man seemed to hold to present well enough, yet yesterday with all it's adventure and love, was still sorely missed in this old mans heart. Again the pen fell softly to the pages below, as the old man fell gently to sleep in his chair.

Yesterday is a memory, more then just a dream
It passes by so frequently, so real it often seems.

The smiles and joys we left behind, are all I want to hold.
The friends which passed beyond the veil, are with me I am told.

You cannot teach me what I know, for life has brought me here,
Just be a friend that I will hold, in the passing of each year.

For dreams and thoughts of all I was, still live within my heart,
and all the people I have known, are found within its parts,

For the past is just as real to me, as the new day which we see,
For all those things of yesteryear, are what have made me - Me.

    The night had seemed strange and unusually long, and the book was the strangest thing of all. When Cap read the pages it was almost like he had stepped back into time and was making all of his choices over again. Tom seemed like he had just been there with him, but he couldn't have been since he had passed away so many years ago.

    He remembered when he walked into Montpelier, Idaho for the first time. He ran into two young men who were walking down the road. They were friendly and they liked to talk like Cap does.

    They taught me about faith, he thought, *those two young boys* with their books. *They said that everything has a purpose, that there is life after death, there is a resurrection. It is hard for me to believe that Tom is gone forever, he was such a good friend, and I want to believe, I want to know, if such things are true, that I will see my friend again some day.*

Cap had let his fire die away, so he took a moment to rekindle it. He then pulled an old kerosene lamp from off his backpack and lit it. He figured he should have done that long ago, the firelight was nostalgic and friendly but not much good to read by.

If that old man comes back here, he thought, *I have some real hard questions for him.*

Grabbing a nibble from a cracker, he lifted the book once more and began to read. The bird, which found the book, still tarried around his small camp and ate what it could find. Another stay at Turnbridge the page was titled.

Dave walked slowly down the wooden walk of this old seaport town. His footsteps resounded slightly with each step like a dull, muffled drum set against the quiet of the early morning air. At first he seemed very much alone but it wasn't long before several people began to emerge from their respective habitations and set in motion their early morning activities.

The surrounding community laid directly on the west or was it the eastern coast of America, and for its' time played an important part in the local fishing industry. As of late, it now served as a great place to put in for dry dock and repairs, especially if the vessels needs were below the water line. The actual dry docks weren't in town, but close enough to walk for anyone who wanted to do so, and most did.

Dave pulled out his pipe and packed it full of tobacco, it had been months since he had last seen Tom, and the pipe had been well used since that time. Popping it into his mouth, he walked slowly along through town, with a light cloud of tobacco smoke drifting along behind him.

People with faces he didn't know, walked busily by him. Yet as his ship began to port here more often, he was beginning to know the people around town more and more. For some folks, he even knew their names, but for others, he only remembered their faces from a passing smile or a brief hello. He had a long way to go to feel like he really knew this community. Many seemed too busy with their work to look and take any notice as he walked by. Some would offer a smile, but most just went on working, occupied with their usual chores. Doing things as they have been done and as their families have done them since the town was first founded. Possibly, for some, the same work which generations of their family have shared from now back to the beginning of time, having life and routine change only with the progression of technology and often that wasn't much.

New faces were not strange here as ships would come and go all the time and often with different crews. Dave himself, like most, had never taken the time to become acquainted with anyone in town enough to say they knew him well. As for Dave, he had visited many ports in his time, met many people. However he knew the ports better then he knew the people. That is to say the sights and smells of each town, wharf, or dock had their own identity and they ingrained themselves deep onto his mind. Dave inhaled the scents of raw fresh fish and tobacco. The wooden planks clonked under foot just so. No matter where the dock was always home to him. Dave looked into the windows of the little wooden shops as he walked by. Trinkets and chests, clocks and compasses, they were all for sale here. He couldn't help but enjoy the dickering of the salespeople. This felt right. For some reason, this community embodied everything he had found pleasant in all of the ports and towns he had liked. This community was a collection of life, all in one package, with everything he enjoyed. There was also an air of community togetherness here, it seemed to be a fun place even without having done anything fun. Dave thought, as he stooped over slightly to read a sign announcing today's town picnic, *and this is the kind of stuff I mean.*

More and more he began to look forward to his stops here and he wasn't even sure why. His dreams at night seem to make this place his home, and he often viewed himself living happily along the shore, just out of town. The perfect place having the world set behind him in all its beauty with the ocean stretching out to meet the sky as his front yard. No matter where he was at during a voyage, his dreams would bring him here, and in them he would be taking twilight strolls through the town. Feeling the peace, which comes from good people of a good community, a place we all hope to live but few ever find.

Today like many other times, as he walked along the roads through the different areas of Turnbridge. He would ultimately find himself down on the old wooden walks near the water. It was here where most of the cargo and catch were brought before shipping, at least for the smaller vessels. Sometimes while passing through this area he would run into a familiar face or two and they would talk awhile. But even if they didn't talk there is always the sense of kinship to those who use the ocean as their way of life. Besides it was always interesting to Dave, to see what others might be bringing in off the water, even a deal or two was struck for seafood or imported goods.

It was here on the docks where Dave could smell the familiar odors and hear the familiar sounds of a fishing community. He supposed that it was a silent, unspoken passion that one day he might find himself owning his own fishing boat and having a small crew. Perhaps it was these thoughts which drew him here each time.

As he walked his senses were filled with the plain and clear aroma of the freshly caught bounty. It was cut, cleaned and prepared for the market by the skilled and callous hands of the fisherman. Mingled in the mix was the occasional scent of new spice, springing up like incense as bails, bags, and boxes were opened from their long journey of far off lands. The sounds of cargo and net as they fed line through pulley and bit, letting go to finally meet the deck with a thunk and the voices of the dockworkers while they managed their skills filled the place. He would watch the crowding of buyers and the dickering of owners, as they inspect their goods, treasures and dreams of profit, and of course the occasional disagreement, which sometimes ended in a fight. But always present in all sights sounds and activities was the mixing of brine, wood and steel, as the tide softly lapped against the pilings and the hulls of moored vessels.

All these things were familiar, and all a part of Dave's life. Making his way up to the main road, less then a half of a block from the docks, Dave inhaled deeply. Fresh baked bread tantalized his nose, he could taste it, covered with just the right amount of butter. Cruelly it emanated from the local bakeries firing up for the day. Breakfast became a sudden and strong temptation as bacon and eggs joined the enticing aromas. Dave found it a most difficult task to choose where to eat at so he decided he would make it simple, it would be the first place he came to.

The roads around town were filled with both automobile and horse drawn carriages. Giving the familiar clanking of hoof on stone, or metal wheel on road as they trod over the uneven surfaces to the symphony of noises already overloading the senses. The intersections would rise and fall in activity, with the progression of the morning, that Dave and others on the walk had to dodge from time to time in order to avoid being ran over.

This was an active community, alive and well kept, the occupants and owners of each resident and business took pride in how things looked. This was what Dave liked, the newness of everything, whether it was found in the people or the land itself.

"Dave!" A familiar voice rang in the air and at once he knew who it was. "Tom," he replied. As he turned about, "I can't get away from you, can I," the two met with a friendly handshake. "How's the youngest captain whoever sailed these seas?" Dave asked.

"Oh, you heard," Tom, answered proudly. "Who hasn't?" Dave replied giving Toms cap a little flip with his finger. "Looks like you beat me by at least a year." "And how about you?" Tom added, "I heard you've taken on a new route. You have command of the Sea Catcher. A fine ship and through Cuba, not bad." He gave Dave a little push and then he continued. " Of course that's how I knew you would be mooring here for the next day or so. So, I decided to make an unscheduled stop just to see ya. Of course my ship and crew understand we needed to port for some difficult repairs, which are real I might add, but perhaps could have waited."

Dave smiled "Nice, but I have the Sea Catcher only for one trip, their Captain died on board just three days out, I heard it was from heart failure, they asked me to finish the run. "Yes I heard" Tom replied "But I didn't know you weren't going to take the ship permanently. "I've got another offer" Dave responded, "but I am more worried about you, how do you make any money with all these emergency stops?" Tom returned the smile, and it was obvious he had figured a solution to that question already. "Well, due to my emergency, I got permission to ship the cargo the remaining distance by rail. That is, if I deem it necessary, and I do. Since the manager of rail lines out of Turnbridge owes me a favor, for saving their cargo last year after that horrible derailment. I'm actually saving a bundle on shipping. I'm also ahead of schedule either way I go, take it myself or send it by rail. So since I'm going to get a bonus for being early, it will make up for the additional rail cost balancing out the ships fuel and crew bonuses. The repairs, as I said, are needed so it's better to have them done now, rather than later when the ship might be in a real fix for time."

Dave grasped Tom's hand tighter, "I can see why they made you a Captain, you think things out well. But, whatever the reasons you are here, it's always good to see you. However, while you're in town you need to be sure you say hi to Wayne Roberts. He's a local resident now."

"What, he moved here?" Tom responded. " I heard he was buying a shipping company out of San Francisco! I figured he would hang around in beautiful California and be a socialite and all. He's truly got the money."

Dave smiled, "No snooty stuff, that's not like him, he's a small town kind of guy. He did buy the company however, and he's offered me a position in it as well. Of course he knows you and he told me when I see you, that you should check with him about a job on one of his ships."

"Captain, I suspect." Tom replied.

"Of course," Dave answered. "What else? I guess I'll be seeing a lot of this place from now on, you could too. For me, he's given me choice of positions, I can float and fill in were ever I want, or I can take a permanent route. Of course since Wayne decided to build his home here, I'll be seeing a lot of him as well. Did I mention he is building a house? You ought to see the plans, it's quite a place."

"I'll make sure I see him," Tom commented, "perhaps you could show me where he's staying later?"

"Sure," Dave responded "I'll do that. I haven't seen him since I got in off our last run either."

As Tom and Dave talked they didn't notice the approach of a large, extremely rough looking individual, whose gaze was intently locked on Tom. It was Marcus, a very burly, and generally angry sort of man, who wasn't overly tall but built bulky and firm. His eyes seemed set in anger and everyone got out of his way. With his massive covering of dark curly hair and his long but large, hairy arms he bore a strong resemblance to an ape. Of course Marcus was very sensitive about being called an ape, and more often, this was how his fights would begin. Of course his fights usually didn't last long and most people new why, he was tough to fight. In fact, it was said he had never lost a fight in his life and the rumor mill had a variety of numbers on how many fights that might be.

"Is that you?" The large figure roared. "Tom McGregor, is that you?" The voice resounded in threatening tones.

Tom quickly looked at Dave, and Dave noticed he had an "Oh No" type of look in his eye. Much like a cat that just realized he had been spotted by the dog.

"Who's that?" Dave queried, while he watched the massive figure fight its way through the traffic and crowds. Tom grabbed Dave's arm and turned, dragging his friend along faster and faster, he started walking briskly away.

"Tom!" The voice called again, "You stop right there!" Dave looked back as he heard the rough voice beginning to curse. Feeling the tug on his arms he realized that Tom didn't want this man to catch him . . . in any way.

"That's Marcus Sternly, and I owe him a bit of money. Just a small gambling debt from when I was a lowly deck hand. Of course I'll make good, but I'm not ready to pay him just yet." Tom said.

"You never told me about this, besides a *little* debt?" Dave shouted. "It looks to me like you owe him your hide, and he wants it, right now!"

"That's what I'm afraid of, " Tom added. "And he's the kind that will peal it off one inch at a time." His voice faded as he hurried.

"Hey" Dave said grabbing Toms shoulder, "You're a captain now, he wouldn't dare mess with you, your crew would tear him to pieces and he would be black balled from work!"

Tom glared at Dave and said "My crew has better things to do then die and if Marcus doesn't care about his gainful future enough to not attack me I'm not going to stop and try and explain to him his career mistakes." Marcus came as close to a run as his massive form would allow, everyone who might be close to his path got quickly out of his way. The glare in his eye, along with his bulk was all that anyone wanted to see of this man's nature. As far as walking, he was making better headway than Tom and Dave. The only thing which kept him from catching up was that Tom and Dave were now running, and they were fast.

"Aboard ship," Tom recounted, "Marcus could lift cargo which three normal men could scarcely heft. As for those stupid enough to come against him in a fight. Well, no one has ever put him down."

"And you gambled with this guy?" Dave asked, in a 'that was stupid' tone of voice. "Come on, the both of us can take him."

"No," Tom said, " I don't think we're enough" Taking a quick turn or two, Dave and Tom looked back and found they had lost Marcus. Even so, they couldn't help the feeling he was somewhere close behind. Tom took another glance over his shoulder.

"If we can avoid him for at least one more hour he'll be gone." Dave looked at Tom with a questioning eye, as if, 'And how do you know this?'. Tom picked up on the question and added. "If you've got someone like Marcus on your tail it's good to know his schedule. His ship sails in two hours."

Dave looked over at Tom " It seems to me you should have paid this guy off along time ago."

"Actually I did, I sent him a letter with the cash in it years ago, I thought all was well and done. I only heard a month or so ago that he never got it and that he was gunning for me. That is when I started watching his schedule.

Dave nodded his head with understanding but added, "Better hope he didn't take leave." Slowing their pace a bit, they continued along down the same road they had begun their retreat on. They didn't know where they were going but it seemed a good enough direction. The only thing that bothered Dave was that there weren't any restaurants on this side of town and he was getting hungry. As they went along, they noticed the buildings getting smaller and fewer and they realized they had been chased virtually out of town. Glancing back from time to time, Tom would check to be sure Marcus wasn't back there. For some unknown reason though, the crowds on the road seem to be going the same direction as Dave and Tom and they weren't getting any smaller as you might expect. Tom seemed to be uneasy about this observation even though no one was paying any special interest to them, he felt that they knew something which he didn't.

"What have we done," Tom whispered, "walked into a funeral or something?"

"Well, if it's a funeral," Dave responded, "they're glad he's gone. Everyone's smiling."

"Yeah, I see," Tom said, turning cautiously around, "and smiling people with no particular reason bothers me."

Tom leaned closer to Dave. "I'll bet they heard that Marcus wants to pound on me and they've all been tagging along to watch me die."

"Could be," Dave answered. "You did attract a lot of attention back in town, I mean with him yelling at you and everything. I'm sure a good fight would be very entertaining," Dave glanced around and added, "that is, to most of the folks from around here."

"Do you think so?" Tom's voice sounding very insecure. He wasn't a coward, but no one would want to fight a bull unless he himself was a bull. However if it came down to it and he was face to face with the monster he wouldn't run either, and that in itself scared him. Dave knew he had Tom going a bit, and what were friends for if they couldn't razz each other once in awhile? Dave was also aware that Tom was a good fighter and showed little fear in a scrap, (no matter how he felt inside).

"Actually," Dave said, "I think the answers right around the corner, I believe the town picnic is supposed to be out here somewhere." Sure enough, it wasn't far before Dave and Tom found a large group of towns people gathered in one area. Coming over a small hill as they walked they saw, scattered in a field, several red-checkered tablecloths which dotted the designated picnic area. People seem to spread out over the field, as they walked about, choosing a spot to make it their own.

As they watched from the roadside, they saw several families setting up tables for a joint picnic brunch. It was quite a sight. The pasture to which the activity was planned went from the road above down a slight slope to the seashore. It was a brilliant green turf, a fit background to the many colored umbrellas which were opening over the picnic tablecloths set against them. Children could be heard laughing and playing all around as the familiar clang of horseshoes rang in the ears of those standing to near. A small wooden ice cream booth was in full swing, while a clown was busy giving away balloons to the kids. A small, almost talented band was playing some of the local favorites. The smell of pies, cakes and fresh bread floated on the air and mingled throughout the growing town gathering. A large wagon filled with watermelons sat near the road and a young boy passed them out to any family who wanted one. Tables were set in two rows and placed upon them was numerous main dishes which were brought by each family to share. Everyone, of course, had plenty to eat, even those who couldn't afford much, it wasn't a time to make money just to share life and each other, even if you didn't know each other well. Above all, everyone seemed to be having fun. Youngsters played in the grass of the field and along the thin shoreline without fear or care. Mindful parents would visit together, but then cast an occasional glance to confirm their children's whereabouts and to see that they were having fun.

Dave took in a deep breath and let it slowly out. "This is what I like " he exclaimed. "Here is a place a man could call home, and feel good about life around him. This is got to be what heaven is, a large portion of peace cut right out of this world, yet set alongside the shores of endless turmoil." Tom looked oddly at Dave; it was obvious he didn't share those feelings.

"You're sounding like a land lover."

"Oh, I love the sea, this is true." Dave answered defending himself. "But one day I won't be young or strong enough to fight the ocean. It will be a place like this . . . that I'll be looking for." "Looks like your looking for it now " Tom observed   "Perhaps I am." Dave responded. Dave looked around at the community gathering and then back out to sea. It was like he could see forever, but he knew the horizon was still the limit of his sight. He turned as if wanting to burn every scene into his memory. In fact he was so entranced that he didn't notice the approach of a young woman, whose path he would soon cross. Tom was also looking around but his thoughts had turned to food, and of course he was still vigilant for Marcus wherever he was now?

In it all, an oncoming collision was developing which none could have guessed or have been aware. It seemed as if fate had set the stage for a meeting, all the players were on the field, the actors were on their marks. No one was conscious of the other and each in a role that they where unable to avoid. It wasn't the sound of crashing metal or breaking boards, only the slight shrill of a young lady as a powerful, young man turned to point out a distant object to his friend and... Swack! The slap of skin against jaw as the backside of Dave's hand fell firmly onto a shocked face. Dave hadn't known how much strength could be behind such a simple gesture as pointing.

The moment lasted forever, and played out in slow motion. For in the moment Dave felt the pain of a finger being dislocated, to his surprise he felt the strength behind the blow which was not intended as an attack, and he felt the shock at not being able to pull his hand back fast enough. The events which followed went hard upon the action. . . blond hair whipped upward, a female figure left the ground and fell quickly back to earth, a tray of rolls went flying heavenward, which many have since wondered if they had ever come down. *Several* items of food, which the young lady had been carrying, took flight along with the rolls and scattered all around the scene in a blast pattern. When most things did return to the earth, gravity and the ground below took its' due upon them.

Dave spun around shaking his throbbing hand as he suddenly realized what had happened. The air became quiet, the whole community seemed to turn and watch. It was like everybody at once had seen what had happened. But how could they? They had all been doing other things, yet they acted like they had seen the whole thing.

Dave and Tom could feel the sudden change of emotions like a tidal pulse, growing on a once calm sea. Several men began to approach them and anger definitely replaced this joyful assembly. Dave felt a firm grip on his shoulder as a raspy voice said, "Hit a woman will you, you cowardly sea scum!" Dave found himself face to face with a large and weather worn man. His face was leathery and pitted, rough with gray stubble. His breath stank from rotten teeth and sour alcohol, but yet in some way the smell seemed appropriate for the way this man looked. His expression showed that he was enraged and in no mood to talk.

Everything again took on the air of slow motion. Dave helplessly watched as the man drew back his large calloused fist. Then with whipping speed, he drove it forward again. Dave could sense the power of the oncoming blow and braced himself. It was strange he thought, how you can think so many things in just a few short moments. Dave also knew if this blow didn't knock him senseless this guy was in for one rip-roaring fight. In the division of moments, and set between thoughts, Dave heard a silent whisper, or was it a yell smothered by confusion? He wasn't sure what it was, not in all the disorder, but it suddenly became clear. It was Tom saying, "Duck!!!"

Suddenly everything sped up and, instinctively trusting his friend, Dave let his weight fall. He felt the fist of his attacker brush his hair as he went down to his knees. Then in response, almost faster than a lightning flash, Tom, who was standing behind Dave, fired two punches to the man's face causing him to stumble backward and the fight was on. Stepping around Dave, Tom became the object of the attack. The rough looking gent swung, but missed on two or three attempts. Tom responded again with several counter punches, putting the would-be-assailant out cold. Turning to Dave who was now standing again, Tom quickly but calmly exclaimed, "Brace yourself, we're in for one whale of a fight and I think it's going to hurt!"

"What's new?" Dave exclaimed "The terrible two are in it again!" He stood back to back with Tom. Dave looked at the unconscious man on the ground and then back up at Tom, "You ran from Marcus?" Tom also gave a quick glance, "Well actually, this should tell you something about Marcus." The crowd looked like a wave moving to the shore as they slowly converged on Tom and Dave.

"Listen everybody!" Dave yelled, trying his best to outmatch the angry voices, "This was an accident!" A short stubby man walked up, he was definitely the town instigator. "Twas no accident, I saw them hit old Jim over there on purpose." "Well yeah," Tom explained

"*He* was on purpose! He was attacking my friend, and I'm sure he wouldn't have started the fight if Dave hadn't hit that girl over there." Tom pointed and everyone looked at the young lady still trying to gather herself up from the ground. Dave, who turned and stood shoulder to shoulder with Tom gave him a nudge, "I don't think your explanation helped much." "You hit a woman!" Someone shouted in the crowd as angry voices raised and the group moved closer. "Yes," Dave said "But no, that's not what I meant, that is, *she* was the accident!!! I hit her by accident." The mass of men took on the appearance of a mob, their collective anger growing as they continued their approach. Dave knew there was no way of getting out of the fight. It was going to be a bad one. He glanced over at Tom as he unbuttoned his jacket, Tom was looking to see if anyone was carrying a rope because this looked tantamount to a lynching party.

Dave smiled at Tom "You were always reliable for a good time, I see you haven't let me down." He said throwing his coat to the ground, he then doubled up his fists and stood ready for the first man. He knew he had done his best to explain, but no one was going to listen. Tom glanced back at Dave. "You're right Dave, nice quiet town you found here. I also think the odds are good that we are going to retire here. The only thing is, I think it's going to be sooner than we wanted." Tom began to laugh as the blows began to fall, however, the humor didn't offset the pain much.

The fight wasn't long and would have become more serious but for one forgotten victim, the young lady. Dazed as she was, she made her way to her feet still rubbing her bruised chin and injured pride. Her vision cleared enough to see the events which were now in motion. Stamping her foot she yelled at everyone. "That's enough!" *Oooooh!* She cringed as yelling made her head ache. "I'm ok." She said again but no one seemed to listen. "It was an accident!" She yelled, but the fight continued.

Actually Dave and Tom were doing rather well against the odds, but suddenly they got some unexpected help. In the midst of their battle they found the same young lady who Dave had accidentally hit fighting along side them. Her long dress was now torn and dirty, but she fiercely began punching and kicking everyone who wouldn't listen to her. She seemed to know everyone who she was fighting by name and she would loudly call those names out just as she kicked them in the shins or stomped their toes with her hard heels.

The crowd thinned with her charge and the only ones left fighting after she had jumped in were those who like to brawl anyway, but she quickly chased them off as well. In the end, all that were left was Tom, Dave, and the young lady, who was then joined by some of her friends. Her friends hadn't come to fight, but to help brush her off and pick up the food tray, which had been scattered where she had fallen. The fall, the fight, and the feet made all the food uneatable so mostly it was a clean up effort rather than a recovery. Fumbling for words, Dave knelt down near her and started to help pick things up.

"I'm sorry," he softly said. Dave deliberately didn't look over at her as he crawled along the ground recovering some of her things. She watched intently as he helped, not knowing what to think or say.

Dave found a basket, and began to fill it.

"You don't have to help," she responded. Of course, right now, what she preferred was that he would just leave. All she really wanted at this moment was to start forgetting the whole thing. Yet in another way this man seemed a pleasant person and she couldn't help herself but like him. She didn't really know why and she hoped it wasn't just because he looked nice. However, she wasn't going to let him know any of that, not after what just happened, that was for sure.

"I know you didn't mean it," She added. "But it's going to take a while for me to get over this." Reaching up she rubbed her jaw. "In more ways than one."

"I know what you mean," Dave responded, gently touching a

bruise on his face. "It will be a story worth telling the kids"

"You have children? "She asked.

"No." Dave responded quickly, " I mean one day, when I have children, this will be a good story for them to hear."

"I would rather forget it." She said, "It's been much to embarrassing."

"I'm sorry." Dave said again "Please," he added, "let me make it up to you somehow. I also feel it an obligation that you should know the name of your attacker. You know, the guy who ruined your day." He smiled and tried to catch her eyes as he spoke his gentle jest. " My name is Dave."

Suddenly she stopped rummaging the ground and sat motionless with a small pyramid of bread rolls in front of her. Looking at the green grass below, she raised her head slowly to gaze into Dave's eyes. His eyes where deep and dark brown, a window to a soul which showed honesty and trust, something she had never seen before in another. Words could never say what she now read within the silence of this glance, nor could mind remember what she now seemed to know. Her eyes were still swollen with tears and she fought the new ones with great effort.

"I'm Linda," she finally said. Her eyes were as green as the new blades of grass that sprout from the spring ground. Emeralds set afire by the sun above and the light which shines from her spirit. Somehow they seemed to burn deep into his heart, right into his soul.

Suddenly a wisp of wind caught her hair, it blew outward and waved softly in the breeze. For a moment Dave caught a glimpse of a sail on the water behind her, and it was filled with the tips of her flowing hair. He couldn't remember what that reminded him of, but it filled him with a strange feeling. Dave realized he had not noticed her before, not in the way he saw her now. Even in a dirt-soiled dress and with mud on her face he was caught up in her beauty. Truly, even with the pain which she obviously felt she was the accumulation of all beauty, beheld in one woman. A warm gentleness surrounded by a feminine strength which seemed to swell behind the windows of her eyes. A familiar tone, or a familiar something, began to pull at the cords in Dave's heart as something seemed to say, 'Eternity'.

An owl broke the silence, his hooting quieting the rush of memories flooding into Caps heart. Those longed for, but feared, derived from the emptiness composed by the many days a man is made to walk alone, those feeling of the heart, which find no hand to hold, no lips to kiss, no life to share. Those things stolen by the grave, leaving behind the empty hole that is left within the soul, yearning for the hope when two once again are made as one.

Caps hands shook, he could not hold the book with these feelings so strong and overwhelming. It fell from his hands, the corner digging into the sand as it landed quietly.

"Lindy." He said softly.

Chapter Three

A New Life Rising

Everything was true which had been read, and he began to cry. He couldn't hold back the emotions battering his chest like swell of the tide, it overflowed down his cheeks and off his chin.

How?, he thought. Even in his log book he had not captured his feelings so well, but here he was, here she was, on the pages of this strange book. Pausing for a bit he watched the book with a curious eye, it now lay upon the ground. He wasn't sure if he loved it or hated it; but he watched it, not always directly, but he always kept it in sight. Sometimes out of the corner of his eye, as he shuffled back and forth in confusion. He would look to see if it would move. Where did this thing come from, how could it be?

The gull, which had been his company during the day, swept suddenly near his fire. This almost startled Cap to death, but when he realized who it was he asked without any expectation of a reply, "Did you know about this?" The birds oddly deep, black eyes looked at him without responding and then quickly ate some of the crackers which had fallen to the sand with the book.

Cap looked around at the limits of the firelight. The old man never came back this way, but it seemed he had to eventually and Cap didn't want him barging in 'till he understood more about this book. He opened the pages and began to read, but he felt the sudden fatigue of the evening upon his body and his strength wain.

How could I feel so tired, he thought, *especially after being so upset by this book?. I have to read more.* But as he read his eyes drifted into darkness where thoughts become reality in dream. He was aboard ship, he remembered the occasion. The sky was gray and the waves were high, the wind was a roar in the ears and the cold spray stung the skin as it pelleted the face. Nature seemed angry or insane as it shook the mighty ship. Even though the torrent pushed at the massive steel body of the vessel it continued on slicing at the waves and lunging forward in the storm. It was late in the day just before evening and the dark skies brought the veil of night quickly upon the deep. Though some light remained, the lightning was now sharper within the heavens. Cap looked out upon the waters over the course they were now on. He thought he saw something at the limits of his sight but he was not sure. Suddenly it was there again. It was in the flash of the lightning, on the crest of a wave, it suddenly struck terror in his heart as he saw a man riding upon the waters like a madman upon a wild horse, laughing as he fought the top breakers in the wind.

His laugh was not of joy but venom and his glare was hatred stitched within the form of a smile. Even at a distance, with only a glimpse of this momentary aberration, Cap could see this being had contempt in his eye as if it wanted their total destruction. Suddenly the sight was gone and Cap wasn't even sure if he had seen it. As he looked about the bridge he noticed that no one else seemed to have seen it.

The spell was suddenly broken as Cap was awaken by the sounds of approaching feet. Closing the book he once again sat upon it. Caps eyes strained to see beyond the firelight, but he couldn't see anyone moving about. Stepping into the light, the old man from before walked up leaning on the shoulders of a much younger woman.

"Hey Cap," he shouted sounding a little drunk. "How about we go into town and bowl a few games? I'll pay for it. I just need some competition and you seem like a guy who knows his way around a bowling alley. Besides Delilah here can't bowl at all." Cap looked over at the old man, he seemed a little younger than he had before but it was still the same man.

"The last time you left here you were calling me a thief and now you want to be buddies?" The old guy sat down on a rock.

"I don't ever hold a grudge," he said, "it steals away too much fun. Besides, I trust you, if you say you don't have my book I figure you must be telling the truth. You are telling the truth aren't you?"

"Well," Cap answered, "I don't know why you figure you can trust me, it's not like you have read a book about my life and know me, right?" Cap looked him strait in the eye, but the old guys expressions didn't flinch. He continued, "But I'll let you know if I find anything, that is anything, I think is yours. But no thanks, I'll skip the game tonight. I just want to sit alone and think."

The old man's face flushed, "You're not very friendly are you? I haven't done anything to you, so I don't understand why you act this way to me. I have been friendly ever since I met you, I only lost my temper for a moment, and I think you can understand my reasons. I lost a very valuable piece of property tonight."

"I don't understand anything," Cap answered, " But I am hoping to before this night is over, so please leave, and let me alone."

"Well ok!" the old man snorted, and he got up and walked quickly away with his companion. From the dark he yelled back "But I'll be watching you, my limited friend!" Cap watched and listened to make sure they were gone, he wasn't sure were they went or how they even got around, but he did finally seem alone.

"I don't know where I am going with all this," Cap exclaimed, " I came here to think, and all I have had are distractions and confusion. Why this book, why the torture of memories long passed into history? Why can't I find peace out here so I can think, I mean, this place is *suppose* to be out and away from everyone?

Cap fell onto his knees. *I was told once to pray, I was told that someone would hear me and answer my prayer. But I don't know what to ask, I'm not sure why I should care about anything except my next meal, and where I will sleep. I mean, I'm not a bum, I have money, but what is money, what is anything when we get old, and where life . . . Time. . , Like a flame has consumed everything we hold dear? And we are then left alone . . . alive . . . but alone.*

The book which had been left barely perched on the log where Cap had been sitting, slipped off and hit him in the foot. He turned and picked it up, dusting off the sand and grit as he did. And, once again, began to read.

Yesterday sits behind me,

tomorrow comes so fast,

but I remember all the times,

as they were, within my past.

I recall the joyful days,

when with you, I once did walk,

We shared our special feelings,

while together we would talk.

I recall your warm embrace

It sometimes seems so clear,

When I can see your smiling face

Those memories I keep near.

And all that's good and happy,

brings you close in many ways,

for I see a clear tomorrow,

when I think of yesterdays.

      Dave sat along the shore and watched the tide make a slow withdrawal from the inner most shores of the bay. Climbing up on a Madrona tree, he let one leg dangle as he watched a dog running in and out of the water down the beach from where he was. Every once in a while a young boy would appear. He would run hard towards the water's edge and throw a stick in the bay and his dog would charge in after it. A muffled bark and a child's voice seem to mix with the sounds of the morning perfectly.

Dave imagined how many times he had passed by just off this very shore while shipping cargo for the lines. In all those times before now he had not even realized that this pleasant community existed and it was just a short distance away from the large ship mooring. He had never considered as he had maneuvered his mighty vessel just beyond the breakers that on shore, just a mile or so across water and land, people played out their lives in Turnbridge. Work, fun, life and death, each person pursuing their dreams in their own way. Not just a few of them, but a whole community which he had never met and in Dave's own positive way he thought, a people he could call friends if he could only get to know them.

Of course the fight the other day wasn't a good start, but Dave felt that everyone had to know by now that this whole event was a big misunderstanding. Dave knew he would never hit a woman, his father had raised him better than that. That first loud mouth individual which Tom had fought, well, he deserved it, and anyone else, who got into the ruckus after it started.

Dave's mind wandered a moment, but he found it difficult trying to rethink things. He had seen many small communities, but nothing had ever taken him like Turnbridge. Of course the place was growing on him each time he visited, but suddenly for some reason it meant more then ever did before. But was it really the town itself or something else? Ever since he met her, the gal he knocked down, he couldn't get her face out of his mind.

Dave looked back at the town. Turnbridge was indeed a breathtaking sight. Looking at it from the water or the beach it had an almost artistic design, something somebody with talent would love to paint. The town set against wooded hills which gently rolled from mounds into mountain peaks behind it. Hills rising in a poetic fashion within and surrounding the buildings and homes scattered upon the communal scene, accented by the small white tower of the local church. It was not a large town compared to most, having only a few paved roads, a few stores, other than those found on the waterfront. The neighborhood homes were mostly all two-story buildings, each being much alike, sat side by side on spacious lots with large friendly porches and great looming trees out front.

Dave remembered the walk he took after the sun had set last night. Deliberately he roamed up and down different roads, and for no other reason than he hadn't gone that way before or perhaps in hope a certain person might spot him and wish to talk. He would walk a zig-zagging course, here and then there, in no real organized fashion. His journey took him through neighborhoods which normally lay hidden from those who only travel the main roads. Perhaps to see something new or perchance, as he thought again, to see *her* one more time even if it was that he found her by accident.

In the silence of the evening the roads themselves seemed abandoned against the crisp night air. But many homes were lit within, as the residences prepared for their evening sleep. All was quiet and Dave could hear the crackle of the gravel under each step he took. Where the road was paved the moist blacken streets glimmered against the escaping light from the windows, or the rare lamp which lit the street. In the night a lone dog would call across the many blocks while another in the distance would answer. Dave saw the dim yellow lights, which gently lit the porches against the dark. They seem to cast a friendly glow on the shrubbery and trees, announcing that a family lives within. His memories stirred and he tried to place a finger on his feelings. He knew in a way he was looking for something, but he wasn't sure what it was yet.

Could it be the people, he thought, *who seem to live together like a larger part of each other's family?* Or was it in himself? Did he have an inner drive to find something more out of life, something with real meaning, something lasting and something secure... he wasn't yet sure, but this place felt good.

He knew one thing had changed in himself after seeing the small town of Turnbridge. The larger port cities which he had come to know in his travels would now all seem much to much alike. But that was last night when he wandered and wondered. This day, so far, had brought few answers to his feelings. Pulling out his pipe, Dave gently filled it. Bringing it to his lips he struck a match, but noticed over the flame a feminine figure walking his way on the beach. He shook out the match and placed the pipe back into his pocket. Dave couldn't yet make out the face but it appeared to be the same young lady he had knocked down at the picnic. Reaching up he rubbed his bruised chin, he remembered her well. As she drew near he saw the discoloration on her face and knew it had to be the same girl.

"Linda," he thought aloud.

"Yes," she answered, as if to say, 'Yes it is me', in response to someone you would know.

Her reply took Dave by surprise, because, number one; he didn't realize he was thinking out loud, and, number two, he wondered how she could have heard him so far away. As she approached he watched, and by the inquisition on her face, he realized, she couldn't tell who he was. Of course, Dave realized he was right and felt a bit disappointed, up and until she finally walked up to him and said, "Oh it's you."

At least it wasn't a cry for help. Dave smiled, "Well, you caught me off guard when you answered me, I was just remembering your name and inadvertently said it aloud. It's incredible that you heard me so far away."

"You remember my name," Linda smiled.

Dave rubbed his chin again, "Believe me... it will be hard to forget."

Linda also rubbed her chin, "I know what you mean... DAVE!" she said loudly with a laugh.   They both laughed, while they reminisced the Battle of the Bruised Chin, as so they dubbed it.

Dave climbed down from the tree and they talked while walking along the shore. They spent time getting to know one another, a luxury they hadn't had in the aftermath of the fight at the picnic. Linda was fascinated with his adventures at sea and Dave learned a lot about this young girl, one who spent her life growing up along the rocky shores of Turnbridge. She seemed to know everything about boating and fishing, which made their conversation with one another fun and exciting. And Dave seemed a master of the deep sea; Linda could never hear enough. They found that they had many things in common likes and dislikes. But more importantly, Dave and Linda found that they both loved life. They loved the world on which they lived, with all its' variety, finding value in every experience, both in good times as well as in bad. They also found that they shared the same habits, in keeping their memories in journals, writing them down, and holding them within the treasure of their minds. Linda had picked up her habit from her father who had also been a seamen aboard a large ocean going vessel. They enjoyed a similar compassion for people, as Linda talked of her many hours at the senior citizens' home. She also would recount to Dave the fun she had, and the training she would gain, from helping Turnbridge's one and only town doctor. Being there when someone needed close watching, especially if care was needed over an extended period of time, was important to her.

    Dave, of course, had been the handy man in his youth, the one who people always called on when something needed fixing. He had become known as dependable, which contributed to his rapid climb to Captain, when he went to work at sea.

    During their walk, Dave learned about the history of Turnbridge, and the surrounding area. He found that Linda knew everyone who now lived or ever lived there. She also had an uncanny ability for recall. During their conversation, Dave learned that several of the men which he had fought at the picnic were actually the preachers' sons and that in the past it was not unusual for this group, along with their friends, to get into trouble. One of the preacher's boys', Zac, had been smitten with Linda for along time. She felt he was only fighting to impress her, which of course it didn't. For Linda, Zac was far too rude to anyone he met and everyone he knew, to ever impress her. He seemed to think that being loud and forceful was a sign of strength, and perhaps that's the way it seemed to some, but to most he was just a bully. At church and alongside his father he was a saint, but at school and at social gatherings he and his friends were the instigators of trouble.

Dave realized from their conversation, that it was going to be difficult for a stranger to find welcome here. Being a friend and moving in as a resident were two different matters to them. It hadn't always been that way, but feelings were made worse when the new shipyards were purposed, most people in Turnbridge had opposed the idea. They knew that such a development would change their lives forever. And, in the end, it would ruin the home they knew, the home their fathers knew. Ultimately, Turnbridge would be swept away by the tide of growth. Most likely by those who had just moved in and had only lived here a few short years.

The port and dry docks were not actually within the city limits, so the town of Turnbridge had to contend with the desires of the whole county. And since the port affected the outlying towns and communities favorably and they of course didn't have to live close to it, they didn't mind having the changes. So the citizens of Turnbridge failed in their opposition. Of course Dave knew, things were going to happen just that way, but he didn't realize what it really meant till now. Wayne Roberts, Dave's boss and friend, was anxious about the changes. For him, he could load and launch his ships from a central point. An improved rail tie was put in because of the location and it would be cheaper when moving some goods to certain points of the country. Wayne had grown up in New York and this town was a pleasant change, even if it did grow. Yes, progress was good for many, and that, in itself wasn't bad. In the end though, the changes would leave only the name Turnbridge where a community once thrived . . . and many had called home.

When the home is very happy
 a pleasant place to be,
 and friends they come to visit
 our joy they often see.

When home is plain and simple

that sometimes is the best,

far from a troubled world

it's there I find my rest.

When home is all my neighbors

and friends I've come to know,

those to whom I have shared my life,

we've watched each other grow.

Then home is my foundation

for then I'm not alone

where ever I might go in life

Where ever I might roam.

For home is all the people

I've come to know from birth,

it is our common place in life,

My corner of the Earth.

      "That was very special," Linda said looking up at Dave. "And I've really enjoyed our walk . . . Will I see you again?"   Dave liked that question, and he was quickly growing attached to this girl.

"You bet!" He answered. "Turnbridge is going to be a regular stop for me from now on. Of course my ship is leaving tomorrow but when I get back maybe we can go out for dinner or something."

"I would like that." Linda answered, as she turned to walk away. "I'll watch for your ship then." Linda gave a quick glance at the sky and immediately grabbed Dave's wrist without warning. Dave was a bit surprised but he didn't mind. With a twist, she flipped his wrist over and looked at the hands on his watch. "Looks like I'm going to be late." She responded to his curious look. "We have had such a good talk, I haven't been watching the time. My mother fixes dinner around this time every day and she has about six hungry fishermen to feed."

"Ok then," Dave responded. "It's a date, when I get back into port I'll look you up."

Linda walked away, and just before disappearing over a bank she turned and said, "Sounds good to me, I'll see you then." Dave stood alone along the beach where they had walked. Leaning once again against the Madrona tree he rehearsed their walk over in his mind. It was all a dream now, and the beach around him seemed so very empty without her there.

Suddenly a cold thought shot up his spine, in all their

conversation he didn't get her last name, he also didn't get her phone number or address. He wanted to avoid appearing to forward, and had thought the topic would eventually come up by itself. Dave also realized he didn't tell her the name of his ship or the date when he would be back. Quickly he ran to the point he last saw her; reaching the sandy bank he looked out into the empty field. Dave wondered how she could have disappeared so quickly.

"How stupid," he thought, criticizing himself. "I could have walked her home." Looking down into the soft mud, he saw the impression of a bicycle tire and realized she was now long gone. Dave turned and walked down the beach for the long walk back towards the docks. He replayed in his mind the satisfying conversation he had just had with Linda once more. But before he got far, suddenly a group of young men came rushing out of the bushes and trees lining the beach. It was Zac and his friends, their impact carrying themselves and Dave stumbling out into the water. Everyone fell forward and almost on top of each other. Zac had Dave by the coat in a tight grip and yelled at everyone.

"Get back, he is mine" The group stood in the hip deep water as Zac began to scream at Dave. "*I* saw you talking with Linda. Who do you think you are coming into town and causing trouble? You think you can run off with one of our local girls do ya? I see you don't have your friend with you, so what are you going to do now, sailor man?"

Dave didn't wait for another word; he knew that nothing of what was being said was going to mean anything anyway. Since Zac kept Dave from getting his footing, Dave wrapped his legs around Zac's waist and pulled his face into Dave's forehead, giving him a painful head butt. Zac let go and fell back, grabbing his nose which started to bleed profusely. Dave stood up and grabbed Zac by the collar, he began pushing him underwater and pulling him out as fast as he could. Several times he slammed his face into the water and then out again, repeating it over and over again. The group of attackers, Zac's friends, just stood there shocked, it had happened so fast.

"Now" Dave said, "Perhaps your ears are clean enough to hear me, as I will say this only once. I will go where I please and see whom I please, we can be friends, or we can be enemies . . . I give you that choice. If I ever act inappropriately to her, by all means beat my brains out. But quit acting like a bunch of school boy's and grow up." Dave let go of him and walked through the small band of friends and back to shore. Straightening his hat and coat, he gave them a quick glance, and then continued on his way. Looking back he saw Zac and his friends walking the other direction and away from him.

So, Dave thought, *this will probably make it harder to get Linda's phone number. But not to worry,* Dave reassured himself, *she seems to know everyone in town, so everyone must know her*.

What Dave didn't realize was that most people in Turnbridge had either heard about or seen his fight with the preacher sons at the picnic, and they knew about "that Dave guy!" Of course none of the boys would mentioned this new incident at the beach, but that didn't matter.

It was also true that the popular version of the picnic was, that the brothers had defended Linda against some unknown, hardened assailants. Rouge, drunken sailors who started a vicious fight in town which spilled out onto the community picnic. Marcus's description fed the fantasy and he wasn't even at the picnic. Of course, the true story hadn't made its' rounds yet and was moving a bit slower than the other. Besides, the rumor was much more exciting to retell. In consequence, Dave couldn't get the time of day, from anyone.

Chapter Four

A difficult call to make

The cold winds of Bear Lake came drifting across the waters. Like a slap in the face, Cap was wakened to the here and now once more. He rubbed his eyes a bit. He had been reading so intently he hadn't blinked enough to keep them moist and clear.

Suddenly headlights appeared behind him, it was a game warden's rig. Cap looked over at his pole and his line was in the water with a float bobbing on the lakes small rippling wakes.

"Hi down there," a voice called

"Hello." Cap answered. A man came into view of Caps lamp and fire; he was a game officer, wearing a uniform and a badge.

"What's up?" Cap asked.

"Well" The warden said, "I have a report of someone fishing down here, and as I can see you have a line in the water..."

Cap smiled, "I had pulled it out of the lake a while ago and I'm not sure how it got in there by itself"

"Well your not suppose to be fishing here at night at all," the warden remarked.

"I know " Cap said,"But I don't have a hook on my line, only a bobber. Let me show you." Cap went to retrieve his pole and added, "I just like to sit and think, a line in the water has always been helpful to me." Cap reeled his line in and when the bobber came into his hand, dangling in the light of the Wardens flashlight was a baited hook. "I don't know how that got there," Cap exclaimed. " I promise you that it wasn't there before." The warden didn't say a word, he just pulled his ticket book from his pocket and issued Cap a citation.

"I'll let you keep your pole, even though I can impound it. It looks like a keepsake, and I'll let things slide that far. But keep it out of the water or things will be much worse next time."

"Thank you" Cap said, "But I want you to know, even though it doesn't mean much, I never put that hook on that line tonight. I don't know where it came from."

"Fine!" the officer said, suddenly angry, "You know, there's one thing I really hate and that is liars. I mean . . . I really get angry when I give someone a break and they think they can talk to me like I'm stupid or something. Just don't forget what I have told you old man, and if you are here tomorrow, we will be talking about vagrancy, get it!"

Cap sat down near the book, he watched as the Warden turned on his heel and walked away towards his vehicle. Suddenly, before he was out of sight and still in the light of the fire, a seagull swooped down and defecated with volume and force, all over the officers uniform.

"Dang you bird!" He yelled, "You must have been saving this up for a month. Look at what you have done! The officer ducked into his truck and came out with a shotgun. He fired it once in the air but missed. The bird swooped back and let him have another load of sticky white bird poop. The game officer ranted and raved as he climbed back into his vehicle and continued on yelling until he could no longer be heard over the engine. He quickly backed up and drove off, disappearing into the dark. Cap tired hard not to laugh at the guy.

Landing softly near Cap, the bird began to poke around for more food and Cap threw him a whole cracker. "There is more where that came from," Cap said to the bird, "as much as you want." Stepping from the shadows, the strange old man came walking into the light.

Cap looked over at him "And I to suppose it was you who set me up with the warden?"

The old man smiled, "Not me, my girl friend did it. She has an odd sense of humor, wouldn't you say? Hey, I can fix that ticket for you if you want me too, I have friends working for Fish and Game."

"No thanks," Cap responded, "I'll take care of it."

"Fine then," the old guy snapped, "but I will take my book back, as I can clearly see that you have it." Suddenly Cap remembered, that in all the excitement, he had left the book lying out in view. Quicker then a flash, the old guy dove for the book, his speed and agility was greater then you would have guessed for a man of his apparent age.

Cap yelled, "You can't have it, and I don't care how much you *say* it belongs to you." Even though Cap was closer to the book the old guy moved swiftly and had one side of the cover in his hands, while Cap had the other. A tug of war ensued, and the old guy began to yell.

"Yes I know about your life, and yes I have read this book. Why oh why would you want it back? It's just a reminder on how you *failed* at life, how you failed those you once loved. *You* let a man die, he would have lived had you been more competent. Your daughter would have survived had *you* been there to get your wife to the hospital on time. Your wife, the woman you say you love *so* much, and pine over so often, how many lonely hours did she spend, while *you* had *your* fun running around the world on your boat? Man oh man, why would you want this book? Why would you want to remember your failures? And then there's your selfishness, which you so conveniently only realized after everyone you loved died. One at a time! You think you are looking for God, well have you ever realized that God might have left you here? Because you have already blown it? You failed! Look at yourself, you're old, and you don't even know who He is. In fact, Sunday school children know more about God than you do, and you think you have time to learn? You think somehow in your feeble old mind, that a sudden dip in the water and a few prayers are going to wipe away a lifetime of mistakes? People are dead! *They* died without your so called love and friendship. Don't you think you might be responsible for just a few of those blunders you call life? Why on earth would you want this book? Let go of it, it is mine."

The old mans words cut deep into Cap's soul, he had punished himself with some of those very thoughts. But like in the storm which brewed it's deadly breath on the high seas, he knew he had to hold onto something, even if it was only a little faith in what he had learned about God, as a F*ather*, and His son the Savior. He also held onto the hope that he had some worth in himself as a man. Instead of defeat, Cap was filled with anger, "This book is *MY* life," he shouted, "The question is not why I would want it, the question is why do *you* want it?"

Suddenly the old man, in his haste and struggle, stepped on the seagull, which had been fighting to stay out of their way. With a loud squawk and a sharp pecking beak to the leg, the bird took as much of a bite that he could get. The bird then hopped into the air and began pecking wildly at the mans face. The old assailant let go of the book with a scream and ran off down the shoreline yelling threats back at Cap. For a great distance Cap could hear the old mans voice, but finally the lake was quiet once more.

Cap stood there looking at the bird with the book still in his white knuckled grasp. " I hope he hasn't gone to get a gun, because I think he would use it on the both of us." After catching his breath, Cap was more curious then ever of what was in the book. So he opened it and read on, keeping a watchful eye at the dark. The words slowly engulfed his attention and he found that he was no longer worried about anything else, only the contents of each page.

Dave powered the small launch towards the large battle ship. It lay quiet in the water not far out of Turnbridge waiting patiently for Dave's boat. Just before Dave's ship left port, he had picked up a few passengers who had business with the Navy. Dave had agreed to their request to transport them out to the naval vessel when they set out to sea. The battleship was underway to some uncertain and unknown destination. And for whatever reason it didn't have the time in its schedule to stop or wait very long. Since Dave's ship would naturally intersect their course while on his normal run, he parted port, and took the personnel on board as a favor to the Navy.

On his original approach, he had maneuvered his ship as close as was allowed to the large Navy vessel, and then used the launch for the remaining distance. Dave would normally have members of his crew take someone out on a launch, but he felt like doing it himself today, along with a couple of deck hands. Besides he liked looking at Navy ships, and this was a chance to see one up close.

As they made the distance between the two vessels Dave wondered about the people he was taxing over, he realized he didn't know anything about them, but he had learned early in his career not to ask. Pulling along side the great ship, Dave's crewmen on the bow received the forward line. As it was tossed aboard it was fastened promptly with a few quick turns around the horn. The crewman on the stern was still awaiting his line when suddenly, and for some unknown reason, the large gray ship backed down on her engines. The bowline of the small boat became taunt and impossible to free, and even with the line turned on the bit for a quick release, it was so tight it wouldn't come loose. Dave thought quickly as he still had control of the vessel, but the danger wasn't fully realized at first. The tension on the forward line became so great that the small boat was suddenly thrown out like a toy at the end of a whip. Against the weight and pull of the two vessels, the man on the bow fought helplessly to free the line, and today for some reason he didn't have his knife. No matter what he did, he couldn't release the simple turns that connected the ship to the boat. Back again toward the hull the small boat flung. The tremendous weight and size of the Naval vessel, along with the rounded curvature of its hull, began to drag the small boat down and under.

Dave stood at the coxswain's wheel, he saw the crewman on the bow still fighting to release the line, but to no avail. He knew he had to act fast, and he only had a moment to do it. The two hulls of the vessels would collide and the smaller one would loose. Either seams would break, or steel would rupture, or the bow would be dragged low enough into the water to let the flood pour into the smaller boat. Of course *this* was the boat that Dave was on, and he couldn't have that. He thought in that instant, *If I am going to sink anytime in my life, it is going to be for far more than a ferry boat ride.*

With a quick jerk on the throttles, he popped the engines forward and then back to astern. Though there wasn't any room to maneuver, and only a few inches between the bows tip and the massive war ships hull, he had to try all the tricks he knew. Dave used all the space available, without even tapping the other vessel. The brief forward motion gave the crewman just enough slack to release the line. With a smack, it fell into the water and with another quick motion of the hand Dave throttled the engine to astern and away from the ship. He was angry, there was no reason for this near disaster. Had the ship just laid quiet in the water they would have tied up, transported their passengers aboard, and then they would have been off. *That would have been just great*, he thought to himself, *I finally meet the neatest girl in the world and I get drowned just a few days later.*

    As the situation now stood, Dave had the Navy vessel lower a net over the side to get their people. With a moving pass along side he had his passengers grab on to the net and climb up to the main deck without the luxury of his boat beneath them. They didn't like it, but he thought that's just too bad. Later Dave billed the Navy for the passengers and the transport. Of course he never got paid, but he felt better by doing so.

    Once back aboard his own ship Dave felt a lot better. Getting back to the bridge, he radioed the Navy ship and talked things out with its' captain. *Not a good start.* he thought as he set back into his chair, *not at all*. Dave realized this was just the beginning of the cruise and his only hope was that the rest of it would be uneventful. These feelings were a surprise to Dave and as he searched his thoughts he realized he had never felt this way before. *Strange, I feel so impatient to get this run over, and that's not like me.*

Cap realized the next page of the book was blank, as if skipping routine moments in his life, but as he looked, it began again in a place almost forgotten:

The ships bow arose with the gentle rolling swell which passed beneath her. A crisp wind blew over the decks, catching an occasional wisp of ocean water and then throwing it up on the breeze. The sky was a broken blue, with patches of solid white and gray clouds and the water reflected the yellow glow of the noonday sun. True clean air and brine filled the nostrils of all who worked on deck, and in their eyes they beheld the horizon where it touched the sky in the distant sea. Dave stood on the port fly deck of the bridge, silently he watched. He loved the sea, and he loved the feelings it gave him. The sounds of the water against the hull, the call of the seagull, or the clang of the buoy bell as it tipped with the wake of a passing vessel or danced with the rising tide, all were warm and familiar in his mind.

Off the stern of Dave's ship flew the albatross, champions of the air and sea. Though they seemed like a drunken man when trying to walk on the ships decks, in the air they would rise and fall with no apparent effort. On guard, they kept a constant vigil for any scrap of food which might get thrown over the sides. But it wasn't just birds, waves, and dolphins, Dave saw the world in a way which most men or women ever do. He found people, at least for the most part, were the same everywhere. Even with customs and beliefs that were different, the common individual was usually a good person. He figured, just watch the kids at play, they are the same all over the world, they only become nuts when they become adults. Even so, everywhere Dave went he had friends that would greet him. And he tried keeping his mind on those very thoughts.

I've just got to think of my current journey or job. He thought to himself, *That will get me through, that is what will make time go by faster.* Yet even with all his efforts, his thoughts would still tug at him, returning again and again, till he was only thinking of "her". His lips gently whispered, "Linda, my lady Linda, my Linda lady, my lady Lindy," He found himself humming to no real tune.

The ship only a few days out of Turnbridge (or in other words, it had been only a few days since they had left.) was on course as they headed for their first stop, a port three hundred miles south of Turnbridge. Dave had thought once out at sea he could put Linda out of his mind, but he was wrong. *Got to get to know her better.* Dave thought, while checking his compass. *Baa, five degrees off course.* He wondered how long he had been daydreaming. Five degrees can mean several miles out of their way if any distance had been traveled on the wrong bearing for long. Quickly Dave corrected his discrepancy and adjusted the heading. Turning to his first mate, he gestured for someone else to take the wheel.

"I can't seem to think," he said as he started for the door.

The First Officer gave a half smile, "Are you ok?" He asked, but silently laughed to himself, he knew what was wrong, LOVE. But he didn't dare say so.

"Yes," Dave responded, "I just have to make a phone call."

The communications room was next to the bridge, and all Dave had to do was to step from one room to the other. The door was often shut because of the beeps and pops that usually emanated from within. Besides, Sparks, whose duties included communications, seem to like the seclusion and often spent his free time powering up his radios.

"Get me a shore land line near Turnbridge, Sparks," Dave said, bursting into the small room. During his visit to Turnbridge he had seen several Ham radio antennas around town so he knew they were there, and since they were a sea going community he knew one or more of them had to have a phone connection. Sparks looked up at Dave from his oversized chair, at least it appeared oversized. Sparks was a thin man and the chair seemed much larger against his lean stature. Some felt he was a bit odd in his ways, always keeping to himself. Though he was a crewman like the others and worked the deck, he seemed to live in his own world, no matter where he was. When at port Sparks would spend his free time taking photos of miniature plants, the smaller, the better. Actually he was quite good at what he did, but to what end no one knew. Even with his oddity, or perhaps because of it, Sparks was a perceptive man. However, today, he didn't have to be a mind reader to tell that something was bugging the Captain.

Sitting up he managed to get a shore station on the radio, it was near Turnbridge and he was glad when he found that the operator had a phone patch and could put a call through on the regular lines.

Looking back up at Dave, the glance was obvious, "What's the number?"

"Oh," Dave thought scratching his head. "I don't know. Let's start with anyone you can get in Turnbridge. It's a small community, and someone's bound to know Linda's number."

"Ok." Sparks said, shaking his head. Silently he thought, *I can't believe this.*

Dave looked down over Sparks's right shoulder as he watched him tune in the radio. Though he never expected formal Captain crewmen type protocol, he thought Sparks was a little to free with his, 'this is stupid,' attitude.

Hours passed, Sparks tried several different numbers; the radio operator on shore would dial and then flip a switch connecting the mike with the phone. But no luck, those who they contacted, who figured out who the Linda was, didn't have the number or didn't want to give it out. The party on the other line did occasionally have another number for Dave to try, one whom they thought "might have that information he needed." So they would try it and find another person who didn't know or wouldn't give out her information.

Finally after several phone calls, they tried talking with the local operator. It was a lady operator whose name was Margaret; she linked them with the only Linda she knew. Linda Martin, an 84 year old retired school teacher and she did live in Turnbridge. Dave figured later that the operator had done this on purpose.

Mrs. Martin seemed pleasant, but she wasn't the Linda Dave was after. For hours she talked, well at least it felt like hours, and Dave couldn't find any way to get her to say goodbye. It wasn't that he didn't like the conversation, but he had to get a hold of his Linda before they lost the connection. Finally he just came out and told her that he was sorry that he had disturbed her, but he had to go. Somehow, this led into several more hours of conversation. During the course of the call, Dave heard the entire history of Turnbridge and was quickly getting to know each individual by description, most of whom though, had already passed away years ago. She continued saying,

"You didn't disturb me, so don't worry about that young man." Suddenly to everyone's surprise and selfish pleasure, the signal was disrupted and the call was cut. Dave was sure the land radio operator must have hung up on her.

Sparks reestablished the connection and tried one of the other numbers they had been given. "I've got one Captain," Sparks said. "This one knows your Linda."

"Quick!" Dave said, "give her to me!"

"Yes." A young female voice answered, "we are best friends, and she has talked about you a lot. I think she wants to see you again." This was Sherry Mikles, she was a few years younger then Linda but they had become best of friends through their years at school.

"Well, that's why I called," Dave replied. "I also want to see her. Do you have her number? I want to call her and tell her that I will back in Turnbridge on August third."

"I have it," the young lady answered. But her tone of voice was like, should I, or I'm not sure I can give it to you.

"I'm not supposed to give it out, " she finally said. "If you give me your number, I will have her call you."

Dave's voice raised, he was frustrated. "I DON'T HAVE A!" he suddenly realized how loud his voice was in the phone. The silent save was the radio operator on shore, who pulled the mike back from the phone, as Dave's voice grew louder. Dave never knew if Sherry had heard his raised voice, but he always wondered what she thought of him because of it. Recomposing, "I'm out at sea, she can't call me, I have to call her."

"Oh," Sherry replied "That does make it difficult." She paused for a moment. "Still, I promised I wouldn't give it out." Dave felt the peaks of frustration once again. He wasn't a violent man, and not prone to anger, but this whole situation was crazy. What does he have to do to get a simple phone number. This girl has it, and right now she stands between him and his Linda.

"I think it is really commendable that you want to keep your promise Sherry, but even *you* said, Linda wants to see me again."

"Yes, " she answered. "But what if you're some kind of nut or something, then it would be all my fault."

Dave scanned his mind for any kind of psychology or trick he could use.

"Perhaps," Dave answered. "But don't you think it is more like Linda hopes, that we might become boyfriend and girlfriend. I'm sure she told you about our walk on the beach and the poems we shared. Well? " He paused, then continued. "You might be the one who actually brings us together, perhaps even in marriage. A ceremony at sea with the ship dipping in the waves, Linda in her white flowing gown and her hair set against the breeze, and I in my uniform standing in bristle fashion along her side. The town's people gathered along the decks and flowers spread along the rails. Leading to the very altar where we exchange our vows. Linda, wife of a sea Captain, living in a large white house, like a castle, standing high above the bay. Windows which open out to an emerald green deep, and a brass scope, set to watch for my returning voyage." Dave heard a sigh over the radio, at first he wasn't sure whether she was crying or not.   "Oh Dave," Sherry answered. "That is so romantic, if she doesn't marry you, I will! Her number is Green Field 8-157. Tell Linda I want to be the bride's maid of honor."

"I will " Dave responded. "However, between you and me, lets give her a chance to get to know me better, at least before we tell her that we have the wedding planned, ok?"

"Sure," Sherry answered. "But remember, if it doesn't work out..."

"Yes," Dave finished. "You've got first dibs."

"Finally," Sparks said, but as he looked up at his Captain his words trailed off. This was the first glance of disapproval he had ever seen in Dave's eye, and he wasn't going to push it. Turning back to his radio he called up the shore station again. However, when they dialed the number all they got was a busy signal. For hours they tried but it always rang busy.

"The radio operator is getting ready to shut down Captain," Sparks advised him. "The next closest one is long distance and I don't think he will put it through for us." Dave felt that old irritation, which never really went away in the first place. There was a moment of relief when he got Linda's number, but now he couldn't get through. He wasn't angry with Sparks. He had been more than helpful, it was just one of those things. Dave just stood there and didn't say anything.

Sparks could see the irritation in his face and silently turned back to the radio, "Lets see if we can get him to try one more time." Suddenly through the light static of the line they could hear a phone ringing. "Hello," a feminine voice answered. It was Lindy, *I mean Linda*, Dave thought. "Hi, it's me, Dave," he clumsily said. "I'm out at sea and "

Linda interrupted, "I know, before you called I was on the phone to the old school teacher Mrs. Martin; we had a great talk. She said you sounded like a delightful young man but thought it odd that you would hang up on her."

"Linda Martin," Dave exclaimed aloud, and then thought, *she knew I was trying to call, why didn't she stay off the line?! Of course, why should I ask?*

"She told me she didn't know you," Dave replied.

"I know, she told me she said that, she misunderstood who you were looking for. Mrs. Martin said you sounded so mature, she thought you had to be looking for someone much older." Dave explained to Linda about how he had been cut off from Mrs. Martin by the shore station, and that he didn't hang up.

"But that's not why I called," Dave said, "I wanted to tell you" Suddenly to Dave's disbelief, the line went dead. A dull deafness seemed to replace the once open line. He hadn't a chance to say anything to her and now she was gone.

"Sparks can you get her back?" Dave asked. But he couldn't,

the shore radio operator had shut down without warning. *Mrs. Martin, Sherry and a hundred other phone calls*, he thought, a*nd I loose the line on the one and only person I wanted to talk to*. He fought to compose himself as he realized he must look like a lovesick schoolboy. "Thanks Sparks, for your time," he added.

Sparks responded with, "anytime ", as he turned back to his black and white photos which he had spread out on the table. Dave quietly made his way out and through the ship to his cabin.

The rest of the journey was a long one, longer then it had ever been before. Dave was on edge the whole way and the crew knew it. Even so, he never let his feelings interfere with the way he dealt with his men. It was the same even-handedness, which he was known for. Even when Sharky Lowery, the lead machinist mate, was found drunk on duty in the engine room and Dave could have slammed him with the most severe disciplinary actions, that is to say, fire him. Being fully justified in any action, while perhaps inwardly venting his own aggravations, he stopped. Dave paused before he reacted, and taking the time to examine the man's work record he found it to be excellent and it went back for many years. Finding the history to be good and with no other signs of problems, he was then left with the task of carefully weighing what had taken place against what he might do to

Sharky. The main steam condensers could have busted pipes, when the water levels fell below a critical point. That would have left them dead in the water. Worse things could have occurred as well, something could have caught fire, or lines of superheated steam could have ruptured. All bad, very very bad, and could have cost lives and equipment and cargo because of this mans incapacitation. But it didn't happen because the chief engineer had been walking through the engine room and found Sharky dead asleep drunk, so he corrected all the neglected machinery *before* anything happened, and then reported the incident. Sharkey of course, wasn't the only man on watch, but during the night the engine room's crew was small and some had to take turns roaming through the vessel checking the many different areas where motor and pump played its part in the mechanical workings of the ship. The condensers were on the lower deck of the engine room and a perfect place to vanish for long periods of time and it was near there where the chief found him.

    Dave had a choice on what he was going to do, because luckily nothing had happened. Had an incident occurred with damage or injury he wouldn't have had any choice. Of course some of the crew already felt that being drunk on duty was to serious in itself for warnings, and this was true when left to itself, when not looking at the whole person, such a case could be made. No tolerance was the best deterrent, but Dave refused to give up his right to judge a situation based on a policy. Written rules are a guideline, he felt it takes a man with his gift of reason to sort out the best course of action, and a fair one.

Dave felt he had to take Sharky aside and talk. He had never had a problem with him, nor did any other captain as the record indicated. But now it seemed in one swift blow, one rather large mistake and without any warnings, he could be fired ending his career forever, because nobody, perhaps not even a desperate tuna boat would hire him now.

Sharky always seemed to be a slob in appearance, and he always kept his feelings to himself. He walked around with a stone cold expression most of the time and few words were ever exchanged between him and any one else. Dave had always felt that his and Sharky's personalities never meshed, so he never took the time to know who he actually was. All he knew was Sharky was a reliable hard worker and he was dependable. Everyone could always rely on him to do his job, that is, up until now.

Now Dave set across the table from him, he saw a stone harden man break down and cry. Sharky had never been one to share his troubles. He felt his feelings have been nobody else's business, no one's but his own. Being a loner and having no friends to speak of, no one even guessed that Sharky had a problem right now. Throughout his life he could always manage things by himself, but now his grief was beyond him. No matter how much of a man he was, this one thing . . . this problem, he couldn't deal with on his own. Sharky's mother was dying of cancer, he had just been told before they left on this voyage. She had kept it from him to spare his grief, facing the challenges herself, that was until she couldn't keep it hid any longer. She knew her son and the love he had for his mom. She was all he had left. When his dad died, those many years ago, Sharky was still young and at home. He was devastated then and his grief was long and hard. It was at this time in his life when most felt his personality hardened, turning inward and forming walls. Because in this young man's heart he couldn't answer the one and most important question. The one that was most crucial to a child, "Where is my dad now?"

    Sharky's mom wanted him to have at least a few years of normal life before he had to face the reality that she would soon be gone as well. She knew the pain and the grief that would come, she just wanted to hold it off as long as she could. *Let sorrow have it's due, but only when it is time, s*he thought. Though he was now a grown man, he was still her boy and he was going to hurt. She couldn't see any reason to let this pain begin any sooner then it had to.

Sharky cried with child like sobs, struggling against the pain to keep it in. This was hard for him, and Dave knew it. Not only the certain loss of his mother, but also the river of emotions he could no longer keep within his heart. Dave rose and walked over to him. Some men need an embrace, some feel they must stand alone, some cry with flowing tears and others hurt with a dry redden eye, and all of them are right.

Grabbing Sharky's shoulder with a squeeze, he silently said, "Your job is safe, and leave is granted with pay." Sharky dried his tears with a slow pass of his dry calloused hands. He looked up at the Captain. "I won't take the leave Captain, not until she is gone. It's what she wanted and I will give it to her. It is what she wanted for me, so her life and my life won't change, at least the likeness of that life. It will just continue as it always has, till we meet again when ever that shall be. You know, like the Christian songs say"

Dave stood silent a moment, the tender love flowing from this man. A man which he had always viewed as void of passion; it took him back for a moment. "Whatever you wish Sharky, but if you stay aboard, no booze, not here, or anywhere. Even though I can't restrict your personal time, no booze on shore leave either. If you do . . . I will fire you on the spot. I know this sounds harsh, but I'm giving you a chance after you made a major mistake. To that, I am being true to you, a man in my employ. If it even looks like you might have another incident, I must be true to the company, this ship, and those who hired me. No matter what kind of pain a man might go through, it is never solved or even made better by alcohol, and when you put lives, ship, and cargo in danger it turns from a personal problem into a disaster for all. So there will be consequences, but for now it won't be your job. Your record is good, and though we don't know each other well, I perceive you're a good man and that's enough for me." Sharky shifted in his chair and looked humbly back into the Captains eyes, "Thank you sir, I won't let you down." He rose slowly from his chair.

"I know you won't," Dave replied. "But before you go," he then pointed to a small room on the other side of his office. "That is my study, it has books, paper and pen. You have my permission to use this room any time you wish, especially at those times when you need to think and be alone. It's hard to find a place like this aboard ship and this is what you need . . . not booze to cloud your thoughts or falsely numb the pain. Just take some time to think and resolve yourself by letting your heart and soul come together. You need to find answers that are real, and those you can live with. I've never been a religious man and this is not a sermon, but sometimes you have to talk to God and let Him know how you feel. Don't expect an answer on your terms, let Him do it in His own way."

Sharky gave a nod of silent thanks, he rose and walked to the cabin door, turning back he said, "It's funny how we always turn to God when we are in trouble, or have to deal with death. I wonder what He wants us to do with our life in-between times?" Dave could see Sharky was re-composing himself; he had to go out and face the crew who would be wondering what had happened. It would kill him if anyone saw the pink in his eyes.

"I don't have the answer to that one, " Dave replied. "Perhaps if we would ask Him every day, we wouldn't have as many problems to deal with." He shrugged. Sharky nodded and closed the door behind him.

Dave's thoughts, as noted in his log for that day:

I remember each year, which has slowly, but ceaselessly brought me to today, the foundation of who I am. I remember the love as it came from my

mother, her shining eyes and happy smile, which was given to me, regardless on how things were in life.

While in youth I recall her arms as they closed tightly about me, the feel of her chin upon my shoulder as she grasped me from behind. The tender care of a loving mother, as she held me in both joy and pain, in tears or with smiles, in every way, she gave her life for me.

She was love, while in daily toil she made my life complete, I never felt so alone or abandoned, nor in the dark so afraid, that she would not be there if I called.

She taught me of God as best she

understood Him and showed me the truth. Though on this path I have not always walked, yet my mom pointed the way.

I cannot believe, that in this great, vast eternity, my love for my mother and her love for me, her son is ever lost.

Cap's seagull began to make a fuss. It was evident that he had run out of crackers, and in some strange way, knew that Cap had promised him all he could eat.

"Ok, Ok" Cap said, "I'll give you some more." Cap closed the book and kept it on his lap, he wasn't going to let it out of his hands again. He looked quickly around the area and then he leaned over and dropped a few broken pieces of cracker on the ground. He thought on how things must appear to the bird, this giant creature leaning over to give it some food. Indeed he remembered what it was like, when all the world seemed so large to him. Cap rehearsed in his mind, every day and every moment, all he could recall when he was young and at home. Memories bouncing back and forth from child, to young man, and when he left home.

"Like you," He said to the bird, "I left home too early, I was too young, still a kid. I would give anything to have spent more time with my mom and dad when they were alive. I guess you didn't have much of a choice, but I did, and you know, we can't go back and do things over again can we?"

Family, Cap thought, *home, you always pick one place in your mind, and that is what, and where, your home was. Filled with mom, dad, the neighbors, and all the kids at school.*

You're sometimes glad when you leave, but you miss all of it, well most of it, when it's gone forever. When you are no longer down the road from where you had lived or on the other side of town, close by. When you are no longer a days trip to spend the night, or have the choice of family for sharing holiday cheer. When choices are lost, like most things we have in life, it is swallowed by the folding events of time, becoming shaded memory, of what life once was.
Happy memories, longed for memories, but memories, which tie us to the past.

I was told once by a wonderful family I knew, that families are forever and when I cross that uncertain bridge from life to death, I hope I find that this is true.

Chapter Five

A New Horizon Rises

At last the port of Turnbridge was in view. The docks made of wood and stone hung silently in the mist over the water. A soft haze rose from the bay, as the large ship approached it's mooring, a mist born of the conflict of the morning chill, and the moods and temperament of nature. To the deck crew the large wooden piers appeared suspended over the light clouds. Drifting in an illusion that they were floating within the rising mist.

Dave stood on the bridge and watched their approach to the docks. He wondered silently as he surveyed the distant town about Linda and where she might be. He could have called her on the way back to port, but it had been a long time since he was here. He couldn't bear the thought, that in the past few months, she might have been dating someone else. After all, there was no real commitment between them, and she is a very attractive woman.

It is better, he felt, to scout things out and find out where he stood or even if she still remembered him. Maybe he would look up Sherry first and get an update on Linda's feelings or what she's been doing lately. Who has she been seeing? *No sense in looking the fool*, he thought. But inside, and very near the surface, he hoped Linda still cared.

The deck crew prepared the ship for docking lines were coiled, and the smaller throwing lines with heavy weighted ends (called monkey's fist) were made ready to toss to the dock workers ashore.

Dave looked down and saw Sharky helping along the lower decks. He realized he had made a good decision. Sharky hadn't touched a drop of alcohol after the incident in the engine room. Since then he and Dave spent many hours talking about several different topics. It appeared that Sharky had overcome his problem with making friends, and he got along with the rest of the crew a lot better. Sharky's mom passed away just a few days before the ship arrived in Portland Oregon; a regular stop for the cargo line which he worked for and Sharky's hometown. Both he and Dave attended the funeral together.

Sharky seemed to deal with her loss better than he had the illness. Dave felt that Sharky had found his resolve, not only through his mothers loss, but his fathers death of those many years ago. It still hurt, as everyone knew it would, but now he knew how to deal with the pain and he learned how to talk about it..

If you only listen to the heart, it will often lie. If you act only on gut instinct, you will often make mistakes. If you approach all things by only pushing ahead, you will sometimes trip and fall. Yet if you put heart, body, and mind together, you usually find your answers. Prayer had done it's part as well. Sharky had used the little room more than Dave had expected, but the results were all he had hoped for.

Facing challenges is best done by considering each of these tools for coping. Sometimes one choice is better than the others, but facing trials in life blindly is not a choice, it is the last resort. Yet often, when faced with challenges, we need someone else to remind us of our options. Pain is like a current, which comes from the sea of our experience. Like the approaching tide it fills the open spaces of our heart, and little can stop it's rising. Pain must have its' due, when it's season is upon us we handle it as best as we can knowing the tide of these feelings will go out once again, as tides are meant to do..

If you shed a tear, it is ok, for tears are the silent ways we say, "I love you' and 'till we meet again." It is that single drop of water, set adrift from the heart and carried across the unknown; that realm which stands between us, and those who've now moved on. Those single silver droplets which say "I love you" and perhaps they hear it too.

The ship was now close to the pier and Dave walked out onto the flying deck. Seeing that his crew was set, he began to shout the orders for the lines to be thrown across. The mighty engines backed down and churned the water in a low dull roar. The ship shook lightly before it moved to a final stop as the throwing lines sailed across the gap to shore. Crews on the dock pulled quickly until they obtained the heavier but stronger shoring lines. On deck turns were taken around the windless, a large spinning spool used to draw in the mooring lines and bring the ship in close to the dock. The great metal body of the vessel squeezed hard against the bumpers of the pier as final bends were taken to secure the lines. The gangway was set across and the last connections were made and the ship was put at rest.

    Dave had been so busy at his work. He hadn't noticed the banner unfolding on the dock. It read "WELCOME BACK DAVE", in large black and blue letters. "Hey Captain," Sharky called out from the lower deck. Dave looked down and saw Sharky pointing at the dock. As he turned he realized what Sharky had been pointing at the banner. He also saw who *had* to be Mrs. Martin, Sherry, and about a hundred other faces that Dave figured were those he had called a few months ago, all crowded around the unfurled paper. Of course Dave shouldn't have known who Sherry was, if it hadn't been for the paper names he now noticed pinned on all their coats. However, Mrs. Martin was exactly as he had imagined her, she was an older gray haired woman with a flowery hat, a wicker basket in hand and a print dress to match her image. Dark woolen stockings covered her ankles, which ended at the top of two small black boot type shoes.

And there was Lindy, he meant Linda, waving vigorously with one hand while the other supported part of the banner. *She is beautiful*, Dave thought to himself. While out at sea he had often envisioned her smile, but now he could see it. It was real and warming his heart, in a way he had never felt before, because her smile was for *him*.

Dave turned and handed the final shoring procedures over to his first officer. Quickly he made his way down to the main deck and emerged out onto the gangway. Linda had moved to the other side and waited. Dave ran across the clunking wooden way, and though it was the same plank as always, each step felt like it was taking forever. He could see her eyes clearly in the morning light, that same green flame gleaming with joy and gladness, everything seemed right. In fact, for this moment, how could anything be any better? Even nature was cooperating, the mist was burning off, the sky above was blue with a patch or two of clouds, the air was clear, clean and crisp. The town and distant hills portrayed the perfect backdrop for this occasion with the rising light of the early morning sun contributed to it's awe. Arriving at the final step, Dave reached to hug Linda, she moved to join his embrace, he thought of just how wonderful a kiss might be right now.

      Suddenly Dave felt himself stumble as his foot caught on the end of the gangway. Reaching for anything he grasped empty air, his forward motion in his haste sent him head over heals towards Linda. His added weight to hers, and advancing mass and forward motion of both of them together, sent them stumbling back into their friends on the dock. Like domino's they fell, over and over, closer and closer to the dock's far side. Joe Peters, an older gentleman who had been fishing along the other side and not caring about having a part in the festivities, one who had been minding his own business, felt himself being pushed helplessly with a human tide. Suddenly he was out in the air and well over the water. Within the fraction of moments, a deep ka-thunk was heard, much like a heavy set kid doing a cannon ball in the local lake. I might add, to Mr. Peters, it felt more like a belly flop. Dave and Linda were lucky enough to keep themselves from falling, as did most of the others. Mr. Peters however, bobbed in the water below like a cork on the end of a child's fishing line. Between gulps of water as he gasped for air his mouth was full of cursing, at least as much as he could gurgle out and each word was directed at as many faces he could make out on the peer.

      Mrs. Martin composed her dignity as she stood up and brushed off the dust, she looked down at Mr. Peters and scolded him, "Now you watch your mouth Joseph, this was an accident and you've got no reason to talk that way. Still! " She paused, straightening out her hat, "You've always had a foul mouth, haven't you? Even when you were a naughty little boy in my class room, more than 40 years ago." Joe slapped the water in defiance and mumbled to himself as he swam for the dockside ladder. Sherry looked around trying to find Dave and Linda, unlike everyone else, they hadn't joined the crowed who watched poor Joe cussing and splashing. She began to ask around, and then everyone else started to look for them.

But all they had to do was turn around, because as the small community crowd turned back towards Dave's ship and they did this together in a strange unison, as if it had been planned and practiced they found them, Dave and Linda, standing close together, in an embrace they had longed for and kissing for the first time. It was a kiss found of legend, tales, and storybooks and one which we all wish we were having, even right now.

The cold night of Bear Lake gave way to the warmth of old feelings. No longer did Cap's memories taunt him, but they embraced him in a loving blanket of things not lost, only set aside. It was as if he could feel Linda near him, enjoying the small campsite together somewhere in southern Idaho. Indeed, he felt the warmth of friends as well, as if they had just finished a long and enjoyable chat. He felt at peace, which he had not felt in a long time.

Deciding to give love a try with someone new can be very exciting, but also very scary, all in one bundle of feelings. It's odd though how sometimes, the someone new feels like someone you have known for a very long time. When life presses on and we leave behind those years, that time when we were looking for a lifetime companion many men and women yearn for those feelings or excitement again. They realize they face *the* challenge, that the game of love will never be as it was when they were young. They want to feel that thrill of uncertainly, the newness of a growing relationship. The first kiss, the first embrace, the feeling of someone else looking at you for that same affection which you are hoping to find.

But love in it's beginning has it's time and place, it's feelings and moments, are but the start of one's life with another. It is the beginning of beauty only and not it's fullness. Like flowers budding in spring, just begging to show it's blossom, it is not in it's fullness until it reaches it's full bloom. It's open blossom is when it's beauty and fragrance adorns the world and completes the treasure. Much like the two finding the fullness of life together and adding to the world a family. But this comes in a time when two have shared life and only if the garden of love is tended and nurtured, as it should be. Many lose sight of how important, how great, how solid life is when it has been lived alongside someone who has made this journey with you. That very soul whose kiss and devotion, was once new and uncertain, but has grown into a trusted strength on the road to forever..

>Two are meant together
>forever's built that way
>That two should walk together
>growing closer with each day.

>Of course there's sometimes sunshine
>But storm clouds do appear.
>Yet life is faced together
>When we draw each other near.

>I am a little stronger, each day which opens new
>I know there's always someone, for me that someone's you.
>You will always see me trying, that I can give my love
>To make your life more happy, like our parents up above.

I'll never feel I've done enough, and this my heart will sigh

But joy I'll find eternity . . . . in every day I try.

Dave paced the bridge of his ship. He had been out to sea for little over a month and he was anxious to get home. Having been married only three months he found this to be the second most difficult voyage had ever been on.

It was a funny thing though, his wedding came off almost like he and Sherry had described it that horrible night when the phone ordeal took place over a year ago now. The main difference in the actual event was that the ship was not underway during the ceremony. But that didn't hurt the event at all. The whole town turned out, even the preacher boys who of course, were on their best behavior. Still, it did help that their dad was paying them to manage the wedding guests, ushers and such.

Before the ceremony, Dave had the uneasy privilege of meeting every man who had a fancy for Linda, but failed to get to the altar. He did wonder how such an attractive woman could have avoided marriage until he finally came along. Some talked about how she was a tough catch, others threatened Dave's life if he failed to make her happy and be a good husband. Dave didn't really feel like they were joking. One old fisherman had his flaying knife out and asked Dave, as he wiped the blade slowly with a cloth, if he had ever seen him at work on the docks gutting fish? Then the old fisherman smiled and said, "I wish you two all the happiness life can give, but if you ever make her cry, you will be baiting my hooks, or I mean, bait *on* my hooks." He grinned crookedly and patted Dave on the back.

Dave was now convinced that the threats were as real as they seemed to be, but also that each man had two personalities and were crazy in someway or another. Because even though they were serious with their words of warning and threats of death, it didn't slow down the fun which they all seem to be having. The town knew how to party, and did so with great vigor.

They would say to Dave once in a while during the gathering, "We just wanted you to know how we feel, that's all."

Linda wasn't to be found as she was getting ready for the wedding, but Mrs. Martin was standing close by clapping her hands to the music. Dave leaned over to her and asked, "Shouldn't the party be after the ceremony?" Mrs. Martin smiled, "It will be"

Dave asked again, " Ok, I was just concerned because half the people are drunk already."

"They're just getting warmed up," she laughed, "You'll see"

Zac, Linda's former would be suitor finally came over to Dave. He had been staring at Dave all day. He was drunk, and almost stumbling,

"Dave, you're a good man!" he said with a slur, and as if they had been buddies for a long time, "How did you do it? How did you make Linda say, "I do?' I mean, I tried *everything*." He began stumbling forward, almost falling into Dave's arms. "Oh excuse me," he said and added. "I mean look at you and I, we're both a couple of good looking fellows, but it's you she fell for. What did you do?"

In Dave's mind he remembered the exact moment he first met Linda, and that was watching her fly into the air after he accidentally hit her. Dave realized that after the many stories he heard this evening, that is from the many men who tried to capture Linda's affection and failed, none of them tried a swift upper cut to the jaw. The irony made him laugh to himself. However, he felt it would be a dangerous mistake to share this little observation with anyone else.

"I don't know Zac" Dave answered "I think, what ever made her see anything in me, must have struck her from right out of the blue, that's the way love is isn't it?" Dave smiled.

Zac shook his head in slobbery agreement. "Your absolutely right my friend," he said "absolutely right. You're a sage, I want to tell ya, a sage." Tom, who was standing near by eating a piece of cake, heard Dave's reply to Zac and almost choked on his food while laughing and trying to swallow at the same time.

Sherry, of course, was taking the approach, "The war isn't over until they say 'I do'," and seemed overly sweet every time she ran into Dave, which she did as many times as she could. Linda knew what she was doing, and was irritated, but she thought, if her love and Dave's love was that fragile, she would rather know it now.

The marriage went without incident. Wayne Roberts had had the deck cleared and he and his wife did most of the decorating. It was arrayed in all the trimmings of a maritime wedding, yet with the flowers and frills of a woman's touch. As the marital event began they stood proudly side by side ahead of the rest, as if Dave had been one of their own sons. It was a wonderful setting. Wayne, who had put on a few pounds over the years, stood erect and beaming next to his slender wife. He was dressed in a black suit which appeared nearly an officer's uniform and she was in a bright yellow dress, one that you might see in the Easter springtime.

Dave stood at the top of the gang plank as Linda walked up the flower laden passageway. The tide was exactly right so the gangway was almost level and not difficult to walk upon for Linda who was now dressed in a long white, flowing wedding dress. She was followed by two little girls also dressed in white and carrying the ends of the long train which followed behind. The dress glimmered as she moved accented with pearl sequins. It flashed and sparkled in the bright light of the noon day sun. It was new, like her love was new and her vow to the man she loved would be new. It was exactly the way she wanted it. Her hair was pulled back and set with a thin white veil, and she appeared to all the glowing beauty which she truly was. Her smile seemed aglow as she approached her intended companion. It was their day. In all the eternities to come, this was when man took woman and woman took man to be the center of their lives and all else that might come.

    The rails along the way upward had been woven in bright white daisies and Linda's presence upon it seem to make the setting complete, or it became complete as she reached to take Dave's hand. The two walked forward through the divided congregation of friend and neighbor. Together they went on a path that leads much further than where the pulpit was now set upon deck. Because beyond the vows and beyond this day they would be husband and wife. Creating a life together out of a world of many possibilities and facing the uncertain course of eternity, together as one.

    The words were spoken, the vows were exchanged in eager

humility. Yet when the preacher said "Until death do you part" Linda felt a momentary uneasiness's, because her heart wanted no end, not to the love she felt for Dave. She wanted no end to their journey. Even if life should be cruel in the fate she and Dave might face, she wanted to face the calm waters of good fortune or the stormy seas of difficulty *with* Dave, *no* end, *no* final scene. Yet she knew that these were the words always spoken at weddings and she would make no fuss against the traditional ways.

Placing the ring upon his finger and receiving hers was to her the sealing and binding of two lives under heaven. With the kiss she knew she was his and he was hers and for now nothing else mattered in the universe. The crowd shouted for joy and Dave and Linda turned to the congregation as husband and wife. Slowly they made their way to the gangway as showers of rice pelted them and the deck of the ship. Tom and Sherry walked up beside their friends and accompanied the wedding party as they walked in pairs down the gangplank.

Tom, being the best man and the life long friend of Dave, was deeply into the celebration of Dave's wedding. Each step he took he wanted to be done just right so that Dave would have the perfect of all ceremonies. In fact he had practiced the night before on how he was going to walk, where he was to stand, and what he was going to say just to be sure he didn't let his friend down. He was that one individual who didn't expect that he was heading for some unfinished business of his own. Business which was about to explode.

Sherry, on the other hand, after accepting the fact that Dave had given his "I do's" to Linda, noticed that there were some very fine qualities found in Tom and began walking a little closer to him than she had done in the wedding practices. This of course, took Tom's attention away from where they were going and who was in their way. In fact, Dave himself was so intent on giving Linda a kiss every other step across gangway and then stopping to pick a flower off the rail and putting it into her hair, that he wasn't looking at who had joined the gathering on the dock below them either. If had they looked at the other side of the walkway, they would have seen Marcus waiting and he wasn't part of the festivities. In fact, it didn't appear that he even noticed that a wedding party was taking place. He just stared at Tom, the unsuspecting victim that was walking right into his reach. Tom, who was too busy trying to get to know Sherry as well, continued to walk without noticing.

Like lightning reaching out from the dockside Marcus grabbed Tom and pulled him over the guardrail. For a moment he suspended him in the air with the strength of his arms and tight grasp. This came as a shock to Tom because he wasn't a small man, nor light in any way. Marcus began to bellow and it was obvious that he was going to give Tom an oral preview of what was going to happen. However, Tom wasn't alone which was something Marcus hadn't considered in his blind rage. Suddenly Dave came running around the end of the gangplank and then dived across the remaining space towards the large brute.

Marcus saw him coming and met Dave with an open hand to the head. Dave stumbled back to the rail as though he had hit a brick wall. Dave looked over at his new wife who stood there with amazement on her face. He wondered if she was going to be angry at him for fighting at their wedding and he was surprised when he heard her say, "Get up! Move faster, tire him out." Dave sat for a moment with a 'what?' expression on his face. Tom, now back on his feet, quickly struck Marcus with two blows to the face, but as he pulled back to give a third blow he realized that Marcus was unfazed by his best shots.

Marcus drew his large fist back to strike, but he found Tom was more nimble than he had expected. But Marcus, after a lifetime of fights, was good at anticipating where his opponent was going to be and caught Tom with a backhand to the head, dropping him like a sack of potatoes to the deck. Sherry shrieked and yelled out "Don't hit his face, big guy, not his face!"

As Tom lay on the ground he wasn't sure what hurt worse, his head, or his hands and he could only give Sherry a broken smile. It seemed that hitting Marcus was almost as painful as being hit by him. As Marcus turned for Tom to continue the assault, Dave managed to clear his head and jump back into the fight. Ducking and dodging, he laid three or four well planted blows to the head and abdomen. His hands were aching like Toms, but he knew he was committed to this fight.

The preacher boys decided they wanted a piece of this fight and of course they sided with Linda's new husband. Sliding down the gang plank rails, Zac came off it like a bullet and straight into Marcus. Wham! The two collided but only Marcus was standing, as Zac was out cold. His brothers went down even faster as Marcus laid out a few good punches and out they went.

Nothing seemed to slow this juggernaut; Marcus didn't tire or respond to pain. Dave suddenly found he was backed into a corner. Tom was still too dazed to help, but at least they, the terrible twosome, were still *conscious*. With all his strength Dave laid one blow after the other, till finally a small cut opened on Marcus's face.

Though many of town's people usually found any excuse to join in on a fight. They all stood and watched, perhaps because their best went down so quickly. Dave figured that some were hoping Marcus would make Linda a widow and give them another chance. In fact he thought he heard the sour mouthed bum from the picnic give Marcus a pointer or two in the excitement.

Marcus paused for a moment, he dabbed his eyebrow and then checked his hand. "Blood!" he said, his voice deep and angry. "Never saw that before!" He looked up with eyes full of rage, deep black coals seemed circled in red, a bull ready to charge. Dave knew he was in trouble and wanted to shrink away but he also knew he couldn't. Linda could also see the tide of destruction moving in on her love and yelled, "Don't let him hit you honey, move even faster." Marcus advanced. Tom rushed up from the ground to help. His head had cleared and he was mad and ready for a fight. It was enough that this man wanted to fight him, but to beat on his friend on his wedding day, this needed some serious pain. Tom laid in one hit after the other, going for every soft spot on a man's body, but Marcus took it all without slowing. It even looked like Marcus was deliberately letting Tom wear himself out. Suddenly Marcus struck with a solid right jab to Tom's face. He fell back, feeling the tingling blackness of unconsciousness trying to take him down.

"I said not the FACE," Sherry yelled angrily but Marcus turned and gave her and evil glare. "Opps!" she said, backing away.

Dave moved forward to continue the assault and give Tom a break, but before he could reach Marcus a sudden blur rushed by him. Someone was grabbing him by the shoulder and pushing him aside and back. Marcus didn't see it coming either, without warning he felt his massive self being pulled to the ground and backwards. Dave watched in wonder as he fell back, but when he was out of the way he could clearly see. It was *Sharky* taking him down! He had joined the fight. His fists flew like a fluttering flurry onto Marcus, who was now staggering from the onslaught.

"Sorry sir" Sharky said as he fought, "I would have been here sooner if I had known, I was on the bridge."

"It's ok " Dave replied, still surprised by his sudden appearance. Dave and Tom were both amazed, because they hadn't been able to make a dent in the giants stamina, and Sharky had him rolling.

"We softened him up," Tom smirked wiping his bleeding lip.

"Yea like a b b gun against a tank." Dave responded, dabbing his brow. "Would have thought it unfair, all of us against him. That is until you have fought him." The crowd around them grew and they certainly became more interested in the battle taking place. Other guests who had been unaware of the fight began to realize what was going on down below and the rails on deck began to fill with on lookers.

Linda, seeing her husband was no longer in the middle of things rushed over to help, while Sherry was doing the same for Tom. Dave thought about helping Sharky, but he realized these two men seemed to be perfectly matched and if he charged in now, he might be doing Sharky more harm than good. Besides every fool knows, you don't jump into a dogfight, even if one of them is your dog. The fight went on for more than an hour or at least it felt that way, but in reality it was 15 or 20 minutes. Bets started to pass among the crowd and when Dave turned to check on Tom, who now sat across from him, he saw a little money passing even from his hands.

As the two men squared off while catching their breath they felt the sudden deluge of water being thrown on them as some on lookers doused them with the water in some wooden fire buckets. Neither Marcus or Sharky was angry about this. In fact it was a needed cool down and like a starter pistol at a horse race they were back at it again, placing one blow after the other.

Suddenly the crowd parted as Wayne Roberts walked up. He was giving Marcus an angry glare, which after a few punches back and forth with Sharky, Marcus finally noticed. It seemed to say, "You better stop messing up this occasion."

Wayne wasn't a large man, but he carried his position well. His mere presence commanded respect and he was Marcus's boss as well. Wayne knew that Marcus was a hard head and he had heard of the grudge which Marcus had for Tom. Even so, he had hired him because he was a walking forklift and a good crewman. All of this just a few weeks before the party, but he never thought Marcus would do this. After all, this was a wedding. Wayne found out, as he had guessed, that Marcus was one of the best workers he had ever seen. He was worth at least two or three men. He knew from the beginning that he would have to keep these two guys apart, at least for Tom's safety. What he couldn't figure was, why was this? Sharky fighting for Tom? But this was mainly due to the fact Wayne had seen how the fight began.

As Marcus looked up from the fight while both he and Sharky paused for another breath, he caught Wayne's eyes in a glance. He saw in that momentary stare, the words that said everything, "Drop it, or you're fired."

Marcus smiled and looked at Sharky. His expression suggested that he would stop if Sharky would. Of course Sharky hadn't seen Mr. Roberts approach, and didn't know he was now standing behind him or that Marcus was getting the stop signals from his boss. As Marcus glared back at Sharky, while giving him his half smile expression, Sharky thought it was an insult or challenge or something, not the first offerings for peace.

Marcus, of course, thought Sharky had gotten his unspoken message and dropped his guard, thinking the fight was over. Like a cracking whip, Sharky's fist broke from his stance and landed firmly on the swelling jaw of Marcus. With two or three spins and a stumbling gate, Marcus fell back, but before he was off his feet Sharky landed another blow for good measure.

Marcus had never been knocked out before. He didn't know what was happening to him, his eyes flickered as they went shut and he fell to the ground. The resounding thud on the wooden deck sounded much like a massive load of cargo falling from a broken net. The crowd roared as they rushed up to congratulate Sharky. Some even went to revive Marcus and dab his wounds, as if this had been a prizefight between two willing participants.

Dave looked around for Tom and saw he was busy collecting his winnings. He looked up and saw Dave's glance, and waved his fists full of green dollars in the air. Tom was grinning with victory 'till he felt Wayne grab his hand and yank most of the money away. Tom followed close behind as Wayne took the money over and gave it to Dave. Wayne smiled as he looked at Tom as well.

"Here you go Dave, some extra cash to spend on your honeymoon. I'm sure Tom's sorry for this interruption at your wedding."

Tom smirked, "More than you know. However I do have enough left to pay Marcus again, maybe that will make him happy."

"Good Idea." Wayne said softly to Tom.

Dave felt a tug from behind and turned to look at the deeply bruised face of Sharky. "Thanks Sharky," he responded sincerely, "I don't know how to repay you."

But Sharky just shrugged his shoulders like it was nothing. "Hey," he added, "ain't nobody beating up on my Cap, except maybe me. Besides, you can add this to the polished brass port hole I gave you as a wedding present."

They started to laugh when suddenly a large familiar hand grabbed Sharky's shoulder. It was Marcus. Sharky turned, expecting the fight to start again, but instead he saw a different look in the eyes of this massive figure. His demeanor didn't look at all like the same man with whom he just fought a few minutes ago. It was humble, even childlike.

"No one ever beat me before," he slowly said. "So I have never felt feelings like these before. I am sorry."

Marcus appeared like a mountain of humility, slowly turning to leave. Sharky reached out and caught his arm "What ya leaving for, there's a party going on inside."

Marcus turned back, "But I'm not invited"

"Sure you are!" Dave exclaimed, "For a while you were the entertainment, so we should at least feed ya."

Tom walked over and stuffed a wad of money in Marcus's shirt pocket, "There's interest in there as well my friend", he said with a smile. "And I want you to know I *did* mail you the money over a year ago, but you must not of got it."

"Oh that was from you?" Marcus said to Tom's surprise, "I got some money in an envelope along time ago, but there was no note in it. I didn't know who it came from."

Tom grimaced, "You mean I forgot to put the letter in with the money?"

"You must have." Marcus said "All I got was an envelope with the shipping company's return address on it."

"You used a company envelope?" Dave laughed. Tom moved closer to Marcus and patted the pocket where he had put the money.

"Keep it" He said and then walked away over near Sherry. Marcus smiled and he and Sharky laughed. Throwing their arms over each other's shoulders, they walked off into the warehouse where the party was just beginning. All the while they were bragging about how hard each other could hit. Linda dabbed at a small bleeding cut in Dave's forehead as Tom commented, "Now there goes a new but odd friendship." Slowly they all walked into the warehouse.

Dave looked at Linda and then kidded, "I was surprised when you didn't join us in the fight." She laughed and grabbed his arm even tighter, "I thought I was giving you good pointers, besides, in *this* dress? Do you have any *idea* how much it cost?" They all laughed as they joined the party inside, and they did party, and they did dance until they dropped.

Yet in the dark of the gangway's shadow, unseen by anyone, Mr. Roberts collected his winnings from an unknown man. It was said the mysterious man smelled like sour mash and alcohol. Later Dave and Linda loaded into one of Wayne's fancy autos and left for their honeymoon in the mountains. It had been a wonderful day.

It's funny how our moments run,

so fast when they are good.

It's strange how many days pass by

seeming shorter than they should.

It's odd how spending time with you,

is never found enough.

And how the days do drag behind

when the road ahead is rough.

But in my heart of yesterdays

I love my time with you.

No matter what the world will bring,

your love will guide me through.

Chapter Six

That others might Live

Cap rubbed his eyes and looked at the sky, he wondered where the morning had gone. Though he joked about the time because the night was passing so slowly, he actually knew how long until morning. From years at sea he came to know the earth and the heavens above in its seasons and he could even tell the time by where the constellations set in the sky overhead.

Though he had accomplished many things before he had met Linda, he never felt that he had lived until she came into his life. Meaning that everything he had done, everywhere he had gone, was just a part of being alive and not actually *living*, until he found her. Having her as part of who he was then and a part of how his future would unfold, put something real into the meaning of being alive.

A cup in your hand means nothing without something to fill it with, or a morsel to share. A book is nothing but paper, until you read its pages and share it's story. A voice spoken in loneliness has no meaning when its words are not heard and understood. To stand and say "The sky is beautiful", shares little wonder when spoken alone. Yet these self same words, when shared with another, causes each vision to take on a greater meaning and it becomes a moment together in the memory of the world you once shared.

Cap thought a moment, *As I consider the words those two boys told me about eternity, calling it the* Plan of Salvation, *I can see from my own experience, how I am made complete with my wife Linda. I can see how it has worked for us here on earth, and why God would have this as the pattern of heaven.*

Cap dozed off again with these thoughts fresh in his mind, dreaming he found himself in the water again, pulling the small boat along. He saw Linda sitting at the bow, but she was not looking at him even though he wished she would. She was looking beyond him, at the horizon. Unlike the other dreams which were calm while he was pulling the boat, this one was not. The water began to swell and the wind began to pull hard upon the rope he was holding. Suddenly over the crest of a wave which rose in the distance he saw a man riding upon the swelling torrent. He was the image of what Cap had seen years ago. This time he yelled, shouting and laughing, as if it was he who was causing the storm. It seemed to Cap that this being was trying to cause the waves to rip the rope from his hands, but he fought with all his might to hold on. Taunting, the angry figure pointed and laughed at Cap's struggle. Cap looked at Linda who seemed steadfast in her gaze of the horizon, as if nothing was happening around her.

"I cannot loose you" Cap yelled, as he woke suddenly from his sleep. Cap looked around in desperation, but calmed as realized where he was.

Suddenly, as if the dream hadn't been enough, the old man from before came charging through the bushes. Cap thought at first the old gent was angry, but his voice was low and humble. "I'm sorry" he said, "Can you forgive me? I should have never been so angry with you. I'll answer any question you have, Ok? Is it a deal?" Cap sat up and put the edge of the book under where he sat. "I do have some questions," He said thoughtfully. "Where did this book come from, how did you get it?"

The old man found a rock and sat on it, "Those are fair questions, and I understand your concern. I mean it sure has been a lousy night, right? And I'm very sorry about that ticket that officer gave you for fishing. I don't know why it's such a crime to come out here in the great out doors and put a line in the water. It's not like your going to empty the lake, or cheat some other fisherman."

"Perhaps " Cap answered, "But I was asking about the book."

"I know" The old man said. "We could learn a thing or two from all those stories. In fact I recall a family out of Dingle who would come here to the lake every year and have a family reunion. They would have everyone in Idaho, Utah, and Montana, camping out right here on this very beach. They would tell stories about family members who crossed the plains and some who starved to death here and there. How some of these pioneers were with the Mormons who were driven out of Nauvoo, and how Brigham Young sent people to this valley to freeze and starve to death in the early years of this nation. I understand they were only emigrants, or at least those whom he couldn't house or find jobs for. You know since we are talking about Mormons, I've heard a lot of horrible stories on what goes on in those Mormon temples. In fact they say there are children and murdered settlers entombed in the walls and in floors of the older ones. I want you to know, I've heard all the stories, and some things, which are just to awful to imagine. But if you live here long enough you hear them all. The thing that bothers me the most is that it would take only one of these stories to be true, and that would be more than enough reason to wonder about these folks."

Cap took a stick and tended the fire, "I don't know" Cap said, "and it's all interesting, but the one thing I would like to know is, where did you get this book from? How can it have my life's stories printed in it? I never let my log book out of my possession in all the years I have lived."

"Book, book, book," The old guy grumbled, "You can't even have a decent conversation can you? Ok, I'll get the things you need you just wait here, and I'll be back. You know that game warden who gave you a ticket, he's a Mormon. They're all like that you know, they will never give a man a break, that is unless your one of them. Anyway, I'll be back in a little while."

"You're going to get what?" Cap yelled as the old guy walked away.

"What you want," He answered as he disappeared. The seagull who had been gone for a while came hopping back into the light of the fire. Cap looked at him and smiled while he threw him another cracker.

"Well at least he didn't have a gun," Cap shuffled a bit and set the book in his lap. "You know, this old guy sure likes to harp on the Mormons. He said many awful things about these people. I wonder if he has ever listen to what they teach? He's never said anything about that. The truth is if we judge any religion by one member or the other, I don't think there would be a single person going to church anywhere.

No, it's gotta be more than that, it has to be the message they pose, the truth they can reveal. Those two boys I met had a challenge, I guess this is where that challenge fits. It's a good one when you think about it, because if God is really there, don't you think he would give us something, some way of knowing? They said pray and ask God if what they are teaching is true, that the Book of Mormon is a true record, as much a record as the Bible. You know it all hinges on that, if the book is true then the work is true." Cap opened his book again or at least the one which looked like his book and his heart felt warm inside while he read on.

Months passed, and Dave was back aboard ship on another cargo run. Everything seemed so far away, the places they were going, and port he called home. After a short stay on the ships bridge, he walked back to his room and plopped himself down into a chair. He decided to write a letter, and he hoped in some way perhaps it might help the melancholy he was suffering but he wasn't sure. With each word he added to the page he found that it did indeed help. Putting pen to paper he started to write about the journey so far, but after a few lines he realized that in some ways his letter lacked his heart and was much like the notations he found in his Captain's log. Dave sat his pen down and thought a while.

What to write, he wondered? *Well she does like poetry*, so he decided to put his heart to open pen and trust that he might get lucky with something good ....

    The moon, stars and sun, shine upon the earth in given order.
    Their tender embrace calls forth the wind that showers the
      land with ocean dew.

    Life breathes the air and takes a drink from the mother of us
    all.
    The earth moves, and with its' seasons, sleeps only to break
      forth in life once again.

    Green leafy explosions, flowers in color robe the land,
    that all that walk partake in humble reverence.

    Our feet tread between the portraits of nature,
    on these paths we walk through eternity.

    We but touch, smell and admire the tapestry woven by the
      hand of God.
    But you and I together... it is made complete.

Upon you I look . . . My Eve.

And added to the glory which I have beheld,

are the entanglements of my heart for you.

For in my eyes, I behold the vision of beauty,

and in my heart I feel its' touch.

For as lightning falls from the sky when clouds sing in rising

tempest.

So is the tender embrace of your arms to my soul.

Like the glass which I take in hand to see the distance more

clear,

My sight is made full, and I am found complete with you.

For the distance which stands between us,

is now but the wind that blows on the embers of my heart,

that love would burn more bright and sure,

But offering in itself, the unanswered yearnings of your touch.

Love embedded so deep, is now revealed,

as that which once concealed it, is now removed.

To be again in the presence of your love,

to feel the grasp of your hand and the warmth of the life within you.

Two souls with a single heart on a road to one destiny.

For what is heaven? It is the eternal light of my eyes

as I look upon you, and you look upon me.

Not just a gift, but a treasure,

as it is found and held within the love of two.

You my lady, are the chalice of my glory,

and I am the light which embraces it.

And together, we are the power of eternity

at the table of our Father on high.

Placing his pen down on the desk, he folded the paper and put it gently into an envelope. Rising to his feet, Dave walked to the bridge and then out into the open air of the morning. The wind felt good against his face; he stood there and gently closed his eyes. Suddenly, a gush of wind took his cap from off his head and sent it tumbling to the water below. His voice of alarm echoed throughout the ship.

A few weeks later in Turnbridge, Linda walked to the large windows of their new home. Still only scantily furnished, mainly due to its size, she knew it would one day be full of the life that she and Dave would share. Sitting into a chair, which allowed her to look out at the sea, she opened her journal to a blank page and began to write. She knew there was no way to send Dave a letter, but at least she could preserve her thoughts and feelings in someway.

This had been Dave's fourth voyage since they had been married, and she was proud of the job he had and the position he held. It did mean many lonely nights, but she was an active person and she knew how to fill the void. Turnbridge hadn't changed much, and many of the things she did before their marriage were still there for her to do now. Walking to the fireplace Linda poked at the burning logs, until a bright yellow light filled the room. Sitting back down she pulled out the journal she had started and wrote,

The evening's silence is broke,

as the night is filled with the rare call of the gull.

A lonely song rides the wind in the darken sky,

but no answer is heard in its' reply

Emerald reflections against the water of dark,

a flowing gown of a million silver fires,

lit from the stolen light of above.

The moon climbs high above the water,

like a pearl set afire, it shows me the horizon

and I wonder if, for you my love...

that in the night, it will guide you home.

    Suddenly Linda heard the kitchen door open. The sounds that followed were clear. Someone was tripping around in the dark. Getting up, she reached for the kitchen light and turned it on, there stood Dave, trying to hang his jacket on a hook. Almost jumping, she fell into his arms and he dropped his bag and embraced her. "Love you honey," she said as she pulled the cap from off his head. However, she noticed right away, this hat was different from the one he usually wore.

"A new hat," She asked, puzzled "I thought you would never let go of your old hat? You even wore it at our wedding." She examined the new one a little closer.

"Yes, it's new," he said. "I lost my other one over the side. A gust of wind caught me by surprise." His voice had the obvious tones of disappointment and perhaps even pain.

"That's all?" Linda questioned. "You took losing that cap better than I would imagine and you know, that shows true maturity." Nevertheless, Linda found that she was still puzzled; Dave continued his expression of disappointment. There was something more than meets the eye, something still unsaid, so she merely questioned him with, "What?"

"Well," Dave continued "When my cap went over, I instinctively yelled' 'cap over board!' Someone on the lower deck heard me, and like any good sailor repeated the call, except he yelled Captain over board. I heard that yell echo throughout the whole ship and with each new voice I felt the deep sensation of . . . oops! . . . Lower and lower I sank as the crew responded to the non-emergency. Well, I was on the fly bridge so I didn't hear the phone ring behind me. Someone on deck was reporting to the bridge, 'the Captain fell overboard'. The helmsman quickly turned the ship to port and backed down on the engines to reduce speed. For a moment, I thought, maybe someone really did fall overboard and that it was a coincidence that my hat was gone at the same time. So I stayed on the fly wing scanning the water for anyone adrift. Inside I figured this whole incident was caused by my spontaneous outburst, but I had to be sure. The whole crew was on deck and I could hear some of them claim that they had seen the Captain fall over. I could see them pointing where they had thought they saw me standing on deck and where they thought I was now floating. Of course this increased my suspicions that someone else had fallen. I tried yelling down from the bridge, but the commotion was so great nobody could hear me and no one bothered to look up. Later I was told that the galley called the bridge to report they had just thrown scraps of meat overboard, those leftover from dinner. They said they had seen a blue shark feasting on the trash. As I turned to enter the main bridge, I heard someone on deck claim that they had spotted me. Selfishly, inside I figured they had found my hat. However, I couldn't see it anywhere. Well, the first officer came out on the fly deck to manage the rescue and when he saw me standing there he almost fell over. When I followed him back to the bridge, they all gasped with surprise. Of course the helmsman informed me that someone had fallen over and they thought it had been me. I advised him that I had heard the call, and to continue the search pattern until all the crew and passengers were accounted for. Of course this gave me another hour to search for my hat but I wasn't going to tell them that."

Linda ran her fingers over Dave's new cap. She felt the swirls of the soft gold thread, which was the insignia of a captain.

"That's too bad, you were getting to be known by that old cap. Oh well, you'll break this one in."

"Indeed," he replied, "but I'm going to miss the old one. You have no idea what that old cap and I have been through in our lives together." Linda scruffed up Dave's hair and then went about fixing dinner. Dave sat in the kitchen, the whole time thumbing his new hat and telling Linda about the trip. But even with everything he said, Linda could see that losing that old hat really bothered him.

"Dave," she said looking him in the eyes. "Forget about that hat. You're home now."

Dave looked over at her as she filled his plate, "I didn't say anything. Anyway, I've only had that cap since my first job aboard a ship and in every place I've ever been."

"See!" Linda said. "You haven't let go of it. Face it, its' life is over as a hat and you buried it at sea." Dave walked over and helped Linda set a hot dish on the table. "Funny," he responded, in a gentle but sarcastic tone. "Listen Cap, I mean Dave, oh, you've got me all mixed up." Linda said breaking into a laugh. Dave walked over and gave her a great big squeeze. "That's ok, the guys aboard ship picked up on my grief, and when they saw I was no longer wearing a hat, I had to come clean, but everyone is sworn to secrecy. They are now calling me Captain Cap. I feel robbed in a way, because most guys get the nickname as short for captain. I think I'm stuck with a far different legacy." "Why would they do that?" Linda asked. Picking up his cup, Dave drew a sip from a hot drink. "Well, I think it's because I had the ship circle for an extra hour, even after we had made a full head count and nobody was missing." Linda broke out in a laugh; "I'll bet Wayne loved you for that." Dave smiled, "I'm not telling him and we made up the lost time along the way. We got to port on schedule." Linda sat down as they prepared to eat; she smiled and looked up at Dave. "Anything else you want to tell me about yourself?" They ate and laughed as the evening past away.

Cap looked over at the bird who had fluffed it's feathers and made a spot to sit and rest. No matter how much value we place on things, simple or complex, nothing on earth is really ours. Things are just props on a stage, and they only have value because we give it to them. Homes, cars, gold, and diamonds are all just things. Even money is just paper and metal, but since we all agreed that it has value it does. People kill for it; thieves will cheat for it, even those who do business will lie for it. It's sad when you realize that many have sold their integrity for a piece of paper or tin.

My old hat was a collection of memories which I hold dear, but even though it's gone I find I still have those memories, I guess nothing was truly lost. When I add up everything I have owned in life, everything I have had, I find the only thing I would really want, that is if I could have it back, is to look into my true love's eyes again. To be with her, to talk to her. I'd like to to see my mother and father again, and to laugh with my friends. When you add up our true treasures in life, we find it always was each other. Knowing that this is true, I find that it is easy to believe and conclude that, in Gods plan, families are forever.

The words on each page of the book seemed to drift off and into Caps eyes once more.

The wind rose and fell in impish harassment, each swell of the ghostly force seemed to grow in intensity. The water darkened as myriads of white-capped peaks whipped in the cooling air. Illuminated by the sun above, the waves were touched by fingers of silver fire, escaping through the broken sky of cumulus and mist. Clouds formed with defined borders, white billows in the sun reaching heavenward. Beneath them, shadowy bellies loomed, laden with their moisture, traveling at a quickening pace as nature drove them forward. In the distance, toward the sea, such clouds were thick and heading inland. Dark veils fell to earth, curtains which opened the scene. Wisps of water, taking flight from waves striking bolder and stone, speckled the large windows of Dave and Linda's home. Seemingly this sight foreshadowed the evening to come, as if in it's own way it announced nature's dreadful intent.

Linda looked out at the rising tempest as she stood upon the observation pedestal that sat before the large seaward windows. Warm and safe inside the comfort of her home she knew what was brewing in the waters off shore. Fear mixed with hope, both beating deep within her heart. She recognized the rising of a storm, she was an ocean-grown girl.

Dave is out there, she thought silently. He was due into port this evening. She knew if the storm was going to be bad enough, he would have to turn his vessel out to sea and ride it out. The whole scene, which now revealed itself in all it's horrible and glorious clarity, meant only one thing, he was now battling the deep and nature itself.

She felt the reassurance that he was a good captain. She

reminded herself of this again and again, he's faced storms like this before. But still the respect of the mighty sea taunted at her and played at all the possibilities of tragedy. Again and again she would fall back to the confidence she had for Dave's abilities and then a silent tear would break free from her eye and roll to a cooling stop on her cheek.

Usually she loved the wind and storms, they were always fascinating, but this one was too close. It's timing was bad, and Dave wasn't home. His strength wasn't there to hold her when the thunder rolled. Of course thunder didn't scare her, it was just that on nights such as these, she enjoyed Dave's strong arms around her as they listened together the passing gale. And when the power would go out it was a special time for them together, as his smile would warm her heart in the flicker of candlelight. His chair seemed dark and empty, alone in the dimming light. Linda couldn't imagine life without him, which only caused her anticipation to grow.

Suddenly, like a mild shock from a loose wire, the phone rang. Linda quickly grabbed it, knowing it couldn't be Dave. Mrs. Martin was on the line, she was concerned about Linda being alone with the oncoming storm.

"I've been through worse than this," Linda answered. However, She knew that Mrs. Martin was aware of that. It was more like she was also concerned about Dave, as much as Linda was, yet she would never say so directly. Linda knew Mrs. Martin was choosing her words carefully, that her intent was to keep her concerns from worrying her even more than she had been. Her call, though sincere, was an attempt to get a feeling for herself on how things were adding up. "Thank you for calling," Linda continued, "but I'll be fine and this isn't Dave's first storm at sea." "Ok," Mrs. Martin answered. "But if you need anything, even if it's just someone to talk to, you know my number. That is if the phone lines don't go down." Mrs. Martin was unusually short on words this evening, normally she talked for hours just to say simple things, this change bothered Linda as well. It was just another event, which made the oncoming evening seem wrong, a bad omen or something.

    The wind picked up in its intensity as the dim evening changed into the dark of the night. The last of the evening's light faded from sight behind the clouds, it left no moon or stars to comfort the earth below. Linda stepped outside the wind whipped at her skirt as she pulled her shawl tightly about her shoulders. Taking one final look out over the sea, she turned and closed the shutters and locked them down. The water roared in the night below as the wind began its familiar howl. She knew she should have done this earlier, but she had lost track of time as she watched the weather. It was now well past the hour which Dave's ship should have docked and he arrived home. He had been gone for two months, an eternity apart, only to be separated by another unexpected delay.

Fixing a hot cup of tea, Linda walked back into the living room, passing her usual chair she lay back into Dave's. As she set her cup down her hand brushed a small pile of letters. They were the ones which Dave had written her over the past several weeks. Half of her wanted to pick them up and read them again, while the other half filled with worry and wanted to hide from the concern. So for a while she sat quietly and sipped her tea. Without thought of her actions, she ran her fingers gently across the surface of the coarse paper. Drifting back into the chair, she hugged it gently as she smelled the familiar scent of Dave's hair upon it. Another tear drifted down and slowly away from her cheek. He was her life, she loved him in a way that no one could explain but only understand. The understanding, which comes only when another loves their companion the way she loved him. She squeezed the chair a little tighter as a soft cry escaped her heart; she finally admitted to herself, she was worried... and afraid.

Suddenly the wind grew in fierceness, sounds of flying debris blew by, some of it colliding with the house. The rain sounded like falling pebbles upon the roof and the sounds seem to blend for a moment into a single rushing force. The surge drifted off into the familiar low howl as it seemed to hide, threatening in its' own way, to rise again. The lights went dark without a warning, not even the usual blink or flutter. Linda calmly fingered the coffee table for matches, and with a brilliant red flare of sulfur, she lit a few candles and placed them into their holders. Clearing the window sill, she placed one of the candles upon it so that the light would shine outward towards the sea.

Picking up the phone she was met by dead silence. It was expected, it usually happened when a storm got this intense. As she sat back into the chair, she thought about the many storms she had seen over the years, this one was not really different. *It is strange,* she thought, *how the same stretch of land and water can be fun and beautiful at one time, and be treacherous and dangerous at another. That on a calm day in summer you can look out and see someone fishing out on the water or along the beach. You might wave at them to say hello, and they may wave back and for a moment, you are having fun. But during times like these, that same spot of water, that same shoreline puts their lives in mortal danger. Even though they are the same distance from the house in each case, it is different. When the danger rises unheeded, you may be beyond rescue, even though you are not far away.*

Without warning, an abrupt blast of wind tore violently around the outskirts of the house. The sudden gust loosened one of the main shutters and it flapped fiercely, pounding the sides of the house.

"Great!" She said aloud then she thought about what she had to do to secure it. The prospect of going outside was very undesirable to say the least. Linda quickly got up and went to the window with hopes that a simpler solution might work. But it was extremely difficult to see through the water-spattered panes, which had become like mirrors from the black night outside and the candlelight in the room. Straining her eyes and placing the light against the windowpanes, Linda saw with relief that nothing was broken. All she needed to do was slip outside and re-fasten the lock. This was good news. She could do it quickly and only get mostly soaked. But she also knew she had to hurry before the shutter beat itself to pieces.

Rushing into the kitchen she retrieved her yellow rubber jacket and boots from the closet, she figured she would at least stay as dry as she could. Making her way back to the living room, she exited through the door closest to the shutters. Understandably, she wanted to do her best to limit her time outside. Stepping out into the night, the air was cold and made bitter by the wind which blew so intently. The rain stung as it hit any and all exposed skin as marble sized droplets were driven into it by the flowing torrent. The surrounding black was as dark as the deepest hole found anywhere on earth. But it wasn't a hole, this was her porch on the seaward side of the house. Linda found that she could only see as far as the beam of her flashlight would shine and that wasn't far. The only other comfort was the dim golden glow escaping from the candles within the house. The sensations of being alone and in a foreign darkness was intense, and it added an awful sense to the sounds of the wind wailing in the dark. It gave Linda a creepy, eerie feeling. The crashing of unseen waves made the whole experience worse. They sounded so close that they sent chills up and down her spine. Like the ocean itself was ready to leave the shore and the violent flood rush inland.

    Linda struggled with herself to compose her feelings, she found herself dealing with the same fears, over and over again. But she was strong, and she could do it, she knew she could. Her foot stubbed against something and for a moment she heard the tinkling, whirring noise of rolling glass. She didn't stop to find out what it was. The rain pounded the ground around her. It drenched everything within its' reach. Her coat would have normally been sufficient to keep her dry, at least if the rain had fallen on its normal course. But when it blows sideways with the wind there is absolutely no protection from it. Even so, Linda ignored the icy fingers of the water as they trickled inside her jacket and down her back. She knew she would only be outside for a moment before she could return inside to cuddle in a warm blanket and snuggling in front of the fireplace.

The shutter was just outside the door, and when she reached it, it was as satisfying as achieving the summit in some great climb. Linda quickly latched it and pushed a nail into the lock to keep it from coming loose again. After checking the other side and finding it secure she quickly turned back to the door. She stopped for a moment and since she was wet already, Linda figured she might as well take a look around. Besides in the dark she had kicked over an unknown bottle somewhere on the ground and she thought she might as well grab it before it got broke, but if it wasn't easy to find she would just forget it. A passing thought crossed her mind as she looked deep into this night of rain and storm. Though unlikely, she thought she might just see the navigational lights of Dave's ship. Inside, she knew this really wasn't likely, after all, if she could see his lights, his ship would be too close to the rocks and in terrible danger. Still, she wished she knew where he was. All she knew for sure was that he was out their somewhere.

The dark was deep and concealing, and Linda placed the bottle that she found into her pocket. She realized it was that old green bottle which Dave had found floating way out at sea on a previous voyage. He had put it outside in the window for lack of a better place. All the while she turned slowly and scanned what she knew was the ocean. She could hear it, but not see it. Unexpectedly a small flicker of white light caught her eye. It wasn't where she expected to see a light, it was too close to the shoreline. As she watched, she realized it was down near the road, just off the beach in the water near the picnic tree. By the lights apparent location, it seemed to be flickering in the wake of the waves crashing along the shore.

    A sudden rush of realization came over her, "Someone's in the water!" she shouted aloud, "This can't be good." Linda watched intently, she saw the light disappear and reappear; it had to be someone signaling for help. For the life of her, she couldn't see why anyone would be out in the water on this kind of night.   The storm hadn't taken anyone by surprise, everyone who knew anything could have seen it coming and that was a long time before it hit landfall. *Of course there's always those who think natures rules don't apply to them, as if they had some sort of special immunity*, she thought. *But what ever the reason, whether foolishness or bad luck, anyone in the surf on a night like this is in bad trouble.*

Linda knew she had to act fast; she couldn't call for help because the phones were out. But if she could get down there with some rope, perhaps she could help. Quickly she ran around the edge of the house to get to the garage; near the door she grabbed a coil of line from a nail. She originally hung it there to be a decoration when they first moved into the house. Linda had never fathomed that she might use it for something real. When she came around to the driveway she found that a large branch as big as a small tree had fallen and blocked the car inside.

This made the situation more serious, because now it would take more time to down the hill. She would have to ride her bike or maybe even worse, she couldn't get out of the weather at all. But someone was in trouble, that was for sure, so she had no other choice. Hopping on her bike, she sped off as best she could for the fork in the road. The driveway had become a river in the rain, and it took forever to go down it. At times the wind gusts came up so fast and hard, it literally blew her off the road. Fighting hard, Linda was able to keep herself upright and after a few bumps and near spills, she was back on the road. The night around her was so dark that the flashlight barely gave off enough light to see her way; the wet gravel below her was her best assurance that she was still on the road.

Of course the dangers of a storm come in many forms. Without warning and out of the dark, the wind brought a large piece of wood, clipping Linda squarely on the head. For a moment she was disoriented and found herself crashing to the ground. She did her best as she went down to control her fall as she slid over wet metal, rubber, mud, and stone. Not moving for a moment, she lay there on the wet flowing surface. Linda knew how dangerous it is to succumb to the cold, so she didn't lay there long. Quickly she rose to her feet, her toes sliding in the mud and gravel, all the while fighting the daze which now fogged her mind. If she was hurt or if something was broken it didn't matter right now, she had to move, not only for those in the water but for herself.. Getting up she grasped the handlebars and straightened out the bike. Her hands ached as she closed them around the slippery rubber grips, her knuckles bleeding from the impact. Retrieving the throwing line which she dropped in the fall, she climbed back on the bike and continued. She was glad to see it still worked after the fall. At least that was a good break.

"Finally!" she gasped, as she saw the tree in the light of a lightning flash. Approaching quickly on her bike, Linda was shocked to see that the tide had come so far inland. In fact the tide was higher than she had ever seen at this end of the bay and now it was pushed by the wind and violent breakers. The picnic tree itself was deep within the water and many of the waves were breaking around it. Driven by the wind they came rolling in hard and covering the tree trunk to about four to five feet in depth.. The road at that point was also in the water so she knew she would have to leave the bike and walk around the shallowest points in order to get closer to where the light was still flickering. This bothered her a lot, because she knew there was a drainage ditch submerged somewhere close by and if she fell in it the stormy water would be well over her head..

Jumping off her bike while it was still moving Linda let it roll away until it fell over. Her feet landed squarely on the ground, but in her forward momentum and sudden stop, she felt something flip out of her pocket and break on the ground. It was amazing she heard it at all in the storms furious lamenting but in this moment of fear and adrenaline everything seemed so much clearer. The crash seemed to almost be directed at her and it sent a shiver of panic down her spine. At first she thought it might have been her flashlight, but she found it had fallen near her feet and was still on. Instant relief swelled in her chest as she realized it was just that stupid green bottle. Collecting her thoughts, Linda squinted as she looked out into the thundering black deep, at first she saw nothing. The light had suddenly vanished. The whole scene was awful, standing so close to the surf it sounded like several hundred lions roaring in Linda's ears. And it was difficult to even tell how close you were, as the borders of the bay would surge and fall back without warning.

With everything she could muster Linda yelled into the dark, "Is anyone out there?" But the waves and wind muffled her voice, and she knew that yelling wasn't going to work. She wondered if the light, or whoever had it, was even still out there or if the storm had taken them out to sea or even worse. With the obvious power of these breakers, whoever was out there could have already been dashed against the rocks, killed and/or destroyed.

But suddenly, as she was ready to start down the shore and check elsewhere, there it was! It wasn't far away, but far enough to be deadly, considering the anger in the sea. Linda prepared to throw her line. It was the only thing she could do. She knew that it would be difficult to toss it against the wind, but she had to try. The end of the line was weighted with a monkey's fist and that was good. It was a regular throwing line, one which Linda had used many times before. She had become very accomplished at tossing them over the years. Often she was the only one ashore when a fishing vessel came in with it's catch at the end of the day and Linda had prided herself on how far she could cast a throwing line, trying each time to reach boats farther and farther out. Of course throwing lines were usually thrown from the boat or ship to the dock, but that never stopped her. However, this was different, in all her days working on the docks, she never had to throw a line against a wind like this.

Fingering the rope, she let some line fall to the ground. She measured how much coil she needed. She would use all her strength to arc it high enough to get it to fall where she wanted it. Bringing the loop back up into her hands and rocking a bit she waited for a lull in the wind, suddenly she flung forward and let it fly. Straight and true it cast into the dark until it's velocity was lost against the force of the storm, then it arced back and down towards the water. Her first throw was good, she made it. The line seemed to hit it's target as it fell right where the light had been. Linda stood there for a moment. She had no idea if anyone was out there, or even if they were capable of reaching the line, she had to wait on chance.

A wave broke close and rushed in the water was now covering where she had left her bike. Linda could feel it rise to the top of her boots. Her legs felt the icy cold water through the insulation and rubber, which separated her from the sea. One thing was for sure, if this didn't work there would be nothing else she could do. She wouldn't be able to go in after them. She backed up a little to get out of the water and to avoid any surprises which the sea might throw at her. Suddenly she felt her foot slide back and down. She realized, with a shock that jumped down to her very heart, she was standing on the edge of the drainage ditch. Luckily she caught herself before she fell in but at least now she knew where it was.

Suddenly the line became tight, pulling outward in her hands as if someone had grabbed it on the other end. Linda pulled, but lacked the strength to bring it in. The rhythmic jerking on the line confirmed in her mind that someone was on the other end. She moved forward and deeper into the water while wrapping the line around her arm for a better grip. Suddenly the tidal surge went out and it pulled Linda off her feet. She fell hard and hit the submerged ground below the water. She felt a sharp pain as something in the mud and gravel cut deep into her leg. The water streamed outward, gurgling and seething, as it built strength for another rush to land. She was drug helplessly in the tidal grasp, out into the dark. The rushing surf had caught her, and she was being pulled outward into the jaws of the wild sea.

Her hand still grasped the throwing line, she wasn't going to let go. She fought to get her footing, but the sand and gravel beneath gave way to the retreating waters of the retreating surf. To her horror her feet became entangled in what felt like a fisherman's net, she tried to calm herself and fight her panic but it couldn't be much worse at this point. She wanted to reach down to free herself, but she didn't want to let go of the throwing line. *I can't let them die!* she thought as she struggled. Someone was out there on the other end. She began to tire fast, it was taking all her strength just to keep from being dragged out faster.

Suddenly she felt some relief in her struggle as she collided with the limbs of the picnic tree. She grabbed on and made a wrap of the line over a branch. The net on her legs was pulling with the weight of the water as it rushed around her. It didn't matter whether it was flowing into shore or back out to sea, the drag was incredible. She realized she must have been caught only by the edges of the net and that the bulk of it was acting like a sea anchor going back and forth in the waves. The constant reversal of pressure was sapping her strength and binding her legs tighter and tighter in the lines. She knew she had to get free before the surf wrapped her up completely. The cold alone was a great danger, even if she wasn't drowning as of yet, the cold would be enough to kill her and Linda knew she had to do something quickly.

Wedging herself on the tree, which had thus far saved her life, she reached down to try and pull the net off her legs. She felt an awful pain in her hand and realized she had been cut by a piece of glass still embedded in her leg. Her sore and possibly bleeding hand gave her a thought and she realized that this sharp glass may be her only real hope. Reaching down along her leg, her fingers crawled carefully over her skin, searching for the object. The wound itself had become numb in the cold water, so she couldn't go straight to it. As she searched she nicked her fingers as they slid over the sharp shard sticking out of her leg. Finally, she grasped the glass as best she could and pulled it out. As the impaled object withdrew the pain returned and she gave a muffled screamed against the wind. The glass was slippery and she knew she dare not loose it, so she grasped it as cautiously but firmly as she could. While holding the glass with her thumb and pointer finger she searched with her pinkie for the net. She began cutting. At this point she wasn't concerned if she cut herself in the process, she had to get free. It wasn't easy, because all the while she worked she had to fight the force of the violent surf and pulling wind. Each movement was either a line cut or a slice to the leg but she continued to cut anyway.

Linda didn't know if it was her effort at cutting or if the net had just broken free, but it fell away from her legs and disappeared under the next wave. It felt so very good to be free, but she knew still had to help whoever was on the other end of her throwing line. The water had receded enough between waves that she could stand up though she was still waste deep in water. She knew she had to hurry and get back up where it was safer, so she took the line off the tree and moved as fast as she could upward and as far from the deep water as she could get.

Pulling with all her strength she dragged the throwing line behind her. She could feel that she was bringing something in. She found that the incoming wave was working with her instead of against her and making the effort possible, but she worried about what was going to happen when it started out again. To avoid losing ground, Linda took a loop around a large boulder and held the rope tight. With each surge inward she would take in the slack and with each draw of the water, she would hold the line firm.

The pain from the wound in her leg and hands was eased by the cold, but her leg felt tight and ached deeply. She knew it was swelling. She couldn't tell if blood was running from her hands and legs or if it was just the rain flowing off of her, but she couldn't worry about that now.

She kept looking for someone to appear but so far all she could see was the rope set taunt into the surf. She knew that who ever it was out there in the dark, he or they would have to do most of the work, but at least now they had a chance.

The water seemed to calm for a brief moment and then it suddenly rushed in from out of the dark. To Linda's relief she saw a white light as it tumbled with the waves onto shore, it was almost here. Looking down Linda realized she still had her flashlight fastened to the pull strings of her rubber jacket. Tipping it up she cast the pale light along the shore, it dimly lit two figures who were fighting in the surf to stay upright. "There are two people," Linda realized with a whisper and she tried to call out to them.

When they were higher on the beach and clear of the waves Linda rushed down to help. It was indeed two men, both wearing life preservers. One of them had a survival light clipped to his life preserver; apparently that was what Linda had been seeing. The larger of the two stumbled a bit as he stood. Reaching down he struggled while picking up his companion. Linda said few words, but helped in supporting the smaller injured man.

"My house is up at the top of this hill," she shouted. "I'm afraid it's going to be an awful climb up the road to get to it, so you need to hang on, stay conscious." It was extremely difficult to hear against the roar of the surf. "We need to get both of you inside as fast as we can!" she again shouted. The large dark figure nodded in the pale yellow beam of her light. Taking the lead from Linda they were off, slowly at first and almost dragging the injured one, they pushed on. Though each step was painful and difficult and their bodies wanted to quit, they didn't stop as they made the agonizing climb up the road towards the house.

It took at least a half an hour to reach the back door and Linda was sure that had it been any further they wouldn't have made it. She was numb with the cold, and she was having trouble thinking and she knew this was a bad sign.

"Just one more step," she kept saying to herself, "One more step." Clumsily, the small group stumbled up the back steps, but as they reached the door Linda realized it was locked. She had come out another way to fix the shutters and now that seemed like days ago when this whole thing began. At that time she had no idea she would be limping back to her house with two strangers under tow. In fact the whole shutter incident may have saved these men's lives, or cost Linda's hers. So far they were winning.

Linda's muscles ached and her hands were openly bleeding and even though the other stranger had born most the weight, it had been an almost impossible task. After giving what help she could in carrying the man up the road, she didn't have the strength to deal with a locked door and she felt that if she let go of him right now, they would all fall to the ground. Using her elbow, she struck the door and broke out a small eight by ten window. Reaching inside she unlocked the latch and swung it open. Suddenly a gust of wind took the door from her slippery fingers and slammed it against the wall inside, breaking the remaining glass of the window pane. The one stranger who was still walking, reached up with one hand and held the door firmly to keep it from slamming again, while with his other arm he supported his friend.

"Sorry for the trouble!" The man said as he struggled to get his friend up the last few steps and in the door. Linda didn't answer, her mind was on what she had to do, and she wasn't thinking clearly yet. Without a word she rushed through the kitchen and through a door on the other side. Disappearing for a moment she returned holding several lit candles in front of her. Strategically she set them on the counters around the table, lighting the room and illuminating her guests. As she turned, she saw the two men still standing in the doorway. Both were dripping wet and covered in sand and dirt. The taller one seemed on the edge of exhaustion as he supported his smaller and yet half conscious companion.

Linda could see in the yellow flickering candlelight, bright red blood oozing and seeping from several lacerations on both men's faces and legs. Without a word or another thought, Linda grabbed up her tablecloth scooping everything into a bundle. Several jars of jelly mixed with jars of preserves and her fine table settings clinked together as she grasped the ends up and set it down in a corner near by. The two men entered the rest of the way and closed the door behind. As they limped into the room, Linda could see that the man who had carried the other, had several bloody injuries himself. Even so, he didn't complain as he strained and struggled in agony. Like on cue, he hefted his friend up and set him onto the table.

He started to say, "Sorry about the window," but Linda seeing the necessity to move quickly, cut him off with a wave of her hand. Grabbing a large box of first aid materials from a cabinet, Linda finally asked, "What happened out there?"

Chapter Seven

Friends are not Forgotten

The stranger drew a breath to answer Linda but found himself coughing violently. Linda knew he was not well but his friend needed attention first. His face wounds looked bad but she knew they were most likely not the worst of his problems. *Facial cuts always look bad* she thought as she looked down around his legs. Linda noticed dark patches on his pant leg, when she touched it she realized it was blood. Grabbing her scissors she cut away the material revealing several deep open wounds. Linda gasped, they were still bleeding profusely so she grabbed the hand of the taller, still conscious stranger and placed it on the wound. "Push hard here, use as much pressure as needed to stop the bleeding."

"You're injured too," the man remarked as he tried to catch a breath. He could see blood on the floor where she had been standing and at first he had thought that the blood on her jacket was theirs, but he realized it was fresh and still dripping. He wasn't much of a sight either. He could hardly stand and his legs and hands were shaking badly.

"So are you" She answered "I'll deal with my problems in a

moment, but if we don't act quickly you two will be in more trouble than me. Lets get your friend tended, and then we can worry about our injuries." The large guy pushed on his friend's wound with a wadded piece of gauze. "I've got the bleeding stopped." he said, "I'll keep pressure on it. You go and get dried off before you fall over."

Linda knew he was right. She could feel the cold taking away her remaining strength. She took his advice and disappeared into another room while the still unknown man leaned in with all his weight on his friends leg.

"My name is Adam," he said into the darkened passages of the house. He was sure she could hear him, but silence was the answer. Adam turned his attention back to his friend and tried to adjust his stance. The bleeding was stopped as long as he kept the pressure up, and that was a good sign.

"You're going to be ok Josh," Adam whispered, but Josh was near unconsciousness, and made no reply. Linda returned holding blankets in her arms and on top of them was a belt., She quickly threw a blanket around Adam, and then used the belt and fashioned a pressure dressing for Josh's leg injury. As she wrapped a blanket around her own shoulder, she watched the wound to see if it was still bleeding.

"Good he doesn't need a tourniquet, we stopped the bleeding without cutting off all the blood supply to the leg." she said in relief. Grabbing some hot water from the stove and adding peroxide, she began to wash the rest of the deep wounds on the half-conscious man. After drying the injuries with wads of gauze, she dressed them with sterile gauze pads she had cut from the roll.

Linda was well trained in first aid. She started with the wounds which were bleeding the worse, and worked her way to the others. All the while she worked, she kept an eye on Adam to make sure he didn't fall over. He had already left the room once, obviously to remove his wet clothes and had returned wearing the blanket only. Adam looked over at Linda while covering Josh with another blanket, "I'm not sure you heard my name."

Linda tied one of the gauze strips down, "I heard it Adam, but I was trying to move as fast as possible for your friend's sake." Adam looked down at Josh and the pile of wet life preservers near the kitchen door. "You saved our lives tonight, not only from the water but from our injuries as well. I've got to say, when I was bobbing in that water and felt that rope sliding over my shoulder, I wasn't sure what it was. I just grabbed hold of it and pulled us in." He paused and then said " I can't imagine what you were going through."

Linda tucked blankets around Josh so he wouldn't roll off the table, "You didn't answer me," she said softly. "What happened? Why were you guys down there in the water?" Linda began tending her own wounds as they talked, sometimes talking from the other room as she cleaned and patched the cut on her leg. *Deep enough for stitches*, she thought, *but that is going to have to wait for later.*

"I think we collided with another vessel," Adam answered. "I would say, it was just off your point out there or at least not much further than that, I'm not sure. Josh and I were on deck securing lines, suddenly the ship jolted and we were thrown overboard. I don't know what happen after that, Josh and I were swept away so quickly. I can't believe we're alive. When we hit the water we just grabbed onto each other and didn't let go. If we hadn't rolled up on the sandy areas of your shore, we would have been ground into bits on the rocks. As it is, we wouldn't have made it ashore alive without your help." After patching the wounds on Adam, Linda checked both men over again, to make sure she hadn't missed any other injuries. "Are you a nurse or something?" he asked. Linda unfolded another blanket and threw it around Adam. Using another, she rolled it up and placed it under Josh for a pillow.

"No," She replied. "Just lots of experience in a small town."

Linda then realized she hadn't introduced herself. She quietly did so while she prepared something hot to drink for them. Stopping for a moment and with a quick glance over at Adam, she had took a moment to think about what he had said concerning a collision. She knew Dave's ship was out there. Against her will, concern began to fill her expressions. "What ship are you from?" She asked. "And who did you collide with?" Turning so that he would not see her face as he replied, Linda adjusted the flame on the gas stove and put the tea kettle on to boil. "We are from the Sea Lark and I have no idea who or even what we hit." Adam could see the flush of concern in Linda's cheeks and realized why she was turning away. "I can tell somethings bothering you. Is it how we came in, and if you should be concerned about us?" "Oh no, it's not that," Linda said. "My husband is the captain of a ship in the Wayne Roberts' cargo lines. He was due in this evening."
"I see." Adam said. "Well, if it's any help, I don't think we struck anything that big. But I can't be sure, it happened so fast." The comment didn't help, but Linda kept herself busy cleaning up the debris and the unused medical supplies.

The hot drinks felt good and Linda went about fixing some soup. In the mean time she had Adam take Josh back to one of the guest rooms. After removing the remainder of Josh's wet clothes and then slipping into some of Dave's hand me downs, Adam made his way back to the kitchen. Linda had a place set for him near the fire, she knew his and her greatest danger was now the long exposure to the cold they had suffered outside. Adam sat and warmed himself while he sipped the hot beverage which Linda provided.

Josh's condition was worrisome, but Adam knew there wasn't much more they could do for him. He would have to ride out the evening here. The phones were still down and the storm was still raging outside. It would be hours, or possibly even a day or more, before any utilities would be restored. Still, he was concerned for his shipmates. They were out there somewhere in the water, suffering an unknown fate, and that bothered him a lot.

Linda's care seemed very effective and, after warming up, Josh awoke and called to Adam. Nothing much could be done for his pain other than aspirin, but Adam fed him some soup and then gave him a run down on the night's events. After the short talk he fell asleep and rested quietly the rest of the evening.

When Linda finished in the kitchen, she walked into the living room and found Adam standing near the windows and staring out the porthole (built into the shutters), which looked seaward. "I need to get help somehow. My shipmates may be in trouble," his voice cracked with concern, turning around, he saw Linda's quiet approach. "There is nothing you can do," she replied, pulling a blanket tightly about her. "Unless Mr. Roberts across the way has his generator going. It doesn't usually work, but he does have a two-way radio and if the batteries have a charge it will still work for a while. However the surf we swam in an hour ago used to be the road; the *only* road out of here. But even if you can get over there, I wouldn't advise it. You can't go back out into the weather so soon." "I can't worry about myself," he replied. "I don't even know if my ship got out a distress call. If your neighbor has a radio, then that's where I've got to go." Adam leaned up against the wall. "For all I know my ship is fighting to stay afloat, or worse. I can't abandon them."

The wind rose fast, as the water began to break over the bow of the large cargo vessel. Dave walked through the small doors of the bridge and found the navigator hard at work trying to guide their ship through the shortest path of the rising storm. Dave had seen many storms at sea and he developed a routine which he followed each time they were caught in one. The first rule was not to get caught, but nature and necessity often had it's own mind and frequently didn't give enough warning to avoid its' intentions. It was clear now that this storm was going to rise into a full gale, but hopefully no further. Even though it was still daytime, the sky was dark. The water began to rise like great mountains of dark liquid. Easily the ship would be lifted to the crest and then fall to the valley of the other side. At times the whole ship would lie between the summits of two waves, riding deep in the trough of passing giants.

    The bridge door opened for a moment, and the wind raced through the small room. The drenched first officer made his way in and fought the storm to get the door closed again Quickly he latched the door and shook himself off. "Found two of the deck hands fan tail jumping," he said with a half grin. Turning, he hung his coat and straightened his sweater underneath. Dave smiled. Fan tail jumping was fun but incredibly dangerous. It was likely and true that most everyone had done this at one time or another, and if you were caught, you usually got a good chewing out. To fantail jump, a crewman would stand on the upper deck of the stern. When the ship was lifted to the top of a large swell and just before it dropped off, he would jump up as high as he could. As you went up from your jump, the ship would fall away from under you as it went down a swell, and for a moment, you would be high above the deck, feeling almost suspended. Before you fell any distance the ship would rise on the next swell and you would land on the deck again. The danger was that the ship might swing out from under you or come up unexpectedly hard, in which case you were either lost overboard, or injured by the collision with the deck.

In Dave's whole career at sea, nobody had ever been lost or hurt fantail jumping. Of course, anyone who was caught doing it was stopped. Everyone knew that if it did happen, and someone went overboard in that kind of weather, that person would probably be lost and better than good odds said that they would die in hostile seas. Because finding someone in the water, in that kind of sea, was next to impossible. Dave looked up at the First Mate with a questioning eye, but before he could ask. "I thought that since these jumpers had spare time on their hands, they could inventory the boatswain's locker." Dave smiled, and turned back to the navigator.

The wind outside grew in intensity as the waves pounded the deck. No one aboard dared to step outside, that is, unless they had too and that was only with a safety line to hold onto. Below, the crew who tried to sleep rolled back and forth in their bunks. Up and down was ok, but the pitch and yaw of the quick jerk to the right and then to the left, was almost too much for anyone to handle, especially those who were new to the sea. The water roared along the bulkhead as the bow plunged deep into the rolling mounds. The sea also would sound against the hull in a rhythmic pattern, not with one voice, but with the course of thunder. If you only had to contend with the sound, without the motion, the sounds might even sooth you to sleep but the motion was always there, you couldn't get away from it.

Those who had to work into the night kept constant vigil over the small floating community. Everyone aboard knows, that the ship is the *only* thing which stands between them and the mysteries of the deep, and everyone wanted to keep those mysteries . . . mysteries.

In the engine room, the machinist mates keep their watch over the power plants which kept the ship moving. Even in the worst of all weather, when the ship's deck would roll and be tossed from the torrent outside, they would go down to the lowest points of the ship and examine the bilges for flooding. The worst place to go, known by all, was the bow, the bilge being several slim hatches down. It was here where just outside a few inches of steel, that the ship fought the sea for it's course. Being in these lower decks was like riding the end of a whip or the tips of long fingers while slapping the water at play, and it was very sickening at times. Most of the watch was spent in the engine room making sure everything was running. During a spare moment, some sailors would stop and let the cool air of the ventilation ducts flow over their face. Often, this was enough to fight against the taunting desire for sleep and the effects of constant motion. Indeed, one large sea valve, which sat alone on the lower engineering deck was often used as a chair. This let those who work in the heat and oil tainted environment stop and rest between rounds. Sitting in that one spot, you could feel the windy cold air blowing from a 12-inch salty tunnel. This air duct, in its' own secretive way, led through the ship in strange forgotten passages, twisting and turning to finally reach the open air of the upper decks. Closing your eyes for a moment, one could almost forget the tedious task of a night watch.

    Dave checked their position on the map. Something bothered him, but he couldn't put his finger on it. He knew the ship could handle the storm, so that wasn't the problem. He had a good crew and could depend on everyone to do their job; still, something was eating at him. It must be Linda he thought. He knew she had be worried, but it must be obvious to her by now that he was going to be late. The course they took home was the best one they could choose. They had to let the storm blow itself out before they could head toward the docks.

    Suddenly empty anticipation filled the stomachs of the bridge crew. It was in everyone's expression. It was that moment when you feel that something was going to happen, but you're not sure what it is yet. The feeling seemed to rise in harmony with the upward motion of the ship onto the next wave. It was like each wave coming at them now counted down to something eminent.

Dave looked out into the dark as far as he could. He saw a small light blip in the distance... in the distance off the starboard side. Bringing up his binoculars he tried to see what the light was. The water spraying on the glass of the bridge made it difficult to see anything. He figured the light wasn't blinking. He could tell it only flashed with the action of the sea. It didn't seem to be a vessel, as it appeared fixed and in one place, but who can really tell in weather like this? Dave scratched his head and thought hard. If he didn't know better he would think he was looking at the lights from his house.

"It can't be," he said, looking at his charts. "That would mean we are far to close to the shore." Dave looked again to be sure, but the light was suddenly gone. It could have been anything, he thought, an illusion in the storm. To be sure, he checked the map to see how far off the coast he would need to be to avoid the rocks on the other side of emerald bay.

But Dave didn't have anytime to make any adjustments on their course, because as the ship passed over the next mountainous swell, an alarming sight came suddenly into view. Another vessel was dead ahead and too close to avoid. How it got there without being seen was unknown, but there it was, and the bow of Dave's ship was coming down on it. "Hard to port!" Dave yelled. "Full reverse on the port screw." The ship's crew lurched to the right with the left sudden spin of the helms wheel. The helmsman responded quickly as he anticipated the command. The massive bow skimmed the hull of the unknown vessel and both ships shook with the impact. Had they not went hard to port it would have been a direct collision. As it was they came down on the other ship, slapping it's stern on the port side. The impact was only a momentary glancing blow. It could have been much worse. The storm could have thrashed each ship about, slamming them into each other several times, but they were lucky. Still, what happened already was bad enough. Yet it was better than slicing the other ship with the bow, from stern to keel, which would have happened had they not acted so quickly.

Dave's ship swung sideways into the waves and rocked dangerously in the surge. It was a perilous angle to be when traversing a storm, but they had no choice, they had to act. On board the alarms sounded, the horns competing with the howl of the wind. Dave ran out onto the fly deck to look back at the ship which they had collided with. But all he could see was a dark, massive shadow in the storm; lit for a moment by a lightning flash then disappearing quickly behind them. Dave opened the bridge door and yelled in, his voice was somewhat muffled by the wind. "We're clear! Helm, straighten us out, take us out to sea." he screamed, "full ahead on all screws."

"Aye Captain!" the first mate responded, "I'm adjusting course 45 degrees and full ahead, Captain," he asked, "should we be at full ahead, what if we're flooding near the bow?"

"Absolutely," Dave responded, "we need a larger gap between us and the other ship! We can't risk being this close while they are adrift, not while the ocean is acting like this." Dave walked back into the bridge area; everyone was doing their job and that was all he could ask for. The engines turned hard as the bow swung swiftly over. The new angle rocked the vessel wildly, as the waves and wind resisted their actions. But they all knew they had to put more distance between themselves and the other vessel. The helmsman quickly turned the wheel to bring the ship around and the first officer adjusted the engine speed and they began to make headway. The large vessel fought hard, being thrown about wildly in the torrent. Suddenly it gave way to the new course and it slid onward, putting the bow head on into the waves. The first officer looked over at Dave, "The other ship sir, no one could have seen them coming. Captain, they didn't even have navigational lights." "I know," Dave said, "It's odd, very odd, but it only suggests that they're in a bad way, and as much as I want to do something for them we can't until we know our own condition and until this storm calms down! The best thing we can do is radio their position to search and rescue. If the weather breaks, and if we not sinking ourselves, then we'll turn back and find them."

On board Dave's men responded quickly to the alarm. As best they could, they moved quickly on a heaving deck. They filed out of their quarters and ran forward for damage control. Coming out onto the open deck, they held tight to the safety lines. Moving in single file they worked their way forward as the storm tossed them from side to side. Dave checked the map and marked their position. At the same time he yelled orders to the bridge crew, "I want as many eyes as we can spare on deck. See if we can get a sighting on that vessel. We know they need help and I don't want to hit them again. Get Sparks going on the radio and contact the Coast Guard. Get me a damage estimate as fast as possible." The whole crew responded. The forward hold was flooding violently. Shoring parties began their fight with the icy fountain of water which was rushing in. The ship began to lisp slightly to the flooding side and Dave knew they had to move fast. The first officer joined the damage control party and oversaw the effort. As they assessed the situation, he grabbed the emergency phone line to the bridge and reported in. "Captain" he called over the phone,"We've got to slow down, our forward motion is forcing the water into breech like a geyser." Dave looked at the clock and in his mind he calculated how far they might have traveled since the time of the collision. He was satisfied with the distance. "We're slowing down now," he replied "I'll bring the speed down to as slow as we can get and still stay in control." "Fine sir," he answered, "Were shoring up the first of the holes now. I don't think we can get the flooding stopped, but we can slow it down enough for the pumps to at least hold their own." "Understood," Dave answered, "Keep me apprised of your progress."

All the while, Sparks was on the radio with the Coast Guard. He advised them of the incident and their need for assistance. They responded to the call and advised them that they were in route with a high endurance cutter. Sparks then tried to raise the other ship, but they didn't answer. So far, they could only speculate to what it's fate might be. After the impact, the other ship had dropped from sight as quickly as it had appeared. Luckily the gale was subsiding and Cap's crew was making some headway against the damage, or at least holding their own.

It was still a black night outside, and the swells were still large, but the wind had died down to a great degree. Dave looked at the clock and knew that dawn was just around the corner. It was about this time that he was able to bring the ship to almost a full stop, and this helped in the work effort below enormously.

For a while Dave thought they could handle things on their own. But without warning, two of the forward control boxes which ran the main pumps shorted out and burned, leaving only one pump to fight against the flooding. This was bad, because the two pumps they lost were the larger of the three forward pumps. As it was, the remaining pump began to whine loudly and they knew it was threatening to freeze up under the load. Without the other pumps, the damage control crews couldn't get to the largest breach, which lay deep in the lower hull. The water was spilling into a medium forward cargo area and hatches couldn't isolate the affected space. The men did their best, and their efforts did slow the flooding, but they had to back off when the water became to deep to work in. They knew if the remaining pump went out, the situation could only go from bad to serious. They knew if they could get the first two pumps running again as fast as possible that they might make it, so this became the priority. The pumps themselves were ok mechanically, their problem was the electric control box and they estimated that this could be fixed with a little time and clever jerry-rigging. It seemed that as the water was now rising in those compartments. The Coast Guard would not get there in time before the water was to deep to save the ship. But as the dim light of morning began to break through the cloudy skies and far sooner than expected, a large 275-foot high endurance cutter came into view and on their way towards them. It was the Wachusetts WHEC-44. When they finally arrived, the Captain came aboard to talk to Dave, he knew he had to be quick as they still had to find the other ship. "What can we do for you Captain?" the Coast Guard officer asked. Dave wiped his hands with a few rags and then shook the Captains hand, "I'm glad you're here. You made good time. Thank you. Let me get right to it, we are taking on water in our forward sections. Our two main pumps have shorted and the smaller one isn't doing the job. So if you can spare them, we need several submersible pumps in order to get ahead of the water."

"You'll have them" the Captain responded, "In fact we're unloading them now from the small boat." The captain paused, "My only concern is that we won't have enough pumps for you and the other vessel."

"I figured that," Dave replied "But if you can give them to me for about three quarters of an hour, I'll have my other pumps up and running. By then I hope you will have found the other ship and then I will make our best speed towards you to give them back and also aid where ever we can."

"Sounds good" The Captain said, "But if you can't get your pumps working by then, I will have to figure something else out for the other ship, at least by then I hope we'll have an assessment of their needs if you have the pumps ready to return in an hour that would be ideal. " He turned without saying more, like a man who just finished his lines in a school play and went back to the launch which brought him.

The other small boat from the Wachusetts stayed only long enough to drop off the submersible pumps and the crew which was needed to set them up. The pumps were small, but combined together and with the last of their own pumps still working, they seem to help a lot. The hope was that the pumps could draw off enough water to allow the repair teams to put a better patch on the interior hull, then perhaps the smaller pump would be enough to draw down the water and keep it down.

The Captain of the Coast Guard cutter radioed over to remind Dave that once he was underway to watch the water for anyone adrift, since others may have had problems in the storm. He also mentioned that with the number of distress calls they had received in the storm, the local search teams and vessels were spread thin and resources were at a minimum right now. Dave acknowledge and expressed his thanks once more. With the addition of the Coast Guard pumps, it wasn't long before the water started to lower in the flooded compartments. A few times, they had to stop and pull the pumps up in order to free a loose rag or two from the strainers, but all in all they appeared to be winning the battle.

The Coast Guard vessel disappeared into the mist of the dawn as it began it's search for the other ship. An hour later they radioed back and advised Dave that they had found them. It was the Sky Lark, a ship Dave was familiar with and he knew the Captain as well. It was still afloat, but only barely. They had absolutely no power and were unlikely to regain it while at sea. They hadn't sunk in the storm because of where the damage had occurred in their hull. Unlike Dave's ship, they were able to seal off more hatches in the affected compartments, at least enough to slow the flooding. They were still sinking because some of the breaches were impossible to shore up, and they had no pumps to remove the water which did flow in. Even though the water squeezed in at a slower pace, the water was rising at a predictable rate and with the time which had passed since the collision, the flood levels were reaching a critical state.

    The Captain of the Coast Guard vessel asked Dave if he could get to their position with the pumps as fast as they could, they might have a chance to save the ship. He also advised Dave that two of the crew of the Sky Lark had been lost overboard during the collision and asked Dave to keep out a watchful eye. With that Dave set their course towards the position of the Cutter and the Sky Lark, although he decided to keep their speed low, so as to not impede the progress of the damage control parties. The flooding did increase up forward and he tried to weigh the flooding with the speed and the time of their expected repairs. He had hoped to have the other pumps working by now and as he checked the progress of the teams who working on it. He was told by his First officer that it wouldn't be much longer before they arrived at the Cutter's position. This indeed was good news. With only hope and still looking for a lucky break, the great white vessel was aided by a search plane. It performed a detailed search for the missing crewmen. Everyone aboard the Sky Lark had been wearing their life jackets during the storm, so there was a chance they survived.

    Dave discovered while conferring with the Coast Guard that

his ship's navigational equipment had not been working properly prior to the accident. He was way off course and not even near where he thought he was, so during the incident he'd been much closer to the shore than they had imagined. Dave realized that the light he had seen truly had to have been his house. What he didn't know was that it had to have been just before the power went down. He realized that having been this close to shore, that even with the course adjustment he was about to make before the collision, it would not have been enough to keep his ship from hitting the rocky shallows just off the other tip of the bay. In a strange way the crash had saved them. Had the accident not occurred and had he not ordered them to steer out to sea after the collision, they would have run aground in the dark. Indeed, it was a wonder why the other vessel didn't flounder on the rocks and in the surf itself, perhaps the impact had helped them both in some way.

While the damage control parties fought the flooding and performed their duties with the skill of seasoned seamen, Dave went about to find out why the ships navigational devices failed. He also wanted to be sure that they were on course now, though with the rising of the sun they could pretty much determine their location from land markers. Also in a way and one which he would never admit too, being off course was an insult to his pride as he was always mindful of his position and of the state of his equipment which aided him in that determination. However, he figured later that the problem must have been deeper in the system than he himself could discover or that the problem had actually occurred with the navigational aids provided by the Maritime system, he wasn't sure. The compass seemed to be working ok. With that, a clock, and knowing your speed, you can chart your position without the need of any fancy devices and this Dave did religiously. However, if anyone on a previous watch had made an error in charting, or if the helmsmen for any length of time had his bearings wrong on the ship's compass and course, being off course even just a few degrees for a given length of time would be enough to get lost. Then they wouldn't know where they were until a time should arise where they could get a true bearing on their position and make the needed adjustments. In fact, it was true that they never found the mystery to this navigational error and Dave had to take the lumps for it during the investigation which followed. For now he couldn't help but think that even though two men were lost and probably dead, this collision may have saved his ship and the lives of his shipmates. And since the other ship was adrift and without power, they certainly would have gone down unknown to anyone with disastrous results. As it were, they were lucky that they themselves hadn't ended up on the rocks that night, running at their best speed directly into them unawares. Considering where they were when they collided with the other ship, it was just short of a miracle that things hadn't been worse. Putting it another way, even though Dave's ship was still under way, it lacked direction and was off course, they themselves might have gone aground in the dark. But together in this accident, the injured and the other ship along with the blind and the lost (his ship), were both saved. Perhaps in life that is why we need each other. Why the sick and old do not always die, why the blind of heart and lost of charity are sometimes found, often through interactions with one another in unplanned and often uncomfortable ways.

Dave made his way forward to check on the progress of the damage control. It appeared that most of the work had been done which could be done while at sea and all that was needed now was to route power for the two regular pumps and get them running. Knowing that the other vessel, the Sea Lark, was by now in an even more desperate need for flood control, and that because they themselves were now under way and that the water was still rising up forward, the first officer had the crew working feverishly on taking the final steps in getting the main pumps back on line.

The power box and the burned lines were determined to be the only real problems for running the pumps. But when they burned, they shorted and burned several lines all the way back to the main power board. It was discovered that someone at some unknown time, had replaced the barrel fuses to those lines with short copper rods, probably a quick fix from another time... a time which someone forgot to correct. Perhaps no one thought to put in the proper fuses because when the pumps were tested everything was working fine up until now and no one had inspected the fuse panel since then. Of course now the damage was far greater than a blown fuse and they where lucky that all it had burned out was the wires and boxes.

To fix this, the crew had to set new cables through the ship all the way to the main power system. A quick fix in a bad situation, kind of a long extension cord through the ship to a control box which was not needed for anything critical. If the wires had not been burned when things shorted out, perhaps they would have just moved the box itself but with the massive damage to the lines this seemed the logical choice of action. Everything was done quickly; lines were thrown through passageways and doors and laid on the deck loosely. All that was left was they had to throw the main current off line in order to make the connections. Since they couldn't isolate the jerry-rigged control box, this meant that most of the ship would be dark while they bolted down the power lines to the grid, but since it would only take a minute they figured the loss of power wouldn't effect much. Sharky assisted the ship's electrician with the cables though he wasn't an electrician himself. He was trying to learn what he could, when he could and besides, at this point everyone needed to pitch in and help and this is where he ended up. Sharky with the help of two others ran most of the lines through the different decks of the ship and then across to the main box and most of this was done before the ship had gotten underway again. They had used all the large wire extension cords aboard ship and they had to pull down some cables here and there and splice them in to make up the needed difference in length.

    The electrician himself worked quickly on the control box to have it ready for when the line made it that far. When all was ready, he waited for the machinist mate to throw the main switch and shut down the power from the control panel. To avoid complications, the trick was to slap the connections in place, tighten them down and power up as fast as possible. So thinking ahead, Sharky set up some emergency lamps to light the area during the short outage. He placed the cable ends near the waiting connections to be ready and had the tools close at hand which he needed. The electrician took in hand the onboard emergency phone to talk directly to the machines mate at the main board. "We're ready," came the word, and none too soon as the ship arrived at where the Coast Guard cutter was and they were more ready to retrieve the pumps if possible. "I'm ready," Sharky yelled to the electrician. "Nobody rush this," he replied, "Lets just do this in turn" Shutting down power to the whole ship wasn't a trivial task; he was trying to go over everything in his mind to see if there was anything he might have forgotten. Sending that much power through a metal vessel can be dangerous and he wanted to be sure everything was ready. "I think were good," he finally said, "shut her down!" he yelled in the phone. The power went out all over the ship and the room was only lit by the yellow glow from the emergency lamps. Sharky rushed forward and slapped the cables over the steel bolts and quickly began to tighten them. "Wait!" The electrician yelled rushing forward. "Let go of the lines, drop them and get back." He had forgotten something, something deadly and silent. But he wasn't quick enough, it was to late. No one had time to react.

  Suddenly to everyone's surprise the regular lighting came back on, power filled the cables from an unknown source. Sparks flew from the arcing wires in Sharky's hands. As his body stiffened he let out a blood-curdling scream. There was a bright flash and a loud pop and

Sharky was thrown from the panel. The lights again went out as the breakers tripped in another room from another emergency system which the electrician had forgotten about in all the commotion and efforts. "Get the power back on!" Dave yelled. "Get some help!" The electrician yelled into the phone for those at the power board to hold for a moment. He ran up and finished tightening the cables to the pumps, he yelled for them to restore power. The lights flickered and came on. The pumps below received their power and began to churn out the water but Sharky lay quiet on the deck. Dave rushed to his side, "Sharky," he said with a loud voice. "Are you all right?" But he knew he couldn't be. Sharky moaned in pain, his hands and arms were burned badly. It was incredible that he could still be alive through all the power that had surged through him. His eyes opened but vacancy looked beyond the gathering onlookers. For a time he seemed to stare into the dark corners of the room.

Struggling to form words Sharky softly said, "Someone's here." But he wasn't talking to anyone. Dave lifted Sharky's head and cradled it in his arms. As he looked up he saw the electrician stood over them watching, his eyes where filled with tears and guilt mixed with worry. He seemed to scan back and forth, looking from Sharky and then back down at the deck. Something was bothering him and it was more than Sharky's injuries. "The generator" he said, his words broken, "I forgot the emergency generator, it's on a power loop. It kicks on automatically when the power goes down. I forgot to turn it off. This is my fault." Seeing that Dave was looking at him, he added, "The Coast Guard doc is on his way." Dave knew what this was going to do to this man for the rest of his life, but right now wasn't the time to think about it. "Keep the pumps running," Dave said, "Have the crew pull the portables and get them over to the other ship." "Aye Captain" he said, without another word, the electrician turned and walked away, with mountains of sorrow on his shoulders.

    Sharky stirred again, "Someone's here," he said again. "Oh " his eyes seem to constrict with recognition. He looked steadily into the empty air on the other side of his Captain. Dave turned around but saw no one there. Sharky tried to lift his head and said, "I knew it would be you, it had to be." "Who's here?" Dave asked. "It's ok Dave" Sharky answered. He had never used Cap's name before, it had always been Captain or Cap. "I knew that we could not love so deeply on earth, to embrace a mothers arms or grasp a father's hand, just to have it fade into darkness at death. Death is not darkness, it is light." Dave brushed dirt away from Sharky's eyes, "Your not going to die my friend, hang in there. Besides you're too darn tough, you traded blows with Marcus. This is just a cake walk." Sharky stirred a little more, "My mom and dad are here and I'm going with them." Dave didn't know what to say, he had no answers for what he was hearing. "Just be still," he said. "Hang on here with us Sharky, help is almost here." "It's ok,"Sharky strained to get the words out in a whisper. His voice sounded cracked and dry, "Happiness is what is important and if it's supposed to be, then it's supposed to be." Sharky didn't seem to be talking to Dave, he seemed to be answering questions from someone unseen, someone which no one else could hear. "If it's time, it's time," he added, as he began to relax. "Mom, I knew you would come. It's been so long since I've seen you. Have I ever told you how much happiness I've had just in being your son?" Turning to Dave, his eyes seem to finally fill with recognition. He was somehow, aware that Dave was with him. "There is something important I have to tell you Cap," he slowly reached into the open air as if to touch something which Dave couldn't see, "something very important, Love is. . . " But before he could finish, a team of Coast Guardsmen rushed into the room, one of them was the doctor. Pushing their way around Dave, they began to work on Sharky but as suddenly as he had sprung to life, he faded and was gone.

Caps eyes filled with tears, he remembered the day Sharky died as clear as if it had happened yesterday. *I sure have missed him since that day,* he thought, *and he gave me a lot to think about.*

    The electrician never recovered from the guilt he had over Sharky's death and drank himself into ruin and an early grave. The investigation which followed, found that he was also responsible for the metal rods that were left in the breaker boxes for fuses. Something he had done and forgot to correct about a year before the accident. Something simple and probably functional for that momentary need, yet it contributed to a string of events which ruined his life and killed another... or perhaps killed them both. He never put to sea again after that voyage, and no one could console him until the day he died. What a loss, not being able to forgive yourself over a single event. Though the results of his mistake could have hardly been worse. A crisis of great magnitude for anyone to endure. Two lives were lost that day. A life sent into the arms of eternity, calling to his mother and others who seemed to be there, while the other life, fell into the pit of despair and remorse, alone and lost.

    Chapter thought: Is there peace from the errors we commit in our life? If it is carelessness or a moment of incompetence, or even a simple lack of awareness in a situation which later becomes critical; can we find peace when we know we have hurt somebody else?

    We know that Christ died for our sins but did he also suffer that we might be free from the remorse of our stupidity? Oh yes, the answer is yes, like unto sin if we seek His peace He will give it. It is there and when we find this peace through trust in Him; we need not let the memory of that day torment us again, because through Him we are freed from it.

Chapter Eight

Hero's

Cap pulled a blanket out of his pack and after adding wood to the fire, he wrapped himself in it and set down to continue reading. He paused to remember when he told a friend about Sharky's death a few months after the accident. The man was quick to tell Dave that when we die we lay in the grave until the resurrection, in a state they call sleep and that the only thing he had witnessed with Sharky was the delusions of a dying brain, nothing more. Dave said to him, "I don't know about such things, but when Shakey died, I was talking with him and so was someone else, someone I couldn't see." Dave had added that he obviously had never seen a man die or at least someone pass from this earth in a way Sharky had done. "I don't have any Bible things I could say to you, but I know what I saw and heard on that day so many years ago." he remembered saying.

Cap shifted positions and began to glance at the pages again. He also wondered when the old man would return with his explanations. But in a way, it wouldn't bother him if he never saw him again as long as he lived. As if his thoughts had brought them, several men dressed like bikers came walking over to Cap's fire. They looked around his campsite and began sitting around the fire. One of them was obviously the leader because all the rest seemed to take their cues from his directions. Yet he himself sat quietly, as a black leather bound grungy looking member of their group got in close to Cap.

"Where's the party old man?" he asked, "Your friend, the other old guy, said you had a party going on over here." "Not here," Cap said, "I'm afraid there's no party left in me and that guy is not my friend." One of the bikers saw Cap's pack and began to reach for it. "Nothing in there either," Cap said pulling his things closer to himself. Another biker grabbed Cap's old logbook and began to thumb through it. "That's ok," said the lead biker, "If you give us some cash, we'll get our own party going and start having fun right here. You don't mind right!" he said in a forceful tone. Cap looked right into the eyes of the large greasy biker, "No party, no money. If you want something from me, lets get to it right now so you can leave and I can have the quiet I came out here to find." The leader motioned for the other biker to sit down. He was distinct from the others because he had blond, but very dirty hair. He stood up and walked over to Cap, "You know, your friend was a lot more fun than you are. But he said *you* have all the money, so I don't think it would be too much for you to help out a little. I mean none of us are going to hurt you and you might say with us here, your safer than you have ever been before." He began to laugh and turned to his friends, "Wouldn't you say so boys?" the gang began to laugh together.

He watched Cap's eyes and smiled. He felt like he had made his point. He reached for Cap's bag figuring that is where he kept his money. But Cap grabbed the young man's hand with his left hand and with his right he made one swift move upward and cut the belt off the bikers pants, using his whittling knife. The pants fell around the biker's knees, as Cap pulled him in closer, "You and your gang can hurt me, I am aware of that. I am an old man now, not even close to what I use to be. But right at this moment in time, right now, I could hurt you if I wanted to. I could gut you like a fish for the pan, but I don't want to." A couple of the other bikers got up and began to rush towards Cap. The lead biker could feel the knife too close to his belly and yelled, "Stop." He knew his friends wouldn't always stop even if they are told to, but this time they listened. Cap continued looking back into the young mans eyes. "Good idea," Cap said "Good for you anyway. But as I was trying to say, I have nothing to give you so just leave, the choice is yours. You feel you have the need to rob me so take what you want, because there is nothing here for you or your friends." Cap let go of him and let him fall back as he put his knife away in his pocket. The biker didn't say a word. He just looked at

Cap, his eyes full of anger. He pulled his pants up tightly with a jerk. He reached out suddenly and grabbed Caps back pack, tearing it away from him. He took the rope off the front of it, which Cap kept handy for his camping needs. Forcefully, with a yank one way and then the next he tied it around his waist to keep his pants up, and then threw the damaged belt into the fire. Throwing Cap's pack back to the ground, he looked at Cap as if he was going to kill him. Stepping forward towards Cap, he reached as if to grab him by his lapels. Suddenly the bushes next to them erupted into a violent storm of loud thrashing sounds. The biker stopped in his tracks, everyone was startled and no one could see who was coming towards them in the dark. Whoever it was, they were coming through with a purpose. "Someones coming," one of them yelled. The rough biker who now held Cap by his coat, let go and he and his friends turned and ran away as quickly as they could. As Cap watched them, he walked down the beach and could see them for quite a way as the moon silhouetted their figures with light from above and from off the lake. They finally disappeared into the dark near the far end and later he saw police lights. In the distance pulling up hard and fast he heard several motorcycles fire up and race off.

They've gone, thank heavens, he thought and at least he didn't have to worry about them coming back to finish him off now. But what was in the bushes making the noise? It was still there and as loud as ever, even though the bikers were now long gone. Cap cautiously turned and went into the dark to see if he could find cause. It couldn't be the old man, he was the jerk who set him up with the bikers, so he certainly wouldn't rescue him. In fact he would more than likely find Cap's struggle and possible beating entertaining. After a few steps he turned to look at the fire. From where he was standing, the firelight seemed to light up the whole area. Cap knew the dark, and he knew if someone was this far from camp they would be well hid, but why scare off the bikers and then *stay* hid? Suddenly from behind him, the bush began to thrash. Startled, he realized he had found the exact bush from which the sound was coming and as he looked he saw it tremble and wave violently again and again. He realized it wasn't something trying to get through the bush, it was something trying to get out. Cap separated several branches and as he did a rush of gray and white almost hit him in the face as it suddenly whizzed by. With a blur it passed near Caps head and he felt his hair ruffle with the fluttering force of this mystery assailant. Cap stumbled back as this screeching creature came plumping to the ground near him. As Caps eyes cleared he realized it was the seagull, his old friend he had been feeding most of the night. "Got stuck did ya?" Cap laughed. "Seems like you have been on my side all night long, I suppose we are kindred spirits in a way, both born to love this old world we live on. But bikers, game wardens, and mean old mean men, I can't figure out why the Stevens family ever moved out here. It sure is a dangerous place. After all that, I can't figure why anyone is worried about the Mormons, so far they've been harmless." Finally settling down he went back to the book, it read.

The day had cleared remarkably compared to the storm which had pounded the shores the night before. However, in the ebb of the long day, most of it's light had faded once again towards evening. Linda stood at the windows as she had the night before. She wondered where Dave might be. She knew he would be late, but not this late. She felt it had to have been his vessel that struck the Sea Lark last night. The only ray of hope which she had, was that after Adam returned from the Roberts, he had news that both ships were still afloat. But the hope was fractured by the report of deaths. While there, Wayne had also used his radio to call for an ambulance. When the weather cleared it arrived and the two men which Linda had spent the night mending were now gone.

As far as the storm went, the skies had cleared to a broken blue and the seas once again beat the shore in its slow rhythmic wake.

The excitement was over, except for waiting, and as time went by this became as hard emotionally as fighting the storm itself. The phones were still down so she couldn't call anyone and the garage was still blocked so she couldn't leave. Even her bike was still down by the picnic tree half buried in sand. She thought about walking but her injured leg throbbed in pain every time she used it. The house was quieter than usual, not even the wind blew to keep her company. An old clock, which Dave brought home from some distant port, ticked annoyingly in the solitude, keeping count the passing of each moment. It took some time but the phones eventually began to work and Wayne Roberts called to check on Linda. He also confirmed to her that it *had* been Dave's ship that was in the accident and that everything was ok. Dave would be home as soon as he could be. He didn't know yet who had been killed aboard ship and the information about what happened was still vague. That Dave was ok was good news, but the silence that loomed after she hung up was still taunting. Finally, in the failing light of this day, Linda noticed the lights of an auto making its' way up towards the house. Linda's hopes were fulfilled when Dave came rushing through the back door into the house. He came running, not walking, into Linda's arms and the two held each other in a long awaited embrace. "It was you?" she asked, a tear forming in her eye.

Dave squeezed her tightly. "You heard about the collision?" He questioned. "I was part of it," she softly replied. "and I thought I might have lost you." Dave looked at her with a puzzled expression on his face. They sat and talked for hours as Linda rehearsed to Dave about the two sailors she found and how the night had unfolded. Dave hadn't heard that the two sailors had been found. He was so glad when she told him, but how strange it was that their two worlds had collided, his ship at sea and their home on shore. He shuttered at the risk she had taken, but his heart was filled with gladness at the person who she is and what she was willing do for others. Dave looked at Linda's wounds and realized that she would need a doctor's care as soon as they could get to town. Silently, as he re-bandaged her leg, he realized the only person who had died that night was Sharky. "It's odd how things happen," he said. "It does make you wonder."

A new Day In Turnbridge:

Several weeks had passed since the accident and Linda awoke to a new day in that large house on the farthest outskirts of Turnbridge. Rolling over in bed, she found that she was alone. Sitting up, Linda looked about the room and paused let her mind clear from the nights sleep. Suddenly she remembered that she shouldn't be alone, Dave's been home for weeks, how could she have misplaced those days and nights? The accident had been a blessing in its' own way. While the ship was being repaired, Dave would be home for months. Except for his time overseeing the repairs and completing the lengthy investigation which follow an incident like this, his job for a while would be more or less nine to five each day.

Linda quickly dressed and searched the house for her wayward husband, but to her despair he wasn't to be found. Puzzled, because it was Dave's day off, she went into the kitchen and looked out the back door, she even tried shouting his name, but no answer. It was then she noticed a small note hanging from the refrigerator, it read;

"About 08:30 you will find this note, so meet me at the fishing pier at 10:00 o'clock sharp! See ya, Love ya Lindy Lady."

Linda glanced up at the old round clock which hung on the wall above the stove. 08:30 she was impressed. Looking at the note again, it was also obvious that Dave had figured her search for him into his timetable and Linda's preference in riding her bike to town. Ten o'clock gave her just enough time to freshen up, change and then travel the distance. She thought for a moment that she might be ornery and drive down, but Linda realized that Dave was planning something cute, so she figured she would just play along. Linda knew that Dave could be devious, so she continued to look for clues to what he might be up to. After changing and throwing her hair into a ponytail, she was off. She figured the sooner she got there, the sooner she would know. During the whole trip to town, Linda considered the possibilities of what he might be up to. *Obviously*, she thought, *Dave has intended on keeping me wondering* and it worked, she was stumped. "What clever plan has he set up?" She said aloud as she peddled along the road. Linda decided it was most likely breakfast at a small cafe near the pier. Obviously Dave figured, that with his mysterious invitation, it would add to the mystique, which of course it did. *But I do have an ace,* she mused, *yes! Sherry.* She would know what Dave was up too and since her house was on the way, she could still make it to the pier by ten. Usually she took her time when riding to town, just to enjoy the countryside, but if she could get to the docks a little before expected, maybe she could add a surprise or two herself.

    It wasn't long before Linda was turning through the gate of the gray wooden fence which surrounded Sherry's home. Annoyingly, as she approached she noticed the home was dark and appeared empty. When Linda went to the door, she found that what she sensed was true, no one was there. After peeking around, she found Sherry's car still in the garage. This was very very strange. Sherry never went anywhere without her car, she hated being trapped so she always drove herself. "So where can she be?" She wondered aloud. Jumping on her bike, she rode to the hill which overlooked the town. Below, Linda could see the piers and docks and the spot where she was to meet Dave. Nothing seemed unusual and everything was quiet and peaceful. The many colored fishing boats bordered the docks lined in rows. The several sailing vessels with their masts secured rose above them as she had seen many times before in her life. At this angle the lines and rigging of so many vessels in one place looked mixed and entangled, yet in truth they were set in orderly fashion. Quietly and gently they bobbed in the water as if waiting in silent slumber for their crews. *Nothing!* Linda thought, *there was no activity at all*. That in itself was odd, there was not even the usual hustle and bustle normal for this time of day. Her anticipation went from pleasure to concern. Slowly the thought of a romantic breakfast was being replaced by concern and an overwhelming desire to rush down and find out what the trouble is. Speeding off she finally arrived at the pier, 10:00 o'clock by the way. The docks were void of life, it was quiet and eerie. In all her years in Turnbridge, Linda had never seen this place so quiet. There wasn't even the usual commotion common around the piers as the boats got ready to go fishing or others returning from long stays out on the water. All the vessels were still tied up to their moorings, all rigging secure. This meant something had happened more dire and more important than work.

Perhaps Dave's note wasn't an invitation; perhaps he was aware of something bad, and rushed off to deal with it? That would explain why he had left so quickly without waking her. And since it was very quiet, what ever happened must have happened at the cargo docks outside of town. A fire or something, an explosion maybe, and that's why he would want to meet her here. It made sense, all the towns' fishermen were part of the local volunteer fire department and that a call to a dangerous fire would be one of the very few things to take them away from their work. But as she scanned the sky she couldn't see any smoke, so she was still puzzled.

Linda took her bike out onto the dock, she figured if she could find someone, anyone, they might confirm or deny her fears. She stopped. It was far to quiet. Her foot slowly left the pedal to touch the wooden planks. She looked about and got off the bike and stood next to it as she slowly moved forward when out of nowhere the air resounded, "BLAM! BLAM! BLAM!" Linda almost fell down with the surprising reverberations as three cannons rocked the air. Suddenly, a band began to play and a crowd rushed out towards her.

Linda saw that Adam, one of the men she had rescued on that stormy night, was leading the on coming procession. Dave was walking along side him a large impish grin, beamed from his face. Beside him was the Mayor along with Sherry; who by the way had Tom locked in her arms and hard under tow. The old school teacher, Mrs. Martin was also there and she was waving a small banner in the air. Rushing over the crowd lifted Linda onto their shoulders and carried her into an old fish processing building near by. Inside the floors had been cleared and a banner read, "To our Hero, The Lady Lindy." She knew right away who worded it.

After setting her on the stand beside several city officials, the mayor addressed the crowd. He was a short potbellied man, who had been the mayor for years, mostly because no one else wanted the job. Like out of a storybook he wore a large, red, white and blue ribbon over his shoulder, and if you didn't know better you would have thought he was getting ready for the Fourth of July. Even so as he motioned in the air with his hands everyone quieted down responding to his cue. "We all know about the tragic collision at sea," he said "and we know that it occurred just off the coast of our quiet, humble community just four and twenty days ago." Mrs. Martin nudged the Mayor with her elbow, her poke was hard and almost took his breath away; "Five and twenty days ago," she corrected him. Turning to Dave, she whispered, "He was like that in school as well." "Ok," he continued rubbing his side. "Five and twenty days ago. We also know that in this tragic event a life was lost and we reverence his memory. And some of us remember that he was the most fighting man we ever saw. Why when he, Sharky, beat down the mountain of a man, Marcus, I made so much' Mrs. Martin jabbed him in again in the side, but this time much harder. He just looked at her and continued. "However," he stopped and looked at Mrs. Martin to see if she was going to jab him again, "We are gathered here today to recognize the efforts of one of our own local girls. For it is because of her that the lives of two of our shipmates of the seagoing trade were saved, Adam Warner and Josh Pullman." The crowed roared with applause. "Had it not been for her," he added, "and her knowledge, courage and dedication to life, they too would have been lost." The crowd began clapping again as, Mrs. Martin, jabbed him again unexpectedly. "We know what she did. Get on with it! The election was a month ago." She softly said to him, all the while keeping a smile and applauding. The Mayor cleared his throat, "Linda, we the citizens of Turnbridge want you to know, we are thankful to you. You are a credit to your town for saving the lives of these two men. But we all know you have been saving our lives for years. Though it might not have been in raging storms or storm tossed seas, it was in your service and your love and compassion, which you always gave freely. From the little old man in the care home, to those of us you watched over when we were ill, and especially again for these two men who would have surely died. While their lives stood forfeit, held fast in the grasp of the angry sea, had it not been for you Linda, the night would have been even darker. Thank you from all our hearts."

The Mayor hung a gold metal around Linda's neck, a brightly colored, red, white and blue ribbon suspended it. He kissed her cheek and shook her hand. As Linda looked down at the metal she noticed that it read, "Best home pastries", but it had a white ribbon across its face that read, "Hero". "Sorry," the mayor whispered in her ear, "it was left over from the fair and this was the best we could do for now." The crowed applauded and shouted with whistles and yells. Adam walked up and handed Linda flowers. A large gold card dangled from the stems and bore the names of all his shipmates. Josh, of course, was still in the hospital several miles away, but his name was at the top in large bold letters. Linda couldn't fight the tears and gave everyone her thanks. A band began to play and they all mingled as refreshments were served. The community laughed, danced, and told stories of their lives at sea and the day slowly faded into evening in song and celebration.

Later that night Dave and Linda sat together in the warm firelight, which flickered from their fireplace. The day was satisfying yet tiring and thankfully was coming to an end. "You know," Linda softly said. "I never thought of myself as a hero. I only did what I needed to do and only what I knew how to do." Dave brushed her hair with his hand and then gently touched her chin and looked into her eyes. "That's all heroes ever are, honey. There is no one definition. If you can be called a hero by those who know and love you and you don't know why, you are probably the truest hero of all." "Yes." Linda answered. "But when you only do what has to be done what must be done, it's hard to call it special." Dave smiled and gave Linda a kiss. "Not everyone can see so clearly, not everyone can react so true. Sometimes the special actions of others help remind us how we should feel and what the worth of others really are. Heroes not only save a life, but often their act stirs our soul and causes us to feel something in our hearts. For a lot of folks, sometimes that is what they need most of all." Linda looked back into Dave's eyes, deeper than she had ever looked before. She knew, really knew she loved this man.

Cap threw a cracker to the seagull, which jumped to his feet to chase it down. "I guess we're not always asked to risk our lives for other people. But if we had too, many people would without consideration of their own lives. Yet to do the easy things we find it difficult and a bother. Easy things like saying hello to a stranger you pass by, visiting a neighbor, even taking care of an aged mother or father. A stranger would jump off a bridge into frozen water to save someone he had never met. Yet we often forget to be a friend, when all someone needed was an ear to listen to them. Yes it seems like it is easier to give up your life for a stranger than it is to give up your time for those you should know better. Sometimes work and responsibilities become so demanding, that we forget why we are working, and for whom we are working. We may say we are working for an employer, or even working for ourselves when self employed. Shouldn't the truth be that we are working for our families to provide and improve their lives over time. In the United States it is said we live to work, while those in Europe like to feel that they work to live. Meaning their employment is to provide a means to live, not become the object of their lives. Dedication to our work is commendable and proper when done in wisdom, but our work should first be to each other and our family. Right?"

"I guess first you have to have a family," a voice said, walking into Cap's firelight. It was the blond biker. He sat down on a rock near Dave. "Look," he said, "I haven't come here to cause you trouble." "Then why are you here?" Cap asked not unkindly. "When you stood up to me a while ago," he said, "if you had been any other old guy we would have chewed you up and left you for bird meat." "Why didn't you?" Cap asked. "I was going too, believe me, but I had time to cool off. Besides, when you looked at me I thought I saw my father in your eyes. You even sounded like him." The biker said. "Your father often cut your pants off?" Cap smiled. "No," he he chuckled briefly, "I haven't seen him since I was sixteen, that's when my mother moved us to Texas. A year later, I had sold enough dope to get my bike and I've been riding with these guys ever since." "Doesn't sound like a very good life," Cap said. "It seemed good at least for us, but not so good for anyone we ran into. Anymore things are not as much fun. I guess you can't live life as if it's one long party and have the fun really last." "Why don't you get away then?" Cap asked "Yeah, how?" the young man wondered out loud. "Change your friends, even if these guys have been your long time buddies. Change something about your life and make it stick. Find out what's good and do it." Cap answered. The biker slid a six-pack of beer near Cap, "You want a beer old man?" "Cap's my name, they call me Cap, and no I gave up drinking a long

time ago." "Bad dreams huh?" the kid smiled. "No, I remember getting drunk with a friend in a Central American country once. He was so drunk he fell down and couldn't get up. We were far out of the regular tourist areas and I knew if we got mugged no one would ever hear from us again. I couldn't rouse him so I sat up all night protecting the both of us. It was the longest night I can remember. I was worried the whole time that some local group of thugs might roll us for our money. By morning he was able to walk and we made our way back to our ship. After that I never wanted to feel so helpless again, especially because of booze or 'social drinking' as some may call it."
"Sounds like a bender, not just a social drink." the biker laughed.
"It always *starts* as a social drink but that's not what stopped me from drinking. I was called over to one of my shipmates home late one evening He was cussing and fighting with his wife and he had hit their 12-year-old son in the face. The whole house was in an uproar. When he sobered up a little, he apologized for what he had done and things worked out for a while. But his pattern of arguments and hitting got worse. The drinking never stopped. They're divorced now. It was so sad. I liked them both, but now the son is drinking," "So that was it?" the biker said, picking up one of Caps crackers from out of the sand and eating it. Cap smiled and handed him some crackers from out of

the package. "No, there's more. I was coming home from the shipyards one night and I saw a car in the ditch, inside two men were hurt badly. As I helped get them out of the car and up onto the road to wait for the ambulance I noticed several bottles of beer in the back seat. It was clear that the two men where very drunk. The car was totaled and one of the men lost the use of his right arm permanently. It wasn't a week later that I saw the fire department going to the local inn. The inn was closed, but some kids had broken in the night before and had been swimming in their pool. They were having a party I was told, celebrating the 21st birthday of one of the boys. I guess he was now old enough to drink so he was taking full advantage of it. When he disappeared that evening, his friends thought he had gone home, so they continued to swim until the manager kicked them out. Well, they found out later their friend hadn't gone home. He drowned in that pool that very night. Since all the pool lights were off nobody knew it. They had been swimming all night with their dead friend below them on the bottom."

"Wow, a really bad experience, yeah, I guess that would make someone give up the bottle."the kid replied thoughtfully. "No that's not it, don't you see?" Cap explained, "Nothing but bad happens around drinking. Nothing good surrounds it at all- death, divorce, destroyed families, lives ruined, nothing but pain ever came of it. The good times, the fun, the friendly socializing, is all part of the same excuse, the excuse that is finally used when a disaster happens. Then we hear the words, 'I'm sorry. I was drunk, I didn't mean it.' People who have the occasional high ball are not taking *chances* with ruining their lives, they have taken the first steps down the road to where their lives *can be* ruined. Life is a course, a destination, one which we choose. If things lead to good then usually happiness surrounds that activity. But if they lead to pain and sorrow and misery, then isn't the answer simple?" Cap emphasized.

"Yeah, I was right," The biker said, as he got up to walk away, "You sound like my dad."

"Thanks, I'll take that as a compliment " Cap responded, "Perhaps you should go and find you dad. Perhaps you will find out how life could be fun again, but in a real way."

"Yeah, I might do that," he said. "But that's a long way to go"

"I know," said Cap, "it will be a long road, but I think you might be happier if you travel it." As the biker disappeared into the dark Cap knew he was alone again, he picked up his book and began to read once more:

Dave sat in his cabin checking some of the final paperwork as his ship sped home from it's final stop. He thought of how good it would be to be back home again after this long voyage. In his mind he recalled Lindy as she stood on the dock while he parted this last time. She was several months pregnant with their first child and Dave really hated leaving her, but he had no choice.

Suddenly like a lightning flash and a thunderclap, Cap's mind was once again back at Bear Lake staring at the book as if it were on fire! "I cannot read this!" Cap said, throwing the book down. The bird took flight in fear and circled the camp overhead. "Not these pages, I cannot live them again!"

Chapter Nine

A Tear Says 'I Love You'

Out of the dark came a voice "What's the matter?" It was that blasted old man again, but this time he seemed to have concern in his voice. Cap was still reeling from the stark, painful reminder of his past and did not think about the fact that he shouldn't answer this one time menace. "It's this book, it makes things too real. I am not only reading it's pages, I'm seeing them, living in the past, I cannot enter this next chapter. I know where it's going." The old mans face looked a little younger and his expressions seemed to show empathy, "I tried to warn you, I was only trying to help when I wanted to keep you from reading this book. I told you that I had read it and I am sorry for this invasion into you life, but since I knew what was in that book, you should have trusted me. I heard what you said to that young man. It was good advice. If something is bad you should avoid it and as we both know the pages which come next are bad."

"They were hard times, I will agree" Cap said. "But not bad in the way you are referring to them. They were sad, the most painful I have ever felt in my heart. What sane person would ever want to feel those feelings again?"

"And that's my point," the old man said, "You have said it so well, those feelings were awful and they cheated you. Your life was never the same, never fulfilled, because of what happened. Trust me now, give me the book and just read your log. Too much of some things are a bad thing. Let go of the book and the story will be finished. Your pain will be over."

"That's it," Cap said softly, "When I faced that era of my life I thought, for me, all the good things were over. I thought I would never have those things in my life again. I believed it, that's why it hurt so bad. Everything felt ended, lost, and helpless. I didn't just cry tears of love, I wept for what I thought would never be again. But I realize I have learned something new tonight, something I have always known but did not see. That is, I have had the clues about life all along. I have been sorting these things out this entire evening. I want to read the book, maybe I am ready." Cap picked up the book and dusted it off. It fell open to the page where he had stopped. He looked at the old guy and said, "Thank you for reminding me."

"Baa," he said "I tried to be your friend, I am sorry you didn't listen. I guess now you will have to pay the price." The old guy, who strangely now looked younger than Cap walked away, vanishing into the dark.

Cap read on:

He recalled Lindy as she stood on the dock while he departed this last time. She was several months pregnant with their first child and Dave really hated leaving her, but he had no choice. Another Captain had been scheduled to take this run but he became ill at the last moment and Dave was the only one available. Wayne hated to ask him. He knew the trip would be cutting it close to Linda's due date, but in the end they were left with no choice. On this trip Dave made sure they made all haste at every stop. Of course the crew was aware of the Captain's situation and pitched in so that everything would go smooth, and it did. Wayne made a fortune from this run and everyone seemed pleased on how things were going. Dave and the crew also stood ready to receive large bonus checks because of all their good work. Wayne added a thought to the next message he sent to Dave, requesting that Linda be pregnant before all such voyages.

Dave sat quietly in his room and slowly he opened a letter from Linda which he got at their last stop. The letters were usually dated because the mail always had to wait at the different ports till the ship arrived. It was impossible to get much mail at sea, so sending a letter had to be plotted out in advance. Dave knew the letter was a bit old but he was glad to get it anyway, it was still a message from home.

Dave my love.

Its' been really difficult without you here, but Sherry has been a real gem. I can't wait for you to get home and you don't know how much it means to me that you will be back in time for the birth of our first baby.

Tom was in port for two weeks and he spent most of his free time helping Sherry put in a nursery. I think somethings going to happen with those two real soon. Sherry said if he takes any longer to ask her to marry him, she's going to do it. Tom always seemed the lady's man but I think when it comes to tying the knot, he's a real chicken.

Anyway, I have a million things to say, but I'll wait to say them to you in person. I'll be there when you arrive, even if I have to waddle out in a wheel barrel. I'll always be there, Dave.

I will always stand to greet you, at the journeys end.

I will wait through darken hours,
I will watch by light of day,
I'll call your name so softly,
from the shores of emerald bay.
I'll hold your image fastly
in the lockets of my heart.
to tell you that I love you,
in those days that we're apart.

On the breeze, that may carry
this message, I do send,
I will always stand to greet you,
upon the journeys end.

  with love to my Cap,

Lindy

Dave knew this was the last leg home on the voyage, but it was going to be the longest one as well, not in miles, but in anticipation. *It will be good to be home he thought,* and he had to ask himself, *Is making these long runs even worth it anymore?* With a child coming into his life, it might be better taking the shorter and more local cargo runs. He liked the idea of being a dad and took it seriously. He knew he had to make both lives, captain and dad, fit as one. It had been a long day to this point and he was tired. With all his daydreaming he began to nod a little.

Suddenly he found himself standing on the deck of his ship. It was night, he was alone, and the ship was underway. Dave looked out into a misty moonlit night. Though it was dark, the horizon was lit by millions of fires in the night's sky. As he watched, he felt a shadow pass by and then drift out and over the water. It was the form of a woman. And as he watched, he realized it was Linda. "Linda," he called out, as he reached to offer his hand. He felt joy and yet wonderment at what this could mean. "Why are you here?" he asked. But she seemed to drift farther out over the water away from him. She said nothing, but her hands waved to him, touching her heart and then her lips, he felt what he could almost hear "Goodbye." "Linda" he called out again, his voice desperate and his hands reaching as far as he could reach. Dave woke to a soft knock at the door, he was shaking a little from the dream. Digging his knuckles into his eyelids, he recomposed himself and said. "Come in." There seemed to be some hesitation to his invitation and he began to wonder if he had been heard. Slowly peaking in the door, Sparks' face came into view. Dave spouted in a pleasant way, "Well, come in Sparks, what's up?" Sparks walked in without a word, he slowly asked Dave to come with him to the communications room. Dave knew it was bad news just by the way Sparks was acting. He got up and walked behind Sparks who sat down in his usual chair.

Sparks grabbed the mike of his radio and said, "Go ahead, he's here" to who ever was on the other end. "Dave, my friend," a voice said over the speaker, Dave realized it was Wayne. "I wish there was another way to bring you news like this. But there is no way to prepare you for this. Dave, today at twelve thirty our time, Linda your wife, died of complications due to her pregnancy. There was no warning. My wife and Sherry were there when it happened and she passed so very quickly. They tried everything they could to save the baby, but they were unsuccessful. I'm so very sorry my friend, I'm so very sorry."

Disbelief and shock slammed into him like an avalanche. Why were they lying to him about something so important? Was this all a bad joke? Deep down, no matter how hard he tried to push it away, he knew it was true and the echo of the dream of just a few moments ago bounced around his head like a phantom. A bitter metallic taste filled his mouth as a rush of grief flowed into Dave's frame like rivers of ice and pain. He fought for composer and took deep breath after deep breath to control his emotions. Gently Dave took the mike and answered, "Thank you Wayne. We're almost home, thank you. I know you will take care of things, thank you." With that he turned to the door and walked slowly back toward his cabin. Before he went in he turned and said. "Thank you Sparks." His voice almost broke and his thanks felt like a lie, but those were the only words he could find strength to say. He turned and walked into his cabin, closing the door behind him.

At first it was unreal, but also painfully real at the same time. He couldn't believe it, it *had* to be some cruel joke. But no one would do something like this, so it had to be true. Emptiness, loneliness, feeling lost, all blended into a river which flowed right through his heart.

"No," he thought to himself. But he wasn't sure what the "No," was for. Sparks walked in and asked if there was anything else he could do, but Dave motioned 'no' and waved him kindly out with his hand. Dave had endured pain, grief and fear in his life, but never before had he felt the surge of helplessness as he did now. He wasn't sure that he could bear seeing the piers of home if she wasn't standing there waiting. He wanted to be home now, but yet he was afraid to be there and find her gone. Out here it still wasn't real, but when he reached port it would all be true, and forever. Dave's heart ached. This powerful man's heart strained as he battled the tears which now fought to escape. In grief, his hand slapped hard upon the desk, the stinging sensation in his fingers mocked him as it confirmed he was not dreaming. "No," he again said aloud. But this time he knew what it meant. He couldn't let grief control him, he loved her too much for that. Snatching up a pen, Dave began to write.

My Dearest love Lindy,

I know that I am sending this letter to an empty house, but somehow I need to reach you and tell you of my love. I am lost inside Lindy, I am lost.

Men on earth have many times said, `I love you,' but this simple phrase only found meaning in my heart when I was with you. Before man placed his foot upon the waters or climbed the highest of mountains, before we were born, and after we are gone these simple three words have found their place for us. As I cannot see the hearts of those who shared love in the past, nor do I know the hearts of the future, in these words which mankind has spoken so many times, I say, Lindy my love no one has ever said such words: "I love you," more truly than when I shared them with you.

Many great loves have found life by poetic hands, both in play and song, for as they have had their birth in the writers hand yet they are just phantoms of truth on a page.

My love is <u>real</u>, our love is <u>real.</u> It is found in each caring act, which we shared. It is found in each tender embrace that was ours. It is felt in the grasp of your hand in mine and as I look into your eyes and you look into mine...it is real.

So very much I would like to say these words to you, but that will not happen. I hope in some way the measure of my life has told you, you are my girl and I am your man. Love is the path we walk a destination for which we make, it flows from hearts which share the common goal of each other. And since all that flows has a course and destination, <u>the</u> destination of my love... is you. I love you, I miss you. I throw a stick into a creek and watch it drift away in the current. It passes from sight, but remains as real as when I sent it on its' way. It also has a destination:

For the stream flows to the river
and the river to the sea,
along its' path it brings my love,
for you, as it came from me.

If it must be carried farther,
to the ocean it will flow,
it will traverse mighty waters
where the whales and dolphins go.

It will gently then pass by you,
and you will cup it in your hand,
like floating thistles on a breeze,
it drifts to softly land.

It will whisper kindly in your ear,
gentle poems of heart filled love
as it came like dew from heaven
 from the sky so high above.

Though, started on that moment,
when I sent it on it's way.
It will reach, to say I love you.
in these simple words I pray.......

I will love you forever
Your Cap, Dave.

      The ship's journey was soon over yet it held in it's wake the darkest hours Dave had ever experienced. At this point there was no quicker way to get him home other than finishing the remaining days aboard ship. Yet he did his duty with little complaint as he held his grief for those nights and days while he was alone in his cabin. The ships mooring lines were set and it was pulled into dock once more. Like a silent movie few voices were heard. No crowd waited on the pier except a few loved ones who came to get their husbands and fathers. For Dave, his friend's were waiting quietly and said little when he finally came across the gangway. Linda's funeral had been several days before the ship arrived, there was no way to wait for Dave's arrival. Loading into Tom's car they drove directly to the cemetery.

      As they arrived Dave looked sadly from the windows of the car at the flower covered plot where Linda had been laid to rest. Dave opened the car door and walked away without closing it. Slowly he crossed the soggy soaked grass to Lindy's grave. The morning was wet but not rainy, the sky was gray and a mist seemed to blow across the ground saturating everything completely. Though unnoticed because of grief, the air was clean and all the colors of nature seemed ablaze under the random passing of the bright cloudy light of the early day. The ground was still broken where she now lie and Dave slowly knelt to touch it. He picked a few green blades of grass and held them close to his eye and then let them fall to the ground without care. His thoughts were of Lindy and inside he could only see her face and her smile shining back. What was next in life he could no longer see, he was alone.

    Sherry suddenly appeared from behind, and Tom was not far behind of her. They had waited in the car to let Dave be alone at the graveside. After a short bit, Sherry decided that this was a mistake and headed over to Dave. In some ways friends were helpful, in other ways they were a painful reminder that Linda was now gone. They ran into each other's arms and for a time cried. Dave finally mustered up the courage to ask, "What happened?" He had already talked to others by radio from the ship, but he knew that Sherry had been there. At first she didn't answer, it took more than a bit to recompose. But as soon as she could, it all spilled out of her as if it were both a torment and a relief to let it go. Linda was just sitting and talking to her like they did everyday. When Linda suddenly stood up without warning, she knew something was wrong and before Sherry could even ask what was going on, she started bleeding badly. It happened so fast and it couldn't be stopped, she got weaker and weaker until she was finally gone.

"I saw her go Dave, I saw her go...." She began to cry with great fat tears spilling down her cheeks and onto her blouse. Tom reached around her shoulder and hugged her tight. He added, "The doctor who responded and went with her to the hospital delivered the baby, a girl, but the baby was also gone and couldn't be saved. They thought they had something at first, but decided your daughter had died before she was born." His face was stone as he spoke, the wearing of emotions evident in his eyes. Sherry started crying harder than ever and Dave held both of them as best he could as her quiet sobs shook her body hard from the inside.

"Thank you for being there," he said. "I'm so glad you are her friends." Sherry dried her eyes and grasped Tom's arm hard. Tom reached over and patted Dave on the shoulder. "We have breakfast ready for you, as soon as your ready, my friend." "Thank you," Dave responded. "I'll be along shortly." Tom nodded, as he and Sherry went back to their car. She sat there with the motor running, her eyes red from tears. She stared ahead, unable to say anymore as they sat and waited for Dave.

Dave reached into his pocket; gently he pulled out a small brass bell. He had intended on giving it to Linda when he returned home. Kneeling, he dug a small hole into the ground near the grave. The inscription which had been scraped into it's side by Dave read:
"Ring this bell for me my Lindy, if you feel I'm far away,
Ring this bell for me my Lindy, when you need to hear me say,
Ring this bell for me my Lindy, in the heavens high above
For in its' simple music, it speaks eternal love."

Dave turned and headed back to the car, Tom had waited for him half way. To Dave it seemed so far away and so uncertain.

Cap looked up at sky and pondered the rising glow which announced the beginning of a new day, the sun was almost there. That faint glow felt just as figurative and personal as it was real and detached from him. He knew that with every night, there comes a new day. Sometimes it's hard to endure the dark hours when we feel alone. But, if we understand heaven, we know that we are never truly alone. Even at his age, and even though he has been alone longer than he had lived with Linda, being without her all these years had never been easy and certainly wasn't now either. But the thought that death was the end of his love or the end of their bonding, that bonding to that one person who made life *and* forever possible, it just didn't feel right. That thought seemed out of place with truth, that very truth which he had learned through his life with experience and understanding.

But how do you argue with death? How do you argue with absence? It seems these events are the final statements of things, when suddenly someone you love is gone. It is then that you face those things you want but cannot change. Where want is compared to what reality actually provides. Eternal life or Death in the grave, Death do us part or Families are forever, God or random Evolution, a heavenly plan for mankind or chance and luck? This is where our faith is tested against events to which we as mortals have no control. We look into the unknown future to which we all shall one day pass and we wonder. We look at our emptiness for our loved one who is gone and hope that one day this void shall be filled again. If it will be, our hearts sigh "could it be tomorrow? " and if it is not does our faith fail? Both at once *and* over the course of the rest of your life you juggle with trying to understand, while taking what you learned in your own experience with life to help you understand, what you want to know. What you *really* want to know is the truth about life and death. Why? Because now someone you really loved has passed through it's portals. Ultimately, you look to faith to see beyond the curtains of death. Inside something speaks of greater things, and you ponder the nature of life and what lies beyond its doors.

Stories and rumors of those who have touched the other side of death's veil sparks interest at first, but later falls behind as you realize they become like a yearning thirst, never giving fulfillment. So we look for another direction to find a truth more tangible and within the grasp of our belief. It is that understanding which comes through the spirit, born of faith, combined with the promptings that accompanies prayer, along with the learning which comes through the lessons of life, and individual study. We find that in the end, we already knew many of the things we were searching for and we now understand the truth that love really does go on forever. That man is not without the woman in the Lord and that families are forever, 'In the Lord', he remembered the missionaries using those very words. To him it meant, 'In the right way, the good way, the way that makes us filled with joy'. So to him it meant, 'Man and Woman must be together to make families forever in the right way to make us filled with joy.' It made sense this way, as he understood it. It fit right with how he felt about Lindy. Cap pondered these things and wrote down a simple thought in poem form on the latest page of his own book. His thoughts were often in poetic form simply because Linda had liked them and he had gotten used to writing for her.

All things reveal a season, when darkness turns to light,
when golden fields of harvest, are concealed by snowy white.
When frozen lands of winter, are turned to sprouting green,
when grown so full in measure, where the fruit of summers seen.
To golden leaves of autumn, that falls on windy days,
to the first snows of the winter, show the pattern of heaven's ways.

Who can measure a life, the days that are needed to cross the seas of mortal existence?
Who can set the days of happiness and pain? Who can show the meaning of trials as they come upon us? And who can change our tears that in every drop we can find joy?
He who made the mountains and cast life upon the earth.

He who caused that two should walk, that life would come from birth.
He who set the world on course, to set his plan anew
Ordained for man that he would live, that one be made from two.
Unto man our Father sent his son, unto man he gave his law,
unto man he taught his truth for us, to sanctify us all

Unto man he gave dominion, on earth he let us grow
He set the course of nature's path, for lessons we should know
Unto man he gave each other, to find eternal ways.
To walk from life together, for these are heavens ways.

Chapter Ten

A new Family Rising

Another page was blank in the mysterious book Cap held in his lap. He knew what days the book had passed over. It was the year after Linda's death when Dave grieved and drowned in a pool of questions and re-questioning. In a sudden insight, he knew it was not included in the book, because it was not just years of loneliness. It was an eternity of pain. He realized that for whatever purpose this book had been created, it was to bring him to a new understanding and not back to the confusion he had felt during that time. The remembrances of that era in his life, had never been forgotten, they *couldn't* be forgotten.

The page opens about two years later.

The county hospital was set down near the water. Their location was ideal because they could receive emergencies from both their own docks and via ambulance by land. For Turnbridge, the hospital was a long drive up the coast and most people didn't make the trip unless they had to. Even though the drive from town was simple, because all you had to do was get on the main road which ran along the coast and head straight to it, the single most deterrent was that the road was narrow and it had many tight bends and curves. So, to most people in Turnbridge, the local doctor and his office was their main source of medical care and well good enough for them. However, as construction began on the new dry docks, the roads along the coast became a priority. They were greatly improved over the last few years, widened and in some cases straightened. Though the intent was to accommodate the new docks, this made the journey to the hospital easier and more practical for residences around the whole county.

Hospitals of course, are an interesting place as they can be a house of healing or a place of passing from life to death. In their walls happiness and sorrow are constant companions. Where on one floor people may mourn the condition of a loved one, on another they may be thankful that they were healed or the surgery was successful. While on another floor pain and concern precedes rejoicing as a new baby cries and takes their first breath. Tonight is a time for joy. Tom rushed from delivery and into the waiting room of the County hospital. Dave sat there half asleep as he had been up all night awaiting the birth of Tom and Sherry's first child. "It's a baby!" Tom exclaimed. Dave smiled and jumped up. "Well, I hope it's a baby, but what kind?" Tom looked back at Dave puzzled. "Like I said, it's a boy!" Dave slapped Tom's back. "Congratulations!" "I was there too!" Tom exclaimed. "I saw it happen. They were going to wheel Sherry to delivery, but they waited to long. They were just getting ready to shuffle me off to the waiting room when Boom! He was born, right there in the hall! It was incredible looking down into those little eyes. Seeing this new little life which just entered this world and my 'son' to boot!" "Wonderful" Dave responded cheerfully "Congratulations!" Tom smiled and said "Thanks". He took Dave's hand and shook it. "So you got to be there for the birth?" Dave asked. "Yes" Tom said, "I never thought it was so human, so real." he added in a hushed tone. "Human? Real? What do you mean by that?" Dave said kinda confused. "Well, we always hear how hard child birth is, but I never thought it was like that. And as I think about it, I never thought there was so much... much-" Tom started to look a little pale. "Much what?" Dave asked. Tom began to look weak kneed, he started to stagger back. "Fluidddddd" he said as he passed out onto the floor. "That's my big brave sailor," Dave smiled as he bent down to pick up his friend. A nurse in the hallway had seen Tom fall and called for a gurney. "What happened?!" she asked as she ran up. "We need help!" She yelled behind her. "His wife just had a baby in the hall " Dave said, but no one was really listening as they ran up and loaded Tom on a gurney. A doctor came running out of the ER treatment room.

"What happened?" he quickly asked. "Well I started to say" Dave tried but he was cut off by the nurse, "His wife is having a baby in the hall and he fell over unconscious. I saw it happen." "Where's his wife?" the doctor spouted. "I don't know, she wasn't here when I came running." "Have the pediatrician stand by and have some one check the halls and find them." The doctor ordered, as they lifted Tom. "No," Dave said, "they are-" but he was cut off again. The ER doctor pulled up the rails on the gurney and they pushed Tom quickly back towards the treatment room. "He only passed out," Dave said, as they rushed down the hall, but like before, no one was listening.

He quickly followed them into the treatment room but he was barred at the door by an orderly who advised him to wait in the waiting room. Dave looked around the large muscular man and saw a full room, every bed had a patient sitting or lying in it. Some were moaning, others just waiting, one of them had a deputy standing by him. This man was obviously a prisoner because the officer never took his eyes off of him. By his manner of dress he was obviously an old salt, a crewman, or a former one of some seagoing ship. But this old salt was obviously pickled, a traditional occupational hazard of sailors. In fact the charge, which earned him a police escort, was drunk and disorderly and it was the disorderly which earned him a large gash on his forehead. Dave looked over where they put Tom and then back at the orderly.

"You don't understand," Dave said, "His wife just had a baby in the hallway and-" The ER doc had been looking into the sailor's eyes using his pen light when his ears perked up as he heard Dave. "In the hallway, yes. Has anyone checked the hallway yet?" the doctor shouted, "Get the other gurney out there and find his wife. Check the parking lot too," he added. "No!" Dave said "They're up on the-" but he was cut off again. "Get that man out of here!" the doctor ordered, pointing at Dave. The room was hectic so Dave could see why the ER Staff might be confused. But not to listen seemed a little too much. The doctor ran out into the hall to see if he could find the woman who was reportedly having a baby.

The Deputy, after hearing that they had a missing person, asked loudly, "What baby?" The drunk seeing the deputy distracted grabbed a bottle of rubbing alcohol off of the counter and began to sip it. The officer turned around and grabbed the bottle but couldn't get it out of the drunk's hands and they began struggling over it. The next ER nursing shift came into the room and that was good, they needed the extra help but the room was getting very full. The nurses going off duty ran out to help the doctor find the unknown woman. The officer and the drunk were now wrestling around the room over the bottle of rubbing alcohol. The drunk kept trying to draw it to his mouth. "You're going to poison, yourself!" The officer shouted but the drunk kept trying to drink it. "One man's poison is another man's trash," He slurred back at the deputy as he managed to get a few drops on his lips. Just then, as if the room couldn't get any more congested, the OR staff came to the ER to take a patient for emergency surgery. Dave had finally given up and waited out in the hall, but as the gurney for the OR came wheeling by he noticed that it was Tom laying on it. "No," he said, "You have the wrong patient." Dave stood in the way of the gurney, and the orderly tried to go around him. After a ring around the rosy, Dave grabbed the other end of the gurney and stopped it. "Get out of the way sir!" the orderly demanded. "No," Dave said, "not till you listen to me!" "This man needs urgent surgery now!" he exclaimed "Get out of my way!" "You're not taking Tom," Dave said. "You know this man?" he asked. "Yes" Dave was about to say, when the ER doctor came rushing up and put his hand tightly on Dave's shoulder. "If you don't leave" he said, "You will be arrested, get out of the way." Dave had enough, that was it. "If you're a surgeon," he said, " I think you will need that hand, because in a moment I'm going to break it off. And this would be tragic, considering how many people need you tonight." Tom started to moan and the doctor turned to check on him. His mind was still fuzzy and all he could see was this hairy face standing over him much to close. "This isn't the right man for the O.R.," the doctor said. "That's what I was saying, but no one would listen!" Dave exclaimed. Suddenly a nurse came running up and said loudly " We, can't find the woman with the baby!" The drunk came running out of the treatment room and began running around the gurney, while the officer chased him. Tom's mind was starting to clear but not quite enough. "You lost my baby!" he said as he began sitting up on the gurney. The orderly tried to keep him lying down, but Tom was still confused and couldn't figure out what was going on. With a quick punch to the face from Toms fists, the orderly started to fall to his knees. The nurse tried to catch the orderly but he was to heavy and they began to fall together. The doctor, seeing them fall, tried to catch the nurse and tripped over the drunk just as the officer was making a football tackle on him. Tom started up off the end of the gurney, causing it to flip up and over them all. As it flipped, Tom slipped off the end and was pushed forward, he fell staggering into Dave's arms. While the rest of the group crashed into a clamoring heap of arms, legs and gurney, right into the middle of the hallway. Tom looked back, as Dave set him upright. "What happened?" Tom asked. "I don't know,"

Dave said, as they turned to walk to the waiting room, "I asked, but they seem to busy to say." "Where have I been?" he asked again "Can't be sure, Tom." Dave replied, "But I was about to congratulate you on your new son." "Oh yeah, thanks" he proudly said, yet still confused. He looked back as the medical staff, and the officer, and the drunk began to sort themselves out. "Must have been an accident," Tom said, glancing back again. "Man, I could never work in a hospital." Dave smiled, and pulled open a box of green cigars and gave them to Tom. "Here pass these out. I figured you were too busy to think about it, so I got these."

"What?" Tom asked and then said, "Not that I'm not grateful, but how long have you been saving these things? I mean doesn't it have to be years?" Dave popped his unlit pipe in his mouth, he looked back and saw that the tangled mess of people had cleared, and nobody was following them. He turned back to Tom. "Don't worry, I just bought them. They're the only brand I have ever liked. So I bought them out of reflex." "Yeah, a reflex I had hoped you were cured of." Tom remarked. "Don't worry! They're not for smoking, especially by me." Dave reassured him, "There for handing out, you know, 'tradition!' " "Thanks" Tom said, and he started handing them to everyone who would take them. But for some reason, a few people shied away from him. All in all, it was a great success. The excitement rose with congratulations and then slowed as everyone took their turns checking out the viewing room to have a look at the new baby. As Tom went in to visit Sherry asked him if he had heard about the excitement. A nurse told her that some woman had come into the hospital and had her child in the hallway and then she and the child just vanished. She couldn't see how any woman could put their child at risk by running off like that. "Perhaps she was afraid of the bill," she laughed. "Also", she remembered, "one of the other women on the ward said there was a riot earlier downstairs, somewhere near the ER". Tom looked at Dave who shrugged his shoulders. "We were down there quite a while, it was busy, but we didn't see anything." The small group visited for as long as they could and then Tom and Dave reluctantly left, leaving baby and mom to rest and recover.

Dave and Tom walked from the hospital to where they had parked. The night air was cold and the stars were bright overhead. The one subject Tom had avoided nagged at him. It had only been a little over two years since Linda's passing and Tom was concerned how this whole occasion was affecting Dave. After all this was how Linda had died, in childbirth. He didn't want to say anything though, he didn't want to bring it up. As they walked Tom fished a bit with his comments but wasn't getting much of a response.

Dave looked over at Tom,"You know, I've seen a lot of babies belonging to family and friends, but these brand new children who just came into this world, they're amazing. When they open their eyes and you look at them you have to wonder. In a way you want to ask them, 'Do you remember where you came from?'."

"I know" Tom said, "That's exactly what I wondered. When I saw my son looking at me, there was a *person* in those eyes. Young, brand knew. Learning, but thinking and taking the first steps to understand." Tom fished around his pockets for his keys and then continued, "Where this little life had come from was more than just Sherry and me. The dawning of a new individual, and totally dependent on what his mother and I can provide."

"You did good," Dave added, "You and Sherry did good." The doors of the icy car resisted for a moment and then came open. Tom quickly started the reluctant engine which finally roared to life. Letting it warm he turned to Dave. "I know what you must be going through," Tom said, "but I'm glad you are here to share this with me. Along with how wonderful I have felt tonight, it has made me think of Linda and of you." Dave patted Toms' shoulder.

"Thanks Tom," he replied, "I figured we both were thinking

about her. But tonight is your night. Yours, Sherry's and your new son's."

Tom smiled. "Yes, but I want to add. I mean, not that I want to, but I figured it might be time that you find someone else and if you do don't be afraid to take hold of it." Dave thought a moment as Tom shifted into gear with a clunk, "Others may want someone else, but I doubt that will ever be me. My Lindy is my life. Once you walk through the gardens of heaven, everything else is just plants."

Tom laughed softly, "Perhaps to every man his wife should be Eve, just like Sherry is to me. But don't sell my idea short, there might be another who could make you happy. Beside you are still young and should have a chance to have a family like me." Dave just smiled, with no real answer. "Besides" Tom kidded, "That nurse in the ER looked like she might be a good catch." "I think she's taken," Dave laughed "What do you mean?" Tom asked "It looked to me she has already fallen for an orderly," Dave laughed, "While juggling a doctor and a cop." Dave continued to laugh, but Tom looked back with a "what" expression on his face.

The two drove off into the clouds of yesterday, as Cap turned the next page. The book skipped through the days which followed. It took up again years later, and Cap was in his old familiar home smelling the scent of years of living and feeling the life that was once within it's walls. Standing at his large bay windows, Cap looked out over the water. It was almost ritual habit he had formed over the years. With his eye to his glass, he would swing over the horizon from one side of the cove to the other.

      He had come to know the changing of the seasons very well, and to him they were much like a family of brothers and sisters both in their harmonies and conflicts. He also knew the land as well, each curve and every stone which lined the beach and lie within the sight of his glass, it was his in it's own way. To Cap, this setting, this beach, and the world about was the masterpiece on the wall as beheld by the artist. It was creation's work, one that never grows old and you never tire to look upon. In all, few things ever changed around the cove, except when nature had a mind to change it. Usually, a new vessel passing offshore, at least one, which Cap had not seen before, was the simple highlight of the day. With a skilled hand he would watch the ship with his glass and sketch it on a pad, glancing back and forth.

      Of course at times, a careless fisherman or an inexperienced boatman would come to close to the breakers below and need to be rescued. Cap, in his early days, would rush out and help. But now being slower and not as strong, he had to content himself with making a phone call. The Coast guard knew him well and even kept his number handy. But *they* would respond and he would watch the rescue through his glass.

Today, though, something was different and something was new. As Cap peered through his glass, he could see across the bay an abundance of activity. It was taking place at the old Roberts' house on the other side. "Someone's moving in," he said in a soft whisper, as he gently adjusting the focus for a clearer view. The Roberts' house sat near the tip of the other crescent which formed the opposite end of the cove, but Cap's telescope had no difficulty bringing the sight in clearly. Of course it wasn't his style to be a "peeping Tom," but up till now he had been the only resident in this area for years.

The old Roberts' home was a tall white house much like Cap's, built by the same builder. When Wayne Roberts died, it was like losing a brother to Cap. Even though the home had stood empty for many years (as Wayne's widow had moved inland to stay with relatives in her elder years) it was difficult to see anyone else moving in. It seemed like a violation to a monument, or an invasion on the past. One against the things which symbolize the life efforts of a hard working and honest man. However as Cap thought about it, he realized this was good in another way, now the home would be cared for, brought back out of the decay. It was a fine house and it would make someone, or some family, happy for many years to come. It's structure was sturdy, built by the finest craftsman, using the best materials. It's foundation was laid upon the same solid black rock which lined this coast for thousands of years and went deep into the earth along the shore. By the lands contour, it set lower and closer to the breakers than Cap's home. But even so, it was high enough to avoid the crashing waves, especially in the passing of seasonal storms.

Cap turned his glass inland to check the roads which led to the two homes. At a certain point there was a common road and then just before the edge of the bay, it broke into a fork that followed the cove to each house. Cap noticed a dusty cloud drifting into a nearby field and as he suspected, he saw two moving vans making their cautious way along the uneven surface. Adjusting again back toward the Roberts' home, he could see two children playing in the yard. A young man and a woman, probably mom and dad he thought, vigorously working and shouldering boxes into the house from the autos.

"Children," Cap thought out loud, he wasn't sure if that was good or if it was bad. He never liked them aboard ship as they always seemed to be bad luck. Cap had never remarried. He never been a father but he had always wanted to be. "Almost," he mumbled, "and what a dad I could have been even if I didn't let them on my ship." He remembered back when his wife had announced that she was going to have a baby. The thrill he felt, the sudden sense of responsibility which over took him, as he thought, *I'm going to be a dad.*

Cap was determined back then that when his son or daughter was born he would give up the long voyages for the shorter routes. He would have given the same up for Linda if she would have asked. But she knew what he was before they were married, a sea Captain, and she never wanted to change that.

"I know I would have been a good father," he whispered, *and then later, the best of all grandpas'.* Just like his grandpa had been to him. He was the greatest, a large friendly man who often bragged he was a full-blooded Frenchmen and proud of it. This was a man who loved life, and always had time for his children and his grandchildren even when life was difficult and burdensome. A firm, but an even handed father/grandfather, one who knew when to be gentle and kind. Cap reflected on the many times he had stayed at his grandparents. He remembered the fun he had had and the happiness they had shared. Grandpa with his strong hairy arms, which he would firmly wrap around his grandchildren as he greeted them or sent them on their way.

Of course recalling the past was not all good. A dull sense of loss accompanied part of it. A reminder that in his life he had missed out, the father he would never be and the grandchildren he would never have. He did, however, have fun watching the children of his friends grow up He was Uncle Cap to many and later Grandpa Cap when his hair turned gray.

Suddenly he realized his telescope was empty and the children were gone from view. As he looked about the house he noticed the movers had arrived and had begun to empty the vans. Looking further south, he found that the children had located the old trail along the road and were making their way around the cove. When they got to the fork Cap noticed they were preparing to climb an old tree, our picnic tree. The poor old thing was older than both homes put together and had stood there for many years. It was the very tree that saved Linda's life those many years ago. *That old tree won't hold them*, he thought as he got up and made for the door. Of course it could have been that he was only looking for an excuse to go down and meet them. Instinctively he grabbed his fishing pole and plopped his hat upon his head. Slipping his jacket on he was gone. It was a quiet walk around the cove and Cap made his way as quickly as he could. He had walked the path a million times and even though the wind and rain would change it, Cap knew each rock and turn as if he had set them in place himself. Rounding a short bend and then through some bushes, he finally could see the picnic tree which marked the middle of the half crescent cove. The tree itself was a large part of the past. Years ago the Roberts' built a picnic table around the tree's base and dubbed the spot the picnic point between the two families. Many times Cap and his wife had met the Roberts' here for lunch or a summer's dinner.

Now, however, the tree was older. It's large branches weak and hanging low. It's trunk now filling the center of the old wood table. It was a wonder it held up against the winds which roared off the ocean from the yearly winter gales. Yet here it was still green, with life on most branches but now with dead limbs mixed within from years of neglect. Below the tree, the table had long since turned gray. It was grown over with the brush of many years coming up through its boards on one end.

As Cap approached, he noticed the tree was empty, the young boy who had been standing on the table, flipping his leg up onto a lower limb, was now gone. Nothing seemed amiss so Cap figured nothing bad had happened. In his journey from the house, he hadn't seen where the children had ran off too. All he really knew now was he badly needed to stop and catch his breath. Slowly reaching the weather worn bench he sat cautiously down and gazed out onto the sea. It wasn't a wasted trip and it wasn't a wasted effort. Even though there was no rescue as far as the children went, the walk had done him some good. Setting his fishing pole down, Cap pulled out his old pipe and gently tapped it against his hand. He rested awhile as he watched the seagulls glide gently above the stony beach.

In the old Roberts' home the light of the early morning sun shone through the windows, which faced out to sea. Shadows of the large cross framed windows slowly crept across the wooden floors of the empty old house, the air within was brisk and unmoved. To Wayne Roberts wife, Anne, this had been their honeymoon home. Though they had been married several years before this house was built, this was the place they built together. All her dreams, sorrows, and happiness were recorded in these walls and on that land. She wanted to walk the halls of not hers, but *their* home, his and hers, and never regard it in any other way. Even empty as it was for years, she wanted to touch the walls and the doors, look through the windows and see the past. To envision the many days they once had together. To walk where they once walked and, in her minds eye, embrace again. To hear, if only in remembrance, the words that they once shared and see the family which sprung from them. But mostly to be with him, on memories stage, her life long friend and companion. Some may view her desires as unhealthy, at least emotionally, but for her, she would say, "I have raised my family, I love my grandchildren, and now I shall have my memories."

Cap helped Mrs. Roberts the best he could over the years after Wayne died. But the time came when she could no longer live in such a large home by herself. Even so, she would never part with the house even against her family's insistence. She held on to the one thing which meant the most to her because that house was part of him and he was part of her, her beloved Wayne. Since those days, she had passed away, and the family had set her to rest together with their father, side by side. In March of this year they decided to put it on the market and sell the home. Even though several of the children had been born in that very house, the memories of the past seemed easier to bear when left behind to be forgotten. For the many long years which the home stood empty, a local gardener had cared for it. Mrs. Roberts couldn't stand to see the place in ill repair so she paid for its keep even though no one would go there for years at a time. However, in the last few years she had been ill and no one was there to check and make sure the old house was getting the attention it needed. In the end, the grounds keeper passed away and no one was hired to take his place. Hence, when the Realtor appraised the home, he found several things which needed to be fixed and replaced. Of course he didn't mention all of them to the perspective buyers, but Mark Stevens had a very good eye for building and spotted each of the problems himself. This all meant that the Stevens' family got a pretty good deal on the old place.

Mark had always loved the ocean, but he never got farther off shore than that of a small rowboat. Annually he would pack up his family and go to the beach for a picnic and each time they camped along the shore they would dream of owning a home by the ocean or a bay. The old Roberts' house was in every way more than what they had ever imagined actually buying. With the exception of the repairs which it needed (but it was those repairs which would make this place financially possible for them) it was a dream come true. Even though some inconveniences would occur such as the long distance drives to town, the power outages, and hauling water when the well pump gave out, they were still happy. Early this very morning the Stevens' family rose to get a quick start. However, even after the long drive, they still had to wait several hours before the first moving van showed up. The kids of course didn't notice the wait at all, they were thrilled about everything. They also thought that everything they found would also be as interesting to their parents, but in reality the, "Come see this and come see that," seemed to be adding to the anticipation about just getting moved in. Teresa Stevens (Mom) could see that the trail along the beach was visible for a long way, and after giving the children some rules about the water and the trail, she sent them on their way.

Of course few people like unpacking but Mark and Teresa were determined to undertake this task alone. They felt it could be special for just the two of them to do it. It was ok at first, but after the vans arrived and left, they thought they would never run out of boxes to unpack. At least the movers had carried in the heavy things and saved Mark and Teresa's backs for other things. Mark walked over to Teresa who was busy at the main windows trying her best to place pictures. Grabbing her up he gave her a tight squeeze and as he sat her down he leaned in from behind and whispered in her ear. "I can't tell you how happy I am. We're lacking only one thing." Teresa looked up at him with a backward glance "And what's that?" she asked, expecting a kiss. "A boat of course," he pointed out at the water through the window. "And just where would you moor it?" She asked also pointing out the white breakers as they crashing against the rocks below. Mark smiled. "I think I saw a spot down by the old tree, you know, the one with the table around it. If the map is right, I believe that area is on our land. If I cut that old tree down, I could build a small boat shelter. From there I could easily roll out a small, let's say sixteen footer and dock right onto the water." Mark bent over a little and made launching motions with his hands as if guiding his boat out into the surf. All the while he watched out of the corner of his eye for Teresa's response. "Oh! So that's why the hugs and kisses," Teresa smiled, "Well, just keep dreaming honey and then you won't be disappointed." "Actually," Mark responded, "it would be hard to get disappointed here." He gave her the quick kiss she had waited for and a tighter hug. The two went back to the long task of unpacking.

A few weeks later, Cap sat at the old picnic tree. An old hand moved across the unwritten pages, trembling with the thoughts of the past. He added to them words which once the paper had lacked. A motion, a story, a tale unfolds in living color upon the dimming white surface and a vision is let go from mind to hand to paper.

The shores of the sea sounded with the ancient rolling roars, emerald floods rising swiftly upon the sand and then drifting quietly away. The water caresses the shimmering face with fountains of life. Ocean birds at wing, as well as those still at rest, sing the ageless ancient songs, passed to them from times long since forgotten. Familiar in a way, yet they called throughout the eons of years when none were yet here to hear. The breeze shares the ocean salt with the land as it is carried like hinting whispers to those who pass near by.

The sky above is blue and clear while the sun warms the rising day as it has in the eyes of the past for days without number.

Cap looked out over the water. Years at sea had left it's touch on his soul the body and spirit. His skin hardened by the salty brine of the many seas and darkened by the sun which rose above them all. Time itself marked its' passing on the pages of old Cap, as if joy and pain were inscribed lightly upon the amiable features of his face. Where he now stopped on his trek was a familiar place to him, a familiar old rock where he sat and always with the same old fishing pole he had used for years. With line in hand he cast his baited hook out over the water. Inside he had no real expectations as to a catch, but he often did it anyway. A large reel set securely on the shaft. It had no fancy name but gently and with care he would turn it slowly. A singular and unique sight, he would appear, if any should chance to see him. The portrait for the painting which never was put to brush, but yet captured in the eye and legacy of those who share the sea, is what he would seem if any did see him standing there. In Cap's mouth sat his pipe, as much a part of him as the clothes he wore. Perhaps, to Cap, it was even more than that. Lifting a flaring match up to the old worn wooden bowl, gentle puffs would let rise small white clouds into the air. Mindfully he still tended his line which drifted upon the water before him while the scent of burning tobacco mixed in the crisp air. The glow of the embers and the taste of the mouth piece, familiar friends he had long come to know.

A small wave capped near the rocks sending a light mist of seawater on the air. The thin crystal shifted in shape as it passed quickly along the sand. Softly it touched Cap's brow with a moist transparent hand. "The feeling of life, that's what this is," Old Cap thought aloud giving his reel a turn or two, "and in this feeling my memories live. Smells, sounds, the gentle touch of the wind, it brings those feelings to life. Thoughts which lie silent, but not forgotten, are reawakened." Cap listened for a moment and could hear the sounds of children laughing and playing along the trail. He realized it was the two whose encounter he had missed a week or so ago. "Linda," a little boy yelled, "here's a really nice one." He was reaching down retrieving something from the sand. It appeared to be something small, green, and shiny. "Let me see Chris," she said, as she ran up to him and gazed at his outstretched hand. "That's just a green piece of glass," she said in a disappointed tone. "No it's not!" he firmly responded, "It's to smooth and round for glass." Chris proudly held it up and let the sun shine through it. Linda looked again, "Nope, its just glass, the sand made it smooth. It must have been here for a long time." Linda's attention shifted from Chris's newfound treasure to the wide green and white caps scattered off the bay. Something had caught her eye but she wasn't sure what it was. "Look Chris!" she exclaimed in excitement. "A huge shark!" "Where?" Chris squinted his eyes in hopes to see what his sister was pointing at. "Didn't you see that? A large fin just popped up out over there on the water!" Chris shifted his position a little, and responded, "*I* didn't see anything, you're only seeing things." His tone was half disbelief and half disappointment. It was clear; he wasn't sure which emotion to feel. Linda found little success in trying to get Chris to look where she now pointed. Cap smiled as he watched. It was fun to watch the adventure the children were having. It was also obvious that they hadn't even noticed he was even there. It was refreshing to watch two young minds as they explored their new world.

Yes, he thought, *New sights in a new land, how exciting it can be?. To travel the world and experience new wonders, to see for yourself those things which you have only heard about in stories or read about in books. Camels walking in the hot desert sun without a drink or fish that can fly upon the wind when cast by a whipping swell. It's the only way to truly know the world is round. It's the best way to know it.*

"There it is again!" Linda exclaimed. This time Chris saw it. A huge dark dorsal fin broke the surface of the water.

"Wow!" Chris shouted in amazement. "I'll bet that's the biggest shark there is." Cap set his pole down and stood up, the children suddenly noticed the old gentlemen near them.

"Those are killer whales," he said. "Watch and you'll see another." Suddenly the whole bay seemed alive with the large animals. The kids shrieked with delight, as they watched the whales rising and falling into the water.

"Looks like they're having fun," Chris exclaimed. As he ran about and pointed at every fin he saw.

"I'm sure they are," Cap responded, "They love to play." Chris looked up at Cap,"You look like a sea Captain, are you?"

"I was years ago, but now I'm just Cap. At least that's what my friends call me." Linda eyes' lit up in response.

"Just like Cap in the Shirley Temple movie! Do you live in a light house?" Cap smiled, he had never thought of himself like that.

"Some have called my house a light house." Cap noticed the young man turn almost formal as he walked over to introduce himself.

"Well, I'm Chris and this is my sister Linda," Linda turned and said hello with her introduction.

"Is your home near here?" Linda asked. Cap turned and pointed up the hill, "That's my house up there, we are just across the cove from each other. I suspect you're the new family moving into the old Roberts' home."

"No," Chris replied. "We've moved into that house over there," Chris pointed to their new home. "At least, mom and dad are moving us in." Cap chuckled a little, "Well, that's the old Roberts' home. They were friends of mine and Mr. Roberts was the owner of the ship I used to be captain of."

"Is our house haunted, I mean, did they die there?" Linda asked, her voice full of concern. Cap smiled, "I don't think so and no, they both passed away far from here. I think you will have a good time living there, it's a fine home and it's in a very good spot. But don't worry, you will be alone, no ghosts."

"Look! " Chris exclaimed, "There's more killer whales! Wow! There's a lot of them."

"That's because they travel in packs called pods." Cap said. "They stay in family groups for many years."

"Families?" Chris repeated. "You mean like mom and dad?"

"Yes, something like that," Cap responded as he made his way back to the bench and sat down. Chris stuffed his pockets with the driftwood he had collected along with the green piece of glass he had found. They all talked awhile and the children listened intently as Cap shared the history of the cove. Cap recounted some of his many adventures and how he eventually came to build his house. At times the children responded with questions and answers of a religious nature, to which Cap thought their response belonging more to a preacher. In fact, Cap felt a lot like he was in a Sunday school class. It was odd how they seem to bring God into every story. At one time, as Cap puffed on his pipe, Linda told him how bad it was for him to smoke and even gave him some reasons why. But Cap only responded with, "Now don't you get started on me." He chuckled, but he put the pipe away anyway. "Hey!" Linda said, as an idea took her. "Why don't you come over to our house for dinner?" Cap grinned again, "I'm sure your parents would like to get settled in before they have guests over." "No, it's ok," Chris, agreed. "Mom and Dad would love to have you come, I'm sure." Cap rubbed his chin and thought. "Ok, I'll be over around six o'clock, but I won't be expecting supper. I would like to say 'Hi' to my new neighbors and give a hand if I can." "Great!" Linda responded. "We'll see you then." The two kids barely said their goodbyes as they ran off down the trail toward their home. Chris was running far ahead of his sister and Cap could hear him call in the growing distance. "Come on Linda, you slow poke."

The day passed into night rapidly as Mark and Teresa opened their last box. It had been weeks since they had began unpacking. Interruptions like work, meals, sleep, and all the normal stuff got in the way. The fun of unpacking had been lost days ago. The kids had come in and played throughout the house when it got dark and like most young children it seemed like nothing was going to slow them down. Teresa paused after running a sharp blade over the top of a large brown cardboard box. "I guess I should think of something for dinner," she said while bracing her back with one hand and standing up.

"Oh, that's right!" Chris said hearing his mother's comments. "I invited Cap over for dinner tonight." In a different setting it might be said that the following parental expressions were priceless, but not at this one. "You invited who?" Mark responded. "Don't you think you should have asked us first young man?" "We're sorry," Linda interrupted, defending her brother. "We thought you wouldn't mind." "You too, huh?" Teresa added as she looked over at Mark, but Mark still had a "Who are they talking about?" expression firmly planted on his face. Linda decided to jump in to explain. "Cap is that old gentleman the Realtor told us about. He lives in the home across the cove." Mark looked over at Teresa just as a knock came at the door and the two found themselves staring at each other. The question was obvious, who's going to answer it? Jumping up before a decision was reached, Chris suddenly whizzed by them. Teresa reached out to catch an arm but missed. Reaching the door, Chris swung it open wide and his parents had no time to protest, but that was sure to come later. It was Cap standing on the porch outside the door. His old form was lit softly by the dim yellow porch light. In his hand he held a large black kettle and a flashlight, which he gently turned off. Mark and Teresa jumped up to greet him. After all, there wasn't much else they could do. "So you're Cap," Mark said reaching out and taking Cap's free hand and shaking it. "Glad to meet you neighbor." "Sorry for scaring you like this," Cap responded. "I'm sure your kids set you up by inviting me over like this. But I thought it a good way to say hello and perhaps, help out by cooking you all dinner tonight." Cap handed the kettle to Teresa as she peaked inside to see what it was. As she opened the lid, a small amount of steam escaped and the mouth-watering aroma of clam chowder filled the room. It smelled wonderful. "Thank you Cap," Teresa responded, "this looks very good." The small group set the table and talked while Teresa prepared a few other dishes. They gathered around the table and sat down to what was their first meal in their new home. Cap reached over to help in serving up the plates but everyone else was responding to a different cue. Bowing their heads, they folded their arms and blessed the food. Mark said the prayer and thanked God for their new home and asked for a blessing on it. He thanked God for their safe journey and then for their new friend, Cap. In closing he asked God that the food would be blessed for their consumption. This was all strange to Cap, but he had figured them to be church going people from talking to the kids on the beach. "You a minister?" Cap asked. "No," Mark answered and laughed lightly at the idea. "But I do hold the priesthood in the church we belong too." Cap sipped his soup and shook his head yes, "I thought so, especially with that wonderful prayer you said." "Do you go to church?" Linda asked. Cap dabbed his lips with his napkin. "Church is a good thing and a lot of people need it, but I have never been one to go. I figure God knows me well enough and I have never done anything in my life that I'm ashamed of." Cap pulled out his pipe and began to tap it on his hand, but when he looked up at all the expressions which read, 'what do we do now' he placed it back into his pocket. Shrugging, he glanced up at the others, "Thought I lost it, but no, it was still in my pocket." Cap gave a nod and wiped his forehead like to say 'thank heavens'. The family began to laugh and the whole group had a great time visiting for the rest of the evening.

Chapter Eleven

Gringo's on the loose

A few years went by and the small family came to know Cap and trust him as the man he was. Chris and Linda Stevens loved exploring Cap's old house. He had quite a collection from his years of travel. Chris stood at the large bay window and swung the telescope from side to side while Linda sat near by examining a large blue glass ball. Holding it between her hands, she turned it slowly. It was a glass float lost from a fisherman's net somewhere across the sea. She ran her fingers over the old worn ragged rope netting that was still wrapped about it, remnants from it's past. Clinging fast to the mesh rope were small white lifeless barnacles. Linda examined them and imagined the day that they were the only passengers aboard a bluish glass ball when it broke free and made the long voyage across the sea to Emerald bay. There seemed to be things from every corner of the earth and the children could identify some of the countries from which the souvenirs had come. In fact it became a game to them and Cap was forced to keep score. However, when needed, he would also fill in the details around each object, especially when debate between the two children got intense.

"You sure have done a lot of stuff Cap," Chris turned and smiled, "And I bet you've been all around the world."

"A couple of times," Cap responded. "and I'm sure by the time you've reached my age, you will have done a lot as well. It gives you something to tell your grandchildren." Chris shuffled a bit and turned back to Cap, "No way. I'm never getting married!" Cap smiled as he pulled his rod from the wall to straighten its' lines, "I'm sure it is safe to say that feeling will change in a few years." Linda set the glass ball down and began to examine some shells, "Chris's going on a mission when he gets older. I might too."

"A mission?" Cap questioned.

"Yes, a mission to serve the Lord by teaching the gospel."

"Oh, a mission for your church," Cap added. Chris turned away from the telescope, "You never said what church you went to Cap." Cap scratched his head, he knew he hadn't been in a church building for several years, but he didn't want to be a bad example to these kids.

"Well," he said "I guess I'm a member of all the churches, because I can find some truth in all of them. But I'm not a member of any particular one."

"I thought so," Chris laughed "Linda caught you by surprise

didn't she? You looked kind of funny with that spoon hanging out of your mouth when she said the blessing." Cap chuckled, "Now, how do you know my religion doesn't say their blessings with spoons in their mouths. In fact it might be an important practice." They all laughed as Linda's attention was drawn to a photo. It was a picture of a young, beautiful woman dressed in a white-laced gown. She held it up to Cap, "Who is this?" "That's Lindy, my wife." Cap answered. "Where's she now?" Linda asked, as she bent down and picked up the things she had collected throughout the morning.

"Oh, she's been gone for many years. Her name was also Linda, like yours, but I always called her Lindy." Cap smiled warmly as the memory of his love showed thru his face.

"Do you miss her?" Chris asked, but Linda quickly scolded him saying it was very improper for him to ask that, of course he misses her.

"That's ok," Cap said, "I like thinking about her. To me there is nothing painful in that and yes sometimes I miss her very much, but it is just my way of saying I still love her."

"I'll bet you can't wait for the resurrection when you can be together again." Chris stated with a smile. Cap looked back at Chris kind of puzzled. However, he quickly realized that what Chris was saying must have been something the children had learned at church. Since he had never really studied any religion he wasn't sure how to respond to this question. He knew what the resurrection was, at least in the many ways it is viewed.

"Well I don't know much about such things," he finally said. "Still, if I ever get to see her again, I would want her to know that she has always been my girl." Cap pulled out his pipe and without a thought, tapped it on his hand. He noticed the children watching intently. Quickly he placed it back into his pocket.

"Still got it." Linda spouted, "You must loose it a lot to have to check it so often." Cap smiled and then bit deeply into his sandwich.

"How did your wife die?" Chris asked. Cap picked up her picture and held it up to see.

"She died while giving birth to my daughter many years ago. It was while I was out at sea. The women who attended her said it happened quickly and that she gently fell asleep and was gone." Cap reflected. "You loved her a lot didn't you," Linda said as she took the picture and gently set it down. "More than I have ever loved in this life. You see that window? She would pace back and forth in front of it waiting for my return from long voyages. That telescope has spied me out more than any other glass in the world. Once I even flew a flag from the highest point of my ship. It read, 'I love you', printed in large red letters. When I got home I found a note on the door it read, 'I love you too, and your flag had best been talking to me'", Cap and the children laughed as Cap related his stories and they sat intently when he told them about Linda rescuing the sailors by the picnic tree. He also told them about Tom and how they ran around together. How they worked side by side on the same ship for years, from deck hands on up, well before either of them made anything of themselves in their carriers.

"Yea, Tom and I would get into quite a little trouble from time to time!" He laughed, entertaining the thought. "Tell us a story." Chris asked as he flipped through Cap's log. "Yes!" Linda added, "Tell us about Tom." "Ok, one more story." Cap agreed. "It was several years ago" he started, but as he continued the vision of his tale became real. It took on form which the children could see as it played on the windows of their minds....

After the ship was fully secured in a small port in Mexico and the deck crews were busy securing the cargo, Dave and Tom decided to go ashore and see the sights. The ship had been delayed a few days because of an important shipment which hadn't arrived. It was to come over land, but reports were that severe rainstorms had held it up. The ship which Dave and Tom worked on had never docked at this port before, mainly due to the size and location of the community. In fact, because of that very reason, few ships ever came to this dock. In it's day, the port area was a bustling business, but like a gold town whose mines are spent, the community dried up and blew away. All that was left was run down warehouses and rusting fittings and fixtures on the dock. The ship, of course, had no choice but to stop here. This side trip had been set up at the freight line office over phone and radio. The necessity became clear when the only way they could meet up with the cargo was to meet and transfer the shipment here. Of course things didn't work out as planned, hence an additional delay. For Dave and Tom, this was the perfect opportunity to check out the new area. Odds were good that they would never stop here again, so the two wanted to make the best of it now.

"Ok!" Dave said to Tom as they walked, "No girls, no booze, lets keep our heads on strait. I don't want a repeat of what happened in Greece."

"Me neither!" Tom responded, "I just want to get a look at this place and perhaps catch a meal." The two entered a small cantina on the far end of town and ate there. They didn't know the language but they did notice a group of men giving them the evil eye throughout their meal. In fact, at one time these men turned their beer bottles over and began to spill their drinks on the ground while mumbling something.

Tom turned to Dave and said, "Either they really don't like the beer or they are saying in some foreign way they don't like drinking with us around. I'm not sure of course, but their expressions tell me it's about us."

"I got that too." Dave answered, "I don't like being the center of attention. Let's finish up and get out of here" The two finished their meal and paid their tab as quick as possible. As they went out the door they looked over at the table were the men had been. Now they were gone.

"I don't think that's a good sign, Dave," Tom said. "Why don't you go out the front and check things out? I have to use the restroom, but I'll be there in a second."

"Ok" Dave replied "but don't be long, I have a bad feeling about this place. "

"Sure. I'll only be a moment. It's just, if something does happen I don't want to have a full bladder when it comes down." Dave walked out into the evening air. It seemed stagnant in a way, kind of hot and stuffy. The sun was still in the sky but descending on the horizon and he knew evening wasn't far away.

Suddenly an old truck pulled up and two men rushed from the sides of the building. They grabbed at him and tried to throw him in the back of the truck. Dave put his foot behind one of the men's leg and sent him over the top and into the truck's bed. As he continued to fight them off, two more men joined in and for a time it looked like a tag team wrestling match. They were persistent and when he would knock one man off, another would grab him. He felt lucky the porch of the cantina didn't allow all four men to be on him at the same time. While the other three were trying to attack Dave, the fourth guy was trying to hit him with a club. It was a heavy stick that looked a lot like a baseball bat. Dave backed himself up against the cantina wall. He would have called for help but he figured no one would come anyway. He also thought it would be best if they didn't know where Tom was yet. Each time a man rushed in and grabbed him Dave would slam his fist into the attacker's belly and then whack him across the face. He grabbed the newest assailant by his clothes and used the stunned man for a shield against the man with the bat. Then with a shove, he threw the man into whoever it was trying to get him next. Over and over again the little routine repeated itself. Dave was getting tired and was looking for Tom when around the corner of the cantina, there he came running full bore into the mob. The first man he slammed into was the guy with the bat. Wham! They collided. Tom took him down bouncing the man's head a few times on the hard unyielding ground. As he was getting up another Mexican, who saw Tom was jumping on his friend, rushed him. Like a spring, Tom jumped up and punched the charging man several times in the torso and then the face. Dave took the other two down with several well-planted punches and Tom laid into the last guy's knees with the bat and he went down with a scream. Dave and Tom were left staring at each other as the Mexicans were moaning and trying to get up.

"I think that scream will bring out the whole town!" Tom exclaimed. "We better get out of here!" Tom dropped the bat and the two ran for the truck which was still running. As Tom began to jump into the passenger side and Dave into the driver's side, they didn't notice four other men coming up behind them. Before they got their bottoms onto the seats, the lights went out as canvas bags were slipped over their heads and they were pulled to the ground. The next thing they realized, after a short trip in the truck, they were being dumped head first onto a pile of straw. As their hoods were taken off they realized they were in a small barn with several armed men looking down were they laid.

"You gringos came off dat big ship?" a small pockmark faced Mexican said. His English was badly broken and he spoke with a deep Spanish accent. "I tink, perhaps, wit da way you are dressed, you are importantte to dat ship." the voice said again.

"I told you," Dave said to Tom "Greece all over again."

"My wallet!" Tom exclaimed, "The thieves have my wallet!" Dave looked up at the man who was speaking. He was a dirty and scraggly haired man. He stank as if he had never taken a bath and his breath was a foul mix of alcohol and tobacco. Tom remembered seeing him in the cantina. "What do you want?" Dave said reluctantly. Looking up at the large bore revolver the man had pointed at him.

"Don't let him get too close, Dave." Tom said, "He will kill you with his smell and who knows what else?" With a grunt the Mexican kicked Tom hard on his legs. A couple of the other men kicked him a few times too. Most of them were aiming for Tom's stomach but Tom was a little quicker than they expected. His face jammed up against Dave's shoulder as he squirmed to keep the kicks in the right places.

"That's all you have?" Tom said, "You kick like a bunch of sissies!"

"What are you trying to do?" Dave whispered, "Let's at least talk to them first."

"Perhaps," Tom said with a devilish look in his eye, it was clear he had a plan, "but if I get them mad enough to fight me I think we will have a chance."

"Not if they kick you to death on the ground first!" Dave responded.

"Yeah, ok, that's possible. I'll wait." Tom said cautiously. The dirty Mexican moved over to Dave as Dave finally got back to his feet.

"You want our ship to pay money for us?" Dave asked.

"Sure." the Mexican said, "You pay fines before you free."

"What fines are those?" Tom asked.

"Fines for causing public nuisance, fighting, and trying to steal José's truck. I could put you in jailhouse, but we are friendly people 'ere."

"What?!" Tom exclaimed, "You're saying *you* are the law around here?" The Mexican pulled out an old rusty badge from his shirt pocket, "Da only law dere is, seignior." Suddenly the sounds of hooves rumbled outside as several men on horses rode up to the barn. They came inside and said several things in Spanish to which Dave and Tom couldn't understand. They were fairly sure *they* were the main topic though.

"I can't speak Spanish" Dave said, "but the argument is over money, that's obvious."

"Yeah, I think you're right. I think someone was suppose to get paid already for our little capture." Tom added, then he laughed, "They didn't take us for free, that's for sure. Look at that guy limping over there. That's my work, I think."

"Perhaps," Dave laughed, "But look at that swelling face over there! That's my work."

"No," Tom disagreed, "I clearly remember him."

"You're crazy," Dave exclaimed, "Look at the size of that shiner. That's my work." The men began to argue viciously about something and the Mexican who said he was the law pulled out Dave and Toms wallets and began laying their money on a large box set up to be a table. Tom took two steps forward.

"Hey!" he shouted, "that's my" but before he could say anything else one of the men pushed him back. "Stop it Tom." Dave cautioned, "It's only money. We have too-" But before Dave could finish he saw them pull his cap out of a bag and put it on the table. Then, to add to insults, they placed his pipe inside it.

"They're trying to divide up what they've taken from us!" Tom observed. Dave wasn't listening, he saw one of the men pick up his cap and put it on and then he raised Dave's pipe to his mouth. That was enough! Dave grabbed the man that was holding his arms and threw him into a wall. In almost the same move, he rushed forward like a charging lion at the man who had his hat and pipe. His left hand grabbed his pipe as his right fist flashed up with an upper cut, slamming into the surprised Mexicans face. With a single blow he knocked him out cold. As Dave's cap fell from their captor's head Dave grabbed it out of the air and flipped it up and on. He turned and slammed the next man into a beam and drove his fist hard into the stunned mans face. Tom knew this was the moment to act and yelled, "It's about time Dave!" With lightning swiftness, he punched the Mexican who was standing near him senseless and then kicked the next closest one with a fast snap to the chest. Dave and Tom realized that the men outside had heard the ruckus and were starting to open the barn door. Since the two large doors opened out the two ran for the doors and body slammed them The force pushed the Mexicans who were coming in off the low loading ramp of the barn and into the streets. Like cowboys, the two jumped on the horses that had been left outside. Kicking them in the sides they lunged forward. Tom's horse reared for a moment and nearly spilled him, as he held on for dear life.

Settling to a gallop, they sped off as fast as the horses would go down the road and out of the small community. Behind them the scattered band made it back to their feet and began to fire what weapons they had.

"I hope they're bad shots!" Tom exclaimed.

"Good or bad I ain't stopping." Dave responded.

"Yeah but," Tom said, disappointed "if this was a proper escape, shouldn't we have something to shoot back with?"

"I'm just glad we have the *horses*," Dave answered, "and my cap and pipe."

"Yeah, and our wallets." Tom added.

"You got your wallet?" Dave asked

"Of course, and yours" he added, "but don't ask for it back, at least not yet."

Dave smiled, "Well I guess we have everything then!"

"Yeah, and we're set. I wonder how much we can get for these horses when we get back to the ship?" Dave and Tom laughed, but the biggest problem now was that they didn't know where they were. They were hooded when they had been kidnapped and brought here. Dave looked up at the stars which were getting brighter as the final light of day turned dark. "This way!" he yelled as they sped off in the direction that Dave knew would be the ocean. From there he knew they could find their way back.

"How do you know where we are going?" Tom exclaimed.

"Always know where you are Tom, and if you don't, the stars can lead you the rest of the way."

"Great, but there is one problem left," Tom exclaimed.

"What's that?" Dave asked

"I don't really know how to ride!" he screamed, as he fought to stay in his saddle.

"Just hold on," Dave chuckled, "and the horse will do the work, besides you're doing fine." The two rode off into a billow of dust rising from the road and into memory.

....

Cap checked the time and discovered it was growing late, and hurried the kids off toward home. They thanked him and couldn't wait for another story.

Again, the old home was left quiet as Cap sat back in his chair, and fell slowly asleep.

Chapter Twelve

A night at Caps

Years had passed and the Stevens family became a solid part of the growing community. Cap became close to his new neighbors and spent a lot of time with the family. The picnic tree was once again used for lunch between the two homes. Mark had revived the old table and cleaned up the brush and climbed the old tree. Twice a month they would all meet and have lunch together. The kids felt like they had a vacation going all the time. Of course Mark never got his boat ramp, but now and then, he and Cap would fish the cove in one of Cap's rowboats. Mark learned a lot from old Cap and became a rather good fisherman. Chris and Linda did as well, but it was usually Mark who would spend his summer days drifting around the cove with Cap. They would catch a variety of fish and Cap would teach them all their names and also a few nicknames. When the tide was low they would catch a fish that was more of a nuisance than fun. Irish Lords, they were called, a small bony bottom fish which had big heads and large mouths, and they were not too good for eating. Of course there was the occasional dogfish, a small bottom dwelling shark. When you got one of them on your line you knew it, and they would bend your pole right over. Chris kind of liked catching those because that fish could pull the boat around in circles if the fishing line didn't snap first.

Once Chris's pole broke along with the line. When the pieces were dragged into the water he instinctively jumped over the side of the boat after it. Cap was shocked and yelled for Chris as he fought to steady the boat, which was rocking back and forth after the boy's sudden lunge. As Cap stood up, kinda half kneed and wobbly, he saw that Chris had grabbed a hold of the bowline and began pulling the boat. "Where do you want to go? " he laughed, kinda dog paddling the boat along. "Back to shore," Cap also laughed, "There's probably no fish around here now!" It was hard for Chris to laugh and swim at the same time so Cap helped him back into the boat. Seeing the boy swimming like a fish and slowly pulling the boat around by the rope had been the highlight of the day. Cap was also wondering why he was having so much deja vu.

Of course through the years not everything was fun. When you have children in a home which wasn't prepared for them one has to accept the hazards, like that of keepsakes falling victim to playful hands. Yet the occasional incident was rare and Cap had been able to repair á broken treasure or two most of the time. All in all they were wonderful children, but children none the less. Cap never wanted to over-react over a broken thing and tried very hard not to get too upset. He never wanted to inhibit their drive for exploration, but he kept a watchful eye to insure they were always safe and having fun. Nevertheless and overall, everything had been worth it. Cap got to be the grandpa he had always wanted to be and became part of a family. After Tom had passed away from a heart condition, Cap didn't see Tom's children much anymore. They had grown into adults and had children of their own. But mostly he never saw them because they had all moved inland and far away, not sharing their father's love of the sea.

    The Steven's kids grew up fast, and as children usually do and they made several local friends. This cut down on visits to Cap's, but that was ok, because the pace became more practical. Cap stayed involved in their lives though and attended the many games of the various sports and activities. He would sit next to Mark and Teresa and root on the team. It was the only time he would wear a different kind of hat, one which supported the team or sport. He looked odd and out of place without his old cap, but it was all in fun. Chris made the football team every year and Linda became an accomplished tennis player. Of course there were school plays and church activities, which Cap would sometimes help with. Especially props for the plays. Cap seemed to be the one who would have the things no one else could find. Linda said to him one time while picking up an antique lamp for a play, "I've got you figured out grandpa Cap, you're a pack rat." She'd picked up a strange object and, while looking for clues about what it was, she added, "A *globe* trotting pack rat."

"Well actually," Cap would reply "I prefer the term Wharf rat, or even Bilge rat. More nautical wouldn't you think?" They both laughed as they loaded the needed materials into the car. Chris and Linda had loved the local schools and as the years passed they both finally arrived at their senior grades of high school. Although their visits to Cap's home weren't as often as it used to be, to them it would have been a crime if they didn't see him in the bleachers during their main games of all the seasons. Of course Cap could still get one of the family to go fishing with him at least once a month. Teresa found that it was a good time to vent any frustrations she might have about one thing or another. It wasn't that she felt Cap might understand a woman troubles, but he was always so positive and calming with his advice. She would sometimes grab a pole and tell Cap they were going fishing herself.

Having had this small family move into the old Roberts' house had been good in many ways. Cap had once felt his adventures were over in life, but for the last ten years the Stevens kids had kept him plenty busy and Mark and Teresa had been the best of friends. There is a simple truth about life, when we meet new people and as we come to know them, they share part of themselves with us and we share part of ourselves with them. Along with the benefits that came to this lonely old man, the Stevens family also grew with *their* exposure to Cap. They got a new perspective about this world we call home, they learned the poetry of nature in the changing of her seasons and they truly found the allure of this land as it is embraced by the sea. The rain of winter used to bug Mark and the snows and ice were always a burden. The heat of summer seemed to be a pest, especially on sultry days. But now they all saw the seasons in a new way. They could all say they enjoyed nature with its own unique ways every day. Because the mood of nature, whether calm or intense, often gave each day it's own identity.

On family home evening night, the Stevens family would take a different window each month and looked out it. They dubbed it family home window night. Each of them in turn would find something beautiful about the world outside, in that particular view.

The lightly lit silver to distant black clouds as the tempest gathered over the sea. The gentle lifting of limbs in trees so anciently born, caressed by the passing breeze. The many colored leaves, as nature touches the forest with her soft hand, and they fall into their winter's sleep. The shore lined with a silver frost as if coated with glass reflecting gently the stolen light from the sun or stars which hang in the cold sky above. Or the golden fields in summer, set against a deep blue sky, warmed by the sun above. To stand upon the hill which overlooks the town, to see the tops of many homes rising slightly above the full green trees. To catch the glimmering pinnacle of reflected sun light as it marks where the community church now stands. To the Stevens family, Cap had made these things clear. This was now home as if they had been born and raised along the shore, their side of heaven.

Mark sat in his study reading a book he had sworn to finish a few weeks ago. Chris walked in and was trying to be quiet, but his natural curiosity caused him to take a quick peak over his father's shoulder,

"What are you reading so intently?" He noticed the outer cover and read, "Warn Your Neighbor?

If you're going to warn Cap, I think you're in for a *long* struggle." His dad looked up blankly, half listening to Chris and half pondering the articles he was reading.

"You know, I never even thought of Cap as someone to warn until you said that.", Mark replied. Chris plopped himself down into a thick chair near his dad, "That's because Cap is set in his ways and they're not *bad* ways either. Besides dad, who would want to change someone like him? Anyway, I could never imagine him without that pipe in his mouth!" Mark smiled. He too enjoyed that old image.

"Maybe that's part of the problem, we don't see him any other way." Chris grabbed a few magazines and kicked back. "Mom's tried to get him to church more than a few times, he just doesn't want to go. He told her once when he dies it's ok for us to do his work in the Temple. He only wanted us to be sure that when we are done with the body, we bury him at sea. I explained to him that's not what we mean by baptism for the *dead*!" Mark laughed as he turned the pages of his book. "This is exactly what I mean, though, I don't think he really knows what the gospel is about. After all, hasn't he spoken often of his wife and the special love they had? I'm sure that, if he understood the principles of eternal marriage, he could gain a testimony of it. I know in my own heart. He would *want* to be sealed to her... if he knew."

"Dad," Chris softly exclaimed in a 'You *so* don't understand' voice, "You're talking about one of the oldest sea dogs we know, and you know what they say about old dogs." Mark sat quietly for a few moments as he flipped through a few more pages. "Still," he paused, "Something inside me... says try."

Cap shifted a bit on the stump where he was sitting. "They did try", he thought out loud to the darkness, "but I didn't think I needed it. I thought I had more answers than they did because I was older. I did more in the first twenty years of my life than they had up to the time I had met them. I lived so long and I have traveled so far, even farther than Mark who once served a mission in Germany. But I realize now I didn't have more answers, I only had more questions. I guess when you figure you have a bundle more thoughts and a thousand more stories than everyone else, you have more knowledge, but the truth ultimately is it doesn't work that way. I know how they tried to get me to church in friendship, without pushing, but I knew what they wanted and I didn't want to give it, not then. I had my memories and I had my trophies of life. I was never going to leave that house and I was going to hold onto what I had till the very day I died. Slowly this time, life not death took this family away from me. Before, mostly death was the biggest thief. Sharkey, Linda, Tom and many many others gone. But now missions, marriage, and jobs would take those who I had come to love far away and gone... and then the passing of time would seal their absence. I miss it so." Suddenly catching Cap off guard, a voice sounded from the bushes.

"You mean 'the family way of life' again," the old man said walking up to Cap. He was looking even younger than even before.

"You're still here," Cap said looking at that old guy's new found youth. "I'm going to have to stop referring to you as old man, I guess? You look younger than me now."

"Of course I'm still here and I'm old enough. But as far as my motives, I have been trying to help you all evening."

"Help? Why's that?

"I said I read the book. I know what's in it. I'm afraid that confusion and lies are going to bring more grief into your life. You're a good man, you have done so many good things. You have earned a break from all of this confusion. You're old, you should be resting in these golden years of your life. Spending your time at the bar, making life fun and happy for yourself and all those poor souls who have never had as much adventure as you. You're strong enough not to drink and smoke if you don't want to. So, it would be story telling and making others smile, a wonderful mission in life, don't you think? Wouldn't this be good?"

"If I want to only understand that I live and breathe, perhaps, but if I want to know *why* I live and breathe, and where I will be, and who I will be with when I die. No, I do not want to see where I *have* traveled anymore. I want to know *where* I am traveling too. I think this book has been showing me that I already believed many of things I have been questioning tonight. Taught by life, through the different stages of each age, I just know. I had already known the truth about those things the Stevens family knew. I just had to realize it for myself. Those are truths which I think most people believe as well, but they, like me, didn't or don't have the courage to put it all together. Most of us didn't want to accept what we thought these truths represent. It would mean that eternity required something more out of us than lip service or than just living as we always have. It forces us to realize that becoming a good person is a change in nature rather than a collection of thoughts. And when you put all that together with faith, that is, faith in God and the Savior and in His work *then* you are following His light, His path. Then our hopes are not just emotional indulgences, they become the blessings of exaltation. What is your name anyway, why do you keep showing up?"

The old guy shifted a bit and thought before he answered, "Like your friends call you Cap, some call me Scratch, perhaps because I am old and flaky. However, I think you are missing the point to all I have been saying. I mean, I respect your right to make decisions, but there comes a time when a person must grow up and face reality. I would think at your age you would be an adult, but you still fantasize about having your wife back and having things like they were when she was alive. You are ill, mentally, because you won't accept that after all these years she is dead. Your daughter is dead and Sharky is dead. And Tom is dead, and Sherry is dead too. That you killed them through your neglect and selfishness and because of that, your friend's children have forgotten you as well. You know they blame you, even though they have said nothing. They are good people because they have tolerated you. That's why you are here, trying to chase down the Stevens' family and see if they even care about you. Ultimately, you will ruin their lives as well." Scratch, as he called himself, said all these words as he walked away and his voice slowly trailed off.

"No," Cap said, "I am here for a reason. Maybe finding the Stevens' family is why I came here, but now I am here. I feel I was guided." The seagull that had been hanging around the camp all night jumped onto Cap's foot and then jumped off. "Well, I guess you trust me," he smiled while he tossed him a piece of bread. Seeing that he was alone again he opened the book and read.

Cap walked about his kitchen and fixed a few things for lunch. He had just pulled a pan off the old gas flame when a knock came to the door, but before he could answer Chris came rushing in holding an envelope in his hand. Cap thought at first that Chris had brought his mail, as he often did, but realized this letter was already opened.

"Want some lunch boy?" Cap grabbed another bowl and set it on the table as he sat down.

"Do you know what this is Cap?" He held his letter up like he would burst if it took a second longer to show his grandpa Cap.

"Draft papers?" Cap questioned. "Sure hope it's the Navy." Cap knew what it was, no other letter could be so exciting, but thought he would let Chris break the news.

"It's my mission call! I'm going to *England*!" Cap could see Chris's excitement. He remembered the feelings when anticipating a voyage to somewhere new and there were few things better.

"England, I remember it well, I spent a lot of time at Portsmouth. You'll have a great time!" Chris sat at the table but he was too excited to eat. Calming a little he took a few sips from his bowl and looked back at Cap.

"You know this is the first time I have left home for real." His voice had the traces of concern. "How did you deal with it on all those voyages you took?" Cap set his spoon next to his bowl as he picked up a piece of bread. He picked at it before looking back up at Chris, "There is no answer which makes it easy. For some people it's no problem, their roots are shallow and they can travel abroad free like the wind across the earth."   "That's not me," Chris said as he ran his finger around the rim of an empty bowl. "I know," Cap smiled. "For people like you and I, who hold onto our family lives firmly, it is always a trial. When you truly step out your father's door for the first time your life is changed. You can never go back and that's what scares us all, but it always seems to work out. At first you are filled with excitement, as your journey lies ahead. But then after you are gone and on your way, you measure the price of your adventure against the time you will be gone, the risk's which lie ahead, and what you hope to gain or do. You then weigh them with things you hold dear back home and see if the journey was worth it. Believe me, after you have been gone for a while things sometimes seem like they don't balance out even if they should. So you shed a tear, you write a letter, and then you do what you set out to do, getting your work done, and adding a vault of memories to your life. You should ask yourself this one question before you leave, 'Is it right?' and if you can say yes, then go, even if you're not sure. Remember the world is a circle and it always comes around to the one place you call home." Chris looked at this aging man who sat across the table from him. He felt a grandson's love for a grandfather. He remembered when he had once felt that he never wanted this man to change, but now he thought how important it is, for Cap to have all the blessings of our Father in Heaven. In fact, he realized how sad it would be if Cap should never have these truths in his life. His dad was right and Chris wanted Cap to know about the Gospel of Jesus Christ. Cap sighed and continued, "After your journey is done and you see the ports of home." Cap's eyes looked out into the room as if he was looking out over the water, "In the distance at first, and then slowly but surely it rises in shape and form right before your eyes, and then you are there. You are then glad you went, but you are also glad that you are now home." "Thanks Cap," he said, as he got up from the table. "You have been the best Grandpa anyone could ever have." Old Cap smiled, "Son, you have no idea how much you and your family have filled my life. It's much like I have lived two lives in my years. I'm the one to say thank you." Chris started for the door, but before he left he sat a book on the counter. On it he had laid the smooth piece of green glass he had found those many years ago, when he first met Cap, and without a word he was gone. Cap walked over and picked up the green glass piece and placed it, like a valued treasure, into his vest pocket. Giving it a pat with his hand as if to check that it was secure. He picked up the book and read the title. It read in bright gold letters: 'The Book of Mormon'

……

The airport roared with life as a small group gathered at gate 10. Chris stood holding a small bag slung over his shoulder as he checked his tickets for any forgotten details. An announcement came over a speaker that they would be boarding in a few short moments and he felt the excitement surge. He was on his way to England to serve a mission and his family and friends were there to say goodbye. Among the commotion Chris continued to look around as if missing something, but then he would turn back to get every last embrace. When finally came the call that they were boarding and a small group formed at the head of the line. As Chris turned to take his place he looked up once more. He had hoped to see Cap, Grandpa Cap, before he was gone. It was very disappointing that he couldn't see him anywhere. He knew it would be two years before he was home again and inside, a silent fear said Cap might not be alive by then, he was very old. Once more he embraced his mom, hugged his dad and gave a quick kiss to Linda on her cheek. Then checking his tickets one last time, he walked over and got in line. Slowly they moved, one at a time, until they passed through the door. Excitement and disappointment seem to mix as his turn grew close. Suddenly he felt a tight grasp on his shoulder and as he looked he found he was gazing into a familiar face, "Cap! You made it!" Smiling Cap laughed, "Of course boy, I couldn't let the best missionary in the world leave without saying goodbye." "It would have been a hard journey if you hadn't." Chris responded. "You never know what a journey holds when you leave because you can only see as far as the horizon, enjoy your adventure", Cap reached out and handed Chris a small wooden carving. Chris examined it turning it over in his hand. He discovered it was the captain's face from off Cap's pipe. He looked up from the carving puzzled. "I have had that old pipe with me for years," Cap said, "It has been like a trusted friend. Along time ago it was given to me by my friend Tom. I'm giving it to you now, not as a pipe but as a token that your Grandpa will always be along side you were ever you might be. And the second thing is it has my blood on it, so in a way a part of me will really be with you." Chris looked puzzled, but Cap added "Don't ask, it's something about old eyes and a sharp knife."

Falling into Caps arms the two of them embraced in tears. Chris turned, grabbed his bag, and disappeared out the door. His journey, his mission, had now begun. Cap stood silently at the empty door and felt somehow he had been lucky, he got to be a Grandpa. Since the Stevens had moved in 13 years ago, he got to be a real grandpa. Mark, Teresa and Linda joined Cap at the window as the large plane soared skyward. First stop, Utah.

A SPECIAL INVITATION

Chris had been gone for some time and the family seemed to have adjusted to the changes. But changes were in the wind, as this day would soon announce. Linda Stevens walked slowly up to Cap's home. In her hand she held a small pink envelope, which she gently set on the screen. Reaching for the bell, she was suddenly startled by a voice from behind her. She nearly jumped out of her shoes as she turned and saw Cap with a garden rake in his hand. She realized he had only said 'hello' and sighed in relief. Cap noticed the envelope at his door.

"What's that Linda? Did you get a mission call also?" Cap picked it up and caught the scent of perfume on the envelope. "I see they like you a whole lot better than Chris, his was just a plain white envelope."

Cap smiled as Linda impatiently said, "Well, open it!" Gently pulling the little card from within, Cap saw it was an invitation to a wedding, Linda's wedding. "Congratulations' sweetheart!" He said as he gave her a hug and a quick kiss on the cheek, "It's a big step, but you will be happy. I know you well enough that this is true. However, I don't recall you asking for my approval young lady!" he laughed softly, "Have I ever met this young fellow?" "You know him, Cap," Linda answered. "He's Dave Peters, the bishop's son." Cap cringed for a moment. The Peters were the grandchildren of the preacher boys' he once had the pleasure to know. He thought it odd though, because in a way it was because of the preacher boys and that fight so long ago that he found the girl he loved. Perhaps if they hadn't started swinging then the fight have never would have occurred. It would have been an apology and a goodbye. And now through their children, the children of those who were a part of Cap's early life, a new Dave and another Linda had come together. It was all too strange.

Dave Peters had been a good kid while growing up. Cap knew him because he was usually on the same football or baseball team as Chris. It was good, he felt looking back at Linda, everything was going to be fine. "You did good Linda," he added. "and I wouldn't miss it. I see you set the date so that Chris will be home from his mission." "Of course," Linda responded, "Chris would kill me if I got married without him being there. We are going to be married in the Temple, so this invitations is for the reception." "Yes, the temple," Cap said. "You have to be a member to go inside. Shame they cheat regular folks from the ceremony." "Well, we get married by the priesthood for all time and eternity. The ceremony is sacred, not secret, so only those recommended by their bishops can attend." Linda smiled. "Of course we can get you baptized and set the temple date a little further down the road." "It's ok" Cap said, "I'm not ready for that and I do understand that folks do things differently. I'll be at the reception. "Thanks grandpa Cap. I just hope that one day you can be sealed to grandma Linda." "Didn't know I still could. Perhaps one day. Anyway, congratulations Linda!"

    Several weeks passed by and life and routine played out the majority of the days. Young and soon to be married, Linda Stevens appeared at the back door of Cap's old home. In her arms were a bundle of blankets and a pillow. Closely behind appeared another much younger girl who was followed by another and then another, till it seemed his whole kitchen was filled with chatting, giggling, laughing young women. Closely behind the small group was Sister Kilmer, the young women's second counselor. Coming to Cap's had been Linda's idea. She had been called as Beehive adviser and, so far, was having a good time at it. Cap watched as they finished unloading their bags and stuff. He noticed Mark Stevens pulling into the driveway. The whole affair was a 'young woman's activity'. Cap had agreed to let them sleep at his house and have activities throughout the evening. Mark was going to be there as a chaperon as well as some of the girl's mothers. Cap's home was perfect, he had built it much larger than he had ever needed because he had planned on having a large family. In fact most of the bedrooms upstairs had never been used for anything, remaining empty and closed since the house was built. Tonight though, they were all opened and after a quick sweep, bedrolls were laid out. They had picked a perfect night, the sky above was clear and the water was a black rolling surge tipped with white rushing waves. The moon was full and it clearly outlined a blanket of clouds which approached from the sea. Cap knew that later that night the wind would pick up and add to the excitement of the sleep over.

The first part of the evening made Cap's home smell like a hair styling salon, but later it moved into a question and answer time... about the boys at school. Refreshments had been served and laid out throughout the evening, and sometime during these events someone found an old picture of Cap from when he was young. For hours all he heard was how handsome he had been, before he got old. Cap chuckled inside, he only felt old when he moved. Cap told them many stories about his days at sea, most of which Linda Stevens had already heard, but even so she was still spellbound with the rest. Of course if he ever missed a part of the story Linda filled in what she remembered from when he told the stories to her. Cap had his usual poetic way, and as he spoke they all journeyed with him into the past. Mark was also entranced and he thought he might have made a good sailor had his life taken a different route. As the story unfolded, being told so vividly, Mark felt he had known these people, Sparks, Sharky, Linda, and Tom. Sarah Star Shepard raised her hand as if she was in school but Cap caught on. Cap loved her middle name as the stars had always been such a part of a seafaring man's life. "What is it Sarah?" he asked. She squirmed a bit but asked, "Does this house have any ghosts?" Cap smiled, but before he spoke and suddenly as if on cue, the wind outside rushed inland off the water and grabbed something loose crashing it into the house. It wasn't large and Cap wasn't worried about it but the timing couldn't have been better, even for a movie. Shrill screams filled the air as Mark rushed out to see if there was any damage. Cap just sat there laughing as the small group finally calmed down. "No," he answered, "I have lived in this home since it was first built and the only person who has died that lived here was my wife Lindy and that wasn't here at home." Sarah didn't feel quite as secure as she had before the wind. "But what about the land before you lived here? Maybe there's ghosts from way back in time." "Yeah," Moriah agreed, "Maybe from some ancient burial ground. They could be Indian ghosts or ghost of old Spaniards who died while seeking gold and treasure!" Mark looked at Cap who sat there amused. They shared glances and he could tell Cap was having the time of this life. Mark figured he would try and bail him out of this question, "Cap has lived here for years. If there were any unpleasant spirits he would have known it by now. Besides, our Heavenly Father instructs us not to dwell on these kinds of things." Without warning, a scream from the kitchen filled the air. It was one of the girls who had been getting a drink. Mark rushed in and found Crystal Kilmer pointing at the kitchen window, "I just saw someone at the window, when he saw me he ran!" "I would run too," Mark responded, but as he looked at her expression he added, "That is if someone yelled at me like that." Mark took that opportunity to retreat and go to the window and look out, something thumped against the wall out side. "See, I told you so," Crystal exclaimed. Mark quickly went outside. He looked all over but couldn't find anything. There wasn't even footprints where the face had been seen or where the thump had been heard. Finding it odd he thought the wind probably blew something into the house. However, it didn't seem that gusty right now. Giving up he went back into the house. Crystal went over and sat next to Linda as close as she could get. She, of course, was huddled with the small group on the living room floor.

"It's his old dead wife coming for revenge!" Moriah spouted, "I'm sure of it." "Revenge for what?" Sarah questioned "For being here in her house," Crystal responded looking around the room. Linda responded in an irritated voice. "Girls, stop it! I have lived around this house all my life, there's no ghost." "Yes, but have you ever spent the night?" Moriah asked. "No." Linda answered, "But in all the years I have known Cap I have come to know Linda, his wife. She would not be a ghost looking for revenge." "Why not?" Sarah asked, "He was such a good looking guy and now there's a house full of girls." Linda explained, "Because she loved him enough to know who he was. She would trust him, she does trust him. I am sure." Cap heard Linda's answer. He was moved by what she said and he would have said the same thing, but the way Linda had described Lindy's love was like she was alive somewhere feeling these feelings. It touched his heart, but he made no comment. "Who wants vanilla ice cream with chocolate sauce?" he asked all the girls. They all rushed up at once. Mark helped

Cap serve the refreshment. "Good way to change the subject." he smiled. The wind picked up through the course of the evening and a lot of things squeaked, banged, and clanged around the house. Cap tried to reassure the girls that these were natural noises, they always happened when the winds blow. But since they didn't seem to want to let go of their fears and in other ways, seemed to be enjoying them, he let it go. Cap began to tell stories of those who died in special ways. He thought if he could turn there fear to a positive thought, such as life after death, perhaps the girls would be more comfortable. Even though Cap was not a member of the church, he could relate to many things which supported the idea of eternal life. He began by relating his first experience with death, Sharky's death. How it happened and the questions it raised in his life. He was surprised how the young women had answers, at such an early age, to the very things he had been wondering all his life. And they were good answers which the girls would share as a matter of fact instead of 'what if', 'maybe', or 'perhaps'. In fact Cap felt like he was learning while the girls were getting a good story. They went on to talk about what a miracle it was when he saw Tom's first child born. Adding, of course, the story about the ER room and Toms near miss with the surgeon's knife. Later they all joined in and shared stories about their lives which were special and happy. Mark told of an old woman he knew back in Ohio. He was at the hospital with a sick aunt and how this lady, which was in a bed close by, seemed to be growing weaker each day. On most of the visits to follow she never awoke from her sleep. Suddenly one day while he was there her eyes opened and she exclaimed she had an important message for her mother who was still alive. She wanted someone to get hold of her so that she could tell what she now knew. No one knows what that message had been because shortly afterward, on that same day, she passed away. Everyone took turns on guessing what that message might have been and most of the comments seemed happy in nature.

After hot chocolate the girls separated for their rooms and the sisters went up with them to make sure they were all bedded down. Cap and Mark found themselves alone in the quiet, staring without words into the soft, flickering light of the fireplace. "You know, Cap," Mark said, breaking the silence, "Even though our homes are built alike, yours seems to have something which mine doesn't, and I guess I can only describe that as history." Cap smiled as he sat back into his chair, "Your home has history, you just don't know all of it." Cap sipped his cup of chocolate and added, "My home may have history to you, but your home has life and that's everything a person builds a home to be alive. You have a wife and children, nothing is greater than those things." Suddenly Cap and Mark heard screams and the pounding of feet running from room to room in the upper floor. Cap looked over and smiled, "Here we go again." Mark rushed upstairs and yelled, "Man coming up!" He found sister Kilmer looking into one of the rooms cautiously. "Everyone ok?" He asked. As Sister Kilmer turned toward him he could see she was a little pale and had an expression of concern on her face, "You know we're a floor up, but the girls said they are sure someone looked in the window at them. They also said that when they screamed and ran this person beat on the walls outside. What bothers me is that I heard the thumps myself." Mark looked puzzled, but knew he had only one option, "Well, I'll take another look I guess." Rushing down the stairs he grabbed a flashlight from his bag. Annoyingly, when he turned it on the light was dim and yellow, he realized the batteries were extremely low. Still, he thought, the moon is full so no real problem and the breaks in the clouds allowed enough light through to almost play a good game of night baseball. While outside, he looked around the house and in the area just below the window. Still he couldn't find anything. Looking up at the second floor he realized it was impossible for anyone to get up to the windows. At least not without a tall ladder, that is unless they could fly. With that he went back inside and tried to calm the fears of the girls. He was really hoping they would listen, because it started to rain and he was getting soaked running in and out. It wasn't over though, throughout the evening several of the girls were sure they had heard voices or seen strange figures out in the hall, but each time it was checked it was nothing. Around three in the morning things seem to calm down and everyone went to sleep. Mark also drifted off in front of the fire and nature outside seemed to calm as well.

    As Mark slept he suddenly had the powerful sensation he was being watched. He felt a cold breeze enter the room which caused him to open his eyes. In front of him floating just off the floor a ghostly image began to form. It was a misty transparent image of a woman and she was pointing at him. Mark jumped up as the image drifted quickly up the stairs and towards the room's where the girls were sleeping. He chased it and yelled 'man coming up', but his voice echoed in what was an empty hallway. "Cap!" he yelled, "Cap come quick, I need your help!" The ghostly figure floated through the first door and Mark threw it opened. The room was empty, everyone was gone! He ran from room to room but everyone was gone. He came out into the hallway and ran downstairs to find Cap. Running into his bedroom, he found Cap standing at an old ship's helm which was strangely fixed to the floor. Cap was turning the wheel and checking a brass pedestal compass. "If you have to go, you have to go." He told Mark when he saw him. "What are you talking about?" Mark yelled, "All the girls are missing, we have to find them!" "No," Cap answered, "Everyone's gone, that's just the way it is. All you can do is stay on course and hope the weather is better up ahead." *He's gone mad!*, Mark thought. Mark ran out of the room and started calling for Linda, his daughter, but she didn't answer. The ghost suddenly appeared in front of him and started walking from room to room as if searching. Mark felt the fear but he followed the image back up the stairs anyway. He ran up to it, "What did you do with the girls?!" he demanded. The image brought its hand up to its mouth and made the sign for Mark to be quiet, 'shush'. It opened a door and Mark could see the girls inside sleeping, everything was ok. "What is going on?" he asked, as he suddenly noticed a face peering in through the upstairs window. Mark rushed down the stairs, the girls had been right! Someone was peeking in the windows and beating on the walls. He rushed out the front door and ran around the house. He found several men in white and red vertical striped shirts. They were pounding the side of the house with large black rubber balls. Mark picked up a ball and threw it at one of the men. It hit him and he fell down dead. The other men didn't say a thing but rushed at him. They grabbed him and threw him to the ground, shaking him back and forth. He fought but couldn't break their grip. He tried to yell, but he couldn't. No sound would come out of his mouth. The shaking got worse and then suddenly he woke up gazing into the face of Cap. "You wanted me to wake you to start breakfast." he said, "and you're a tough guy to wake." "You know Cap," he said as his head cleared, "I don't think I'll camp out with a bunch of girls again. Just too scary." The dreams the girls had that evening were varied, from walking through the halls of a haunted house, to those of riding the waves on sea going ships and standing at the helm, some with sails unfurled in the wind or watching the sea break in rushing wakes port and starboard along the wooden hull as the ship's bow pushes forward on the sea. Some said they dreamed the stories which Cap had told, others went off on adventures of their own. When the morning sun arose they all packed up and made preparations for going home. After a quick breakfast, which the adult leaders provided and a few goodbyes, the rides were there and as fast as they came, they were all gone.

  Mark was still curious about all the thumping and supposed faces the night before. He had to confess that he had heard something thumping a time or two as well. He figured it was that thumping that sponsored his weird dream. As he looked around, he realized there were no other footprints but his own. But as he walked around the house, he began to examine an old tree standing near by. It was obvious that it's branchs didn't touch anywhere but suddenly he realized what the ghosts had been. Underneath and hanging from several limbs, were at least a half dozen large cork floats. Mark realized that with the length of each of the ropes and with the swing of the branches in the wind, at times the corks would have been carried into the house or in front of a window. They must have swung in the wind until a gust was strong enough to carry them into a wall. Mark laughed as he went back into the house to get Linda and after letting those left know what he had found and then, thanking Cap for everything, he loaded up and drove off for home. The ghosts of Cap's seaside house were finally at peace.

A year passed in the town of Turnbridge. Linda's marriage went off well, everyone had fun and was moved by the occasion. She and her husband moved out into the county closer to where he worked. They bought a small house and seemed to be happy. As planned Chris came home off his mission in time for the wedding. It was a wonderful homecoming, but he was home only long enough to say goodbye and he was off again for college. Mark Stevens was transferred to Logan,

Utah by his work. They were devastated with the news, but his employer was losing too much money in the area so he downsized the Turnbridge office. At least he still had a job so they packed up and moved away.

Chapter Thirteen

I know where I am

All the goodbyes were difficult and no one wanted to be parted. Promises were made to keep in contact, but letters became only cards with a note or two and time separated Cap from the rest.

Cap realized that he had been part of an adventure and never had to leave his home. Those years had been wonderful. But he was alone again and here he would stay until he died. His home was filled with memories from his youth and now added to those, were the years he was called grandpa. The Roberts' home was empty again, but Mark and Teresa kept their ownership with hope to come back some day. Cap would never leave this home and now he would ponder his new memories along with the old. Sitting by the fire he added a few more stories to his logbook and then he fell asleep with his old pipe in his hands. When his old eyes closed on the silent scene of his living room it was the last time his eyes would see his home as he had built it.

Cap set the book on his lap, this part of the story wasn't so long ago that he would need to refresh his memories with a book. The old house was gone. It had been the treasure trove of his memories and the vault which held the tokens of his life. He turned back in the book to another time when the large white walls still stood. When the building itself was a land mark for all those who lived within it's reach. Again this new book read like it was about him rather than from him. He read words he wrote many years ago:

    Since his youth, this was the only house which Cap had ever lived in, at least to which he would call his own. Other than this, it was apartments and ships that had housed him. Built in his younger days for his wife Linda, they had hoped to spend all their days together in this home. They had wanted to raise a family, watch them grow and then go out into life on their own, then to grow old together here. The goal was was to create dreams together as life would take it's natural course. It always does and that's ok when you are happy. In the end they shared what years life had given them. Now a time had come, much sooner than Cap could imagine, when he would be alone for the rest of his days on earth. Cap had kept claim on his home and property for all the years which followed. He would never leave this place, it would be leaving way too much behind.

    Many of the sea going folks who lived near by shared a

different kind of love for his home and, of course, for other reasons. In consequence Cap's house had been unofficially christened with many nicknames. In several ways, it's size and location made it much more than a simple dwelling. Cap's home had become a visible marker for those out on the water. A land marker which lead anyone navigating their way inward to the first of several sea buoys. Those are set as channel guides to guide boats around the shallows and then home to the inland water ways. These markers, which when on their own were often hard to find, were made elusive when bobbing in the high caps of frequent white waters. After a hard days work what most fishermen looked for was an *easy* path home and Cap's large chalky home provided that. Once you saw it's white walls or it's lighted rooms you continued north for a small space and then you banked your vessel hard for a quick run up the channel to port. During the daylight, the tall white walls of his home reflected the sunlight from many angles and could be seen miles out on the waters. In the evening, the light from the upper windows acted much like a beacon, at least to those who knew what to look for and most who sailed and fished around these parts did. Many have remarked after a long day of fishing, with tired eyes and sore hands, that in the dimming and often dark skies of on coming night the flaming yellow-white glow of Cap's lamps could be seen like an old friend, standing watch and leading them to their homes. The house was to Cap's friends, like an unofficial lighthouse set against the misty fog of the eventide. For this reason Cap had always left a light lit in the seaward most rooms. Fishermen, many of which had known Cap a long time and some were even the children of past friends, used his home to guide themselves along the coast. Consequently, anytime he needed to throw a coat of paint on his walls all he had to do was go to the hardware store and buy some paint, then without saying a word the whole community would mysteriously show up at his house for a painting party.

      Stories were often shared around town about the large white house. Somewhere desperation had been turned to hope from those who were lost or in trouble offshore. They would speak of times when they were caught by the sea and had nothing left to give in their defense. They would catch sight of Cap's home, standing tall against the storm or lit in the black night of a cloud cast sea and they suddenly knew where they were and made a new effort to make it home. Sometimes sailors would make a ghostly account. That as the mist would rise off the waters in a specter haunting fashion, when it would gather on the bluffs of the rock cliffs just below Cap's house, when markers would disappear under the white blanked of the misty fog.

There Cap's home could still be found set on the rocks, just high enough above the fog that it would seem to be floating on clouds. In fact, on one occasion, a clever fishermen happened to have a camera with him when he got lost in the fog. As he drifted about helplessly for hours, he finally came out into a semi clear area on the water and there was Cap's home, like a dream or a fairy tale floating on the clouds. His picture made the front page of the local paper the next week. Cap had always kept a copy of it on his wall. He tells everyone who asks it's proof that he lives in a dream home.

  At Bear Lake, Cap paused in reading, he remembered that photo, but his smile of remembrance went quickly to a solemn look because now the photo was lost Everything was lost. He didn't want to think of that. He wanted to remember instead. Opening the book, again he read on:

  His love of the sea was mirrored in its construction and his love for a special lady was carved in every curve and design. It was the same for her. Truly for them both that special love, the true love which everyone hopes to find in their lives. It was his love for her which caused him to build this home and the love they held in common to have it built in this place. Because here in this setting, everything which they held dear was one, together as a whole. From the breaking of waves below to the endless horizons beyond. It was the warmth of the fire within and each other just being together. The tender love of his wife for him and his loving touch for her, her shadowy form at the window and his rush through the door when he would return home. Sounds, silence, events, and all that was wonderful was found here at this place.

Cap turned to the seagull. He flipped back to the page where he would have been had he just continued to read. "I know what is coming up next, and I think I understand why now. This is the night my house burned down. In fact, I not only lost my house, but my garage and sheds as well. *Everything* burnt down that night, even the old trees. I was wakened by breaking glass. A large framed photo of Linda and myself fell onto the floor and woke me. I could barely open my eyes. I had to force myself to move. It was just in time for me to get out alive. I was choking from the smoke and my eyes were burning. I grabbed what I could, but that was only my backpack, my logbook, and few things which were inside my coat pockets already. Everything burned. It was so hot nothing survived except my old refrigerator and since I kept my money inside the freezer at least I had some cash when it was all over. Not to mention what I keep buried in the yard in a few secret places.", Cap opened up his backpack as if to show the bird. It was full of money mixed with his personal things. "Guess the bikers could have had a good party." he smiled. "I was afraid it was all going to spill out when he grabbed the rope off of it." he laughed, "But if they knew what I still had buried around my property back at Turnbridge, I think... well you know. Yet in the end, it is just money and I would give it all just to have my old house back ." Cap pulled the top tight on his pack and threw it back on the ground, "No one came when my house burned, no one called the fire department. I don't know why or how someone didn't see my house burning but no one came. Nothing was on at the Robert's home, no phone, no power, so I couldn't go there for help. The Stevens' had already moved away, I was alone at this end of the county. My car was destroyed because I couldn't get it out of the garage in time. I had spent too much time trying to rescue anything I could. So when the house and everything finally burnt out, and I saw there was nothing left, I gave up. I started walking. I thought I would walk until I died, I was sure my heart would give out. I walked up the coast and back down it. I lived on the streets here and then there. But I never died, even at my age. I made every mile and every step until I ended up here at Bear Lake. When I met those missionaries in town, those two young boys, they reminded me of Chris. I wanted to talk with them so bad. They told me things I had heard the Stevens family say for years, I felt like an expert at their religion. But here and now I was finally *hearing* the words, learning the lessons which are found in the words. The message Mark, Teresa, Chris, and Linda wanted me to understand, but I would not apply to myself." Suddenly breaking Cap's thought as he talked with the bird, Scratch came charging from the bushes. His eyes were evil and intent, "You can give me my book right now! I have tried to be patient with you because you're an old man. But now I am mad and I *will* hurt you if I have to put up with any more nonsense." Scratch grabbed the book, but Cap held on tight. "You know this book is not yours! Are you a thief? Do the Mormons like thieves? Can you get baptized as a thief?" Scratch yelled. Cap struggled to hold onto the book. He felt he did not dare let go at any cost to himself, "I realize now that the book was never yours, it *is* mine. It would only be yours if I would give it to you! I know who you are now. Leave me!" Cap said loudly. "Yeah and who do you think I am?" Scratch smirked. "At sea I thought I knew you. I thought I heard your roaring voice in the thunder. I thought I watched your evil hand turn the breaking swells to torment men as they fought the ocean for their lives. I thought I saw forks of lightning in your hand as you hurled them at the sea or lit the blackened storm in your rage. I thought it was your looming presence churning the tempest with malignant intent, hiding the stars and covering the moon. But this was not you. You were not there. I found you in the whisper of lies, the act of deceit. I heard you in the voice of hate and the artificial friendships of predator and thief. You are the author of false pleasures which lead men to the stagnant spirals of life that descend ever downward. I know who you are! Leave me I say again!" Cap exclaimed. "You know huh? I'll leave, when I'm done with you! You think you are *so* smart, you think you have it all figured out. If I am who you think I am, can you imagine how much danger you are in right now? Not just of your life, but *I* will take your immortal soul down to the flames, down to torment forever!" Yanking the book from the hands of old Scratch, Cap turned away and said, "I will not listen to you any more, by the power of God leave me!" Scratch followed Cap as he walked around the campsite trying to avoid him. Scratch smiled confidently,"And exactly what power is that? Do you think because you have had some sort of epiphany you are suddenly a prophet or something? Perhaps someone forgot to teach you the spell, the proper pronunciation, you know, the chant that will cause me to run away?" "By heaven then and all the angels about me- Leave me!" Cap again said. Scratch mocked, "I must say that sounded very good, you called on heaven. I think you even expect that I would turn tail and leave you now, but see I am not! This is *my* world, they haven't told you everything, you know. You *are* in danger, drop the book and run. You know nothing! You're lost and you are mine, so you might as well go back to life and have as much fun as you can before I have to come for you. I'll leave you alone, at least till then, I promise."

"Why don't you leave?" Cap yelled as he fell to his knees, knocking his old logbook off the stump. "Why, oh why can't I be free from this tormentor?" As Cap sat there wondering what to do he glanced at his old book which now laid spread out on the sand. A tear fell from his eyes and hit the sand. It fell near a picture of Linda, which had fallen out of the books pages. He had thought he had lost all of his pictures in the fire, he had thought there was nothing left of his treasures on earth. And here it was, a photo of Linda smiling at him, from all those years ago. He picked it up and kissed it and said, "You are right Linda, I have been talking to the wrong person."

His spirit swelled inside and his words were filled with heart and soul, "Thank you Father in heaven, for this simple gift. Thank you for all the things I have learned this night and in my life. Thank you for my wife and the friends I have had and all the opportunities and blessings you have given me. Thank you Father that I should live long on this earth, long enough to learn these simple but great lessons of life. I know that my Redeemer lives. I know that You have placed on earth men, called by You, with authority from heaven. I wish that my heart could express my feelings more fully, so I say to thee again, thank you Father."

When Cap looked up the old man was gone. He was far down the beach walking away, quiet and without incident. No thunder, no lightning, no wind, except the breeze which came from off the lake. To mortal eyes Cap was alone, but to heavens eyes he was circled about by the spirit of God, in the presence of all those he had ever loved. Cap turn the photo over and found words written on the back, it was a message from Linda, it read:

My Love Dave,

I picked up this empty log book today, Knowing that one day you would use it to record your life within it's pages.

I figured that by the time you get to this page in your life, we would both be old, gray grandparents. I do not know what the future holds for the two of us, I only know that where ever you are when you read this, I love you, for always and forever.

May these words and this picture remind you or give you strength if the seas are dangerous and threatening. Knowing that somewhere at your journeys end I am waiting, to greet you home.

Love forever, your Lindy

Knowing his Father in Heaven was but the start and accepting his Savior was the beginning of knowledge, he felt suddenly filled and whole. He realized that knowing the words, knowing the truth has no power until it comes from the heart. A heart now changed, willing to grow and actually walk in the light of His love was what he had ultimately wanted and needed. Though time had taken all he had held dear nothing was really lost. It was only beyond the next horizon, awaiting him at home, in his Father's care.

Sunrise broke the night and light overcame the darkness. The morning sun flamed into life as it broke over the mountains. The lake lit with a beautiful turquoise display in the morning light. Cap's campfire had burned out and the seagull was gone. It had joined its friends searching the beach for available scraps of food. Cap packed his belongings and headed to Montpelier. When he arrived, he did his best to remember the last address he had for the Mark and Teresa. He knew that Mark worked in Logan but for some reason decided to live in Montpelier. As far as his map shown, Logan was a long way away from Montpelier perhaps he got it wrong. He wasn't sure so he went up to the first address he thought was theirs. It wasn't them and they didn't know who he was talking about. But in Montpelier I guess you can get a north mixed up with a south or and east and west. He knew he had only three more neighborhoods to check. However, a scruffy old gentleman running around town knocking on doors can raise some suspicion. He never made it to the third address before a police car pulled up and stopped him.

"Excuse me sir," The officer said. "Will you talk to me a moment?"

"Why yes," Cap responded, "perhaps you can even help me."

"Are you saying sir, " The officer asked, "that you need some sort of medical care? Do you want me to call an ambulance?

"No, no," Cap said, "I am looking for an address." as he said this he noticed another officer sitting in the passenger side. He was listening, but his eyes were on some document he was working on intently.

"Do you have any identification sir?" the officer asked.

"No, I lost it all in a fire."

"Really," the officer said snidely. "What's your name?"

"My name is-" But before he could finish, a voice yelled.

"Cap!" It was the officer's passenger. "Cap!" the voice yelled as he jumped out of the car. It was Chris! He ran to Cap and held him tightly. "I was told you were dead." His voice broke, "I was told you were killed in a fire. Cap you're alive!" he sobbed and shook Cap back and forth.

"I'm ok Chris," he said holding his young friend, "I was looking for your dad and mom's place. When I lost my house I didn't know what to do so I just walked."

"Walked where?" Chris said stepping back.

"Through all the years of my life," He answered with a shrug, "and it lead me here. I was hoping to find your parents, but I'm glad I found you."

"You don't know. They aren't here, they moved back to Turnbridge a few months ago. Dad got his position back. You can't imagine what we all thought when they found your house gone, burned to the ground, and no one had any answers. No one knew what happened. It's only luck you have found me here! I was heading to BYU tomorrow."

"Police work, huh?" Cap smiled

"Well, criminal law." Chris answered, his eyes reflected his thoughts, "Cap, I need to get a hold of Mom and Dad. We've all been torn to pieces thinking you were dead."

"I would like that," Cap said, thinking back at the night he had just had he was ready, even though a burned patch of land was all he had left there. "And I would like to go home," he added, " but I want a favor from you my former missionary. I would like to be baptized as soon as permitted." Chris gleamed with joy,"Always a missionary grandpa Cap, always a missionary." The two enjoyed their day together as Chris made arrangements for Cap to be flown home. Mark met him at the airport and took him home to their house. He lived upstairs for several months, planning to get his land cleared as soon as possible. Later he wanted to build a small cabin where his house used to stand. He figured he didn't need much more than that at this stage of his life.

Cap took the lessons from the missionaries and he was baptized by Chris not long after. A year later he was sealed to Linda and soon after he had Tom and Sherry's work done. Later he did the temple work for everyone else he could do and was able to do. Tom's children and grandchildren became interested in the church and the Stevens family became fast friends with them as several became members in the same Stake. Cap even had a calling in his Ward, he was assigned to open the gospel doctrine class each week and he did this gladly, taking his calling seriously.

    His cabin was never built, but he did live in a mobile home on his old homestead for the years that followed. Cap no longer had to turn the pages of his book, he was now writing them anew, stuffing them into the end of his old ships log.

Chapter Fourteen

Another Horizon

Like many times before Cap stayed for dinner at the Stevens residence, but he excused himself as it grew late. He felt the need to head home. It was good to have Chris back even though it was going to be a short stay. Linda and her husband came over to eat and to visit too. Chris and Cap had shared their stories about England and of the things which happened while Chris was away on his mission and a few stories about college. Mark wanted to drive Cap home and so did Chris, but he felt a need to walk. After thanking them several times for their offers, he finally was able to get his coat and head out the door. Of course this was after he promised he would call when he reached home.

The trail was quiet and the moon above was full. Pale silver rays lighted the path and the water was calm. There were sparkles on the gentle dark deep. It was filled with millions of shining stars ever moving and ever changing. The shadows were dark and well defined, black to gray they cast their inky cloak. Cap slowly walked up the trail and he looked out over the waters as memories tugged at his heart's strings. It was like the sea held in a glass, all the life he had known and the shores he now walked were the stage in which all had played. Now though, it was different, he saw it differently in someway. Like light in a darkened room he knew all who he had once loved, still live. As he made his way by the picnic tree it was if he was passing by the children, Chris and Linda, young laughing and playing, pointing out the whales in the water. He could see Chris out in the water pulling him around in the boat as he swam holding tightly to the bowline. He could see the waves as they must have been when they wrapped around the old tree and Linda was holding onto it for her life and the lives of the two men in the surf. He could see himself off shore holding Sharky as he reached for a family which waited for him on the other side. Cap continued to walk making his way up the final steps of the path. Ahead he could see Tom as his face gleamed when he announced his first child and how silly he looked slipping off the gurney into his arms. But further ahead at the house he could see Linda waiting for him, waving for him to hurry.

The play is not over, he thought, *it waits for the curtain to rise once again. And in that scene, or in that act, I will embrace the arms of* the woman I love and the hands of those who called me friend. Right now, Cap thought, *I am here to help those who are still on this stage, at least until my turn on earth is up.* Cap knew inside that the gospel was true. The plan of salvation was so clear and simple. It was not just knowledge, it was the simple feeling that satisfied the soul and brought peace to his heart. A peace that did not have its origins in Cap, but came from the spirit of truth that shined within.

As he looked out as far as the darkened night would permit the water touched the sky. The horizon of evening is limited, but he now knew he could see beyond it. Eternity itself didn't seem so far as it once had been, nor was it so strange that he could not comprehend. No longer a subject for only preachers, it was now the understanding of man. He shuttered at the fleeting thought that he might have missed it if the Stevens' family hadn't moved next door so many years ago. That he might not have embraced it had he ended his journey too soon.

It was good to be alone for this walk, for somehow inside Cap felt he saw the love of God. As Cap stood at the door and looked down the hill at the Stevens' home, he noticed foul weather brewing off the bay. It didn't look like a major storm, but he knew there would be a lot of wind and rain. Cap, of course, was right and as the evening drew nearer the storm seemed to rise as the wind and rain combined to beat along the shore. Cap lit a candle anticipating the oncoming power outage. He stood by his window, it wasn't near as nice as his old windows were, but they were windows none the less. Below he could see the headlights of a car which sat motionless by the old tree near the fork in the road. Odd he thought, swinging his new telescope onto the site. He couldn't see much in the dark but it was clear that the old picnic tree had fallen and it was on top of a car. *I thought the old tree would last forever,* he thought. *Pity.*

Cap watched intently to see if anyone was moving, but all he could see was the steady headlights beaming out over the water. Grabbing the phone he found the lines were dead and he realized the tree must have struck the telephone lines as well. Grabbing his coat, he jumped into the old Ford pick up which Chris had found for him and raced down the hill. Reaching the tree he saw it was Mark's car. He was outside it and pinned below a branch. Cap rushed over and found that he was ok, the mud below him had cushioned the trees' weight, but he was still pinned tightly.

Cap grabbed an ax out of his truck's bed and started to hack at the branch. It didn't hurt Mark till he had cut nearly through and the wood started to vibrate with each blow. He was exhausted and Mark kept telling him he should go and get Chris. But as he looked up at the power pole, he saw the fallen tree had weakened it. It seemed to whip violently in the wind and he was afraid the power lines might fall. Suddenly the branch snapped where Cap had been chopping, and Mark felt the relief as he was freed from the weight. Cap stumbled back and fell to the ground with his last blow. Mark wasn't hurt bad so he got up and loaded Cap into the old Ford as his own car had been completely disabled by the branches of the old tree. He knew he had to get Cap inside fast. "Hang in there, Cap." Mark said as he put the truck into gear and pressed on the gas pedal. The tires spun for a moment and then they slipped and slid down the road toward Mark's home. Cap was breathing hard as he whispered, "Don't worry about me, it takes more than a little rain to wash away this old salt." Mark was still worried. In the dim light Cap looked bad. The wind rushed through the door as Mark came bursting in. Fallen leaves and icy rain followed them, driven by the storm which raged outside. The home suddenly cooled by the torrent until the door closed behind them. Mark struggled to support the weakened form of Cap who slouched in his arms, barely able to stand on his own. They stumbled for the couch as Chris rushed up from his chair and helped them the rest of the way. "Call an ambulance!" Mark shouted, but Teresa was already at the phone. Linda, on cue, quickly disappeared into the bedroom and brought out blankets and a heating pad. Teresa looked up while tapping on the dial, "The phones are down. I can't even get a dial tone." Mark looked back at her, his eyes said it all and it looks bad. Setting the phone down Teresa rushed into the kitchen for some warm liquids and the first aid kit. By now Cap looked almost gray and Linda felt tears welling up as she saw him fading away. He looked like he was nearly gone already and the thought of losing him hurt and burned deeply. "Stay with us Cap, don't go." she softly said. Cap looked up from the couch and into Linda's eyes. His voice was weak and broken, in a whisper he spoke soothingly, "All things pass my dear and because of you I know it's not forever. We will be together again some day. I don't think I'm going to make it back this time. Be strong, I love you. I love you all." Cap seemed to fade and the color in his face became pale. Teresa came back into the room and embraced Linda fiercely. He was dying and they all knew it. His breath became shallow and more uneven by the moment. Suddenly, with an unexpected light, he opened his eyes once more and in a quiet humble voice whispered. "You have been my family, the one I thought I would never have. Thank you." His voice trailed off to silence, his eyes shifted to empty space, and he was gone. "Goodbye, Cap." Chris said softly to himself as he gave a final check to Cap's pulse and pulled the blanket up and over his face, "Goodbye, Grandpa Cap." Tears replaced his words as he turned to his family. Silently and unseen by mortal eyes on the other side of life the darkness became light. Pain and weakness fled and love prevailed. A golden light of presence which cast no shadow shown through all things.

"Tom, you old sea dog!" Dave said, looking up at his friend. Tom reached down and helped Dave up from the couch. As he rose from the couch his body no longer hurt and he felt strength as if it had never been gone. "How are you doing Dave? Welcome home." The tinkle of a small bell filled the air as Dave noticed someone moving behind Tom. Emerging from around his friend Dave could see it was Lindy, his wife, smiling as she reached out for his embrace. They fell into each other's arms and wept for a time. It was pure joy!! The joy of being together again overflowing from their very centers. Lindy pulled slightly away to look up into Dave's eyes.

"I accepted the gospel Dave, at the baptism which Teresa did for me in the temple. I was there with you. We are sealed for all time and eternity, you and I." Dave smiled as he hoisted her high over his head, his arms stretched out, holding her fast. Bringing her back down their lips met softly, sweetly the first kiss in eternity. Together again among the stars of heaven. He had always known he loved her and she always knew she loved him but never before had they felt the pure love flow through them as they did now. This was Love free from the shackles of worldly cares. This was Love which radiated like a light for all eternity to see and it was theirs.

Turning back Dave saw the family which he had adopted as his own. They were gathered around the body of old Cap. Though they knew he was now happy, they could not fight back the tears which broke free from their eyes and they held onto each other for strength. But crying was ok, it is always ok. It's how we say, from the very depths of our hearts, "Goodbye. I love you always. 'Till we meet again."

"I understand now," Dave said both to himself and to those around him, "how my joy will be great with theirs in all eternity. When they too travel through this door on their way to immortality we will share a new kind of joy together." Dave turned away and slowly before him the skies opened like a vast field of clouds and in them he saw Sharky and Wayne Roberts and even the old school teacher, Linda Martin, who was not so old anymore. The whole town of Turnbridge seemed to be there. His mom and dad joined them on a path he now walked and his grandfather also who held in his hand, the hand of a young girl. Dave looked at her and studied her face. He knew he should know this girl, but didn't exactly remember ever meeting her. Of course! This was his daughter, the one who died with Linda those many years ago. Old Cap hadn't been sure if she had ever been born as he wasn't there during the birth. But she *had* been born and he remembered it was Linda Stevens who *insisted* that he be sealed to her. She had said, "I have a feeling Cap, I can't explain it, but you have to give your daughter a name and be sealed to her." They did and young Linda had stood in at the sealing with her mother, Teresa, for Cap's wife. It had taken Cap a good long while, but finally he settled on the name Hope Linda

    Lindy reached and took her daughter's hand and the three walked into a large gathering of family and friends. They were gone from the grasps of this earth. Gone until the time was that they should return. Their family reached back into the clouds as far as the horizon and at it's head was One who shown brighter than them all. All generations stood together to welcome him home, this Captain of the sea.

    At the wheel stood I against the earth and the sky.

    to govern the course I should take.

    A chart in my hand and a compass to see

I cross through the life that I make.

I am born from the port with the sky in my eyes

but the horizon is all I can see.

And even though waters are calm on the start,

In life, this shall not always be.

For the metal of souls is tested in trial,

and quality, in crews we do take.

The waters we pass, the choice of our port,

the path, as it falls from our wake.

And as all have a start, we all have an end,

'tis the same port of call, we then go.

Though vastly parted away, or on straight course near by,

our ship's flag in this bay... will then show.

In joy from ashore a shout will call

to the vessel who's made its' way home.

In joy we embrace, in memory cry,

in this way our love is then shown.

For in yesterdays past, we said goodbye,

today we greet with a tear,

for they who once had left our side,

are now, once more found near.

        The Earths end, Eternity Begins

        With Love, Your Eternal Brother and friend,

                Randy

Dedication

We look for inspiration in life for characters and stories that may provide the story of our hearts intent. Those closest to us, those who inspired us, those who protected us, those who taught us by example. They are those who painted on the canvas of our memories the horizons of which our internal eyes focus. None better in my life then that of my father and my mother. It is true my brothers and sisters added to the balance of who I am. Thus it is they, father and mother I attribute much of my learning and understanding which started my mortal experience on its way. I know it is my Father on high who cares for the course of my life, but I recognize it is He who gave me what I have today including the gift of agency which allowed me to make mistakes of which I do not hold Him or my earthly parents responsible. Thankfully He gave me and all of you and repentance and redemption as well.

I am dedicating this book to Gerald Harry Shepard. I could easily add my mother Margret Alice Lilley Shepard Peck as they together provided the garden from which I sprung.

In my father's youth, dad cared for his family, grandpa and grandma, brother and sister, during hard times of the early years of the 20th century.

When World War Two shook its ugly head, my father answered the call. He joined the Navy and gave of his time for the defense of the United States of America.

He served as a corpsman aboard ship and later on a secret island locations of the Aleutian Island chain. Because of the secret nature of his assigned base you might say he fought WW2 for free. Each month when he received his pay he would send it home to my mother to help her live while everything was being rationed back home.

He hoped she was saving some of the money for their life after the war, and she was thinking he was saving the money at the base till he got home. But when he returned home they both found they were wrong. Someone in the postal chain between his duty location and his home in Washington state had been stealing every dime he had sent home. So he fought the war for free, except for the cost and hardship it put upon my mother during that time.

When the war ended Dad applied for an early out on his enlistment, but the Pacific Islands were still active as it took time to inform the enemy that the war had ended.. Dad's best friend was shot and killed by a sniper while on patrol while trying to wrap up the problem Islands. Out of his grief, he wanted to go back into the post war world but this time as a combat paratrooper. Luckily for us who came later in his life, there was no need for his continued participation and he was released from duty. Sharky in the story is based on this friend though historically I only know of their friendship.

When dad found faith in Jesus Christ in the early 1960's, it took! He became a man of Christ as he came to know Him. It provided another avenue for his natural self to become teacher, caregiver and friend. He never filled a calling of great importance, however he did what most fail to do. He lived as a man of Christ in all that he said and did. Was he perfect? What man is? But because he was who he is, I know Heavenly Father is well pleased. It is the silent average son, man, father, husband not recorded in history who are the building blocks of the true unwritten history of God's plan on planet earth. When dad was ill unto death, the Veteran's hospital remarked they had never seen such a procession of friends honoring a single man.

If you would like to contact us

Randy and Char Shepard

christmasten@gmail.com